INVITING BEDLAM

DEMON BOUND
BOOK 2

GRAE BRYAN

PROLOGUE

Nix

Nix stretched out on the sandy cave floor, briefly bemoaning the rock grit that was going to end up in his gorgeous hair.

The Void was the *worst*.

Absolutely no creature comforts to be found, and wasn't that just a kick in the pants for the four creatures trapped here? Nix's bed was made of dried *leaves*, for fuck's sake. They couldn't even summon changes of clothes—they were all stuck in whatever clothes they'd been wearing when last completing a contract.

How exactly was he supposed to uphold a sense of fabulousness with these kinds of constraints?

And true, none of them exactly needed creature comforts. They didn't need to eat or bathe or even sleep when in limbo—but what fun was there in only getting what one *needed*?

Life was about want.

And Nix *wanted* back in the human realm pronto.

"I'm bored," their little chaos demon lamented, echoing Nix's own sentiments. He was perched on a rock across the cave from Nix, the viewing portal between them, resting his chin on clenched fists. "So, so bored."

"I know, baby," Nix soothed, turning his gaze from the cave ceiling to give him a sympathetic look. "You wanna change the channel?"

They could turn the viewing portal to whatever part of the human realm they wanted, one of the few actual benefits of the Void. Nix was personally a fan of peeking into porn shoots (and wasn't that a fun aspect of modern times?), while Chaos's tastes were a little more...varied. Last week (Or was it last month? Time moved so strangely here.) he'd been all about forest fires.

"No." Chaos's lower lip pushed into a pout. "I'm sick of watching. Always *watching*."

So was Nix, for that matter. Real sick of it. How long had it been since he'd had a contract? He would have thought their Book was lost forever, if not for the fact that Kai had been summoned a few days ago. Which was ridiculously unfair, since he'd been the last one summoned before that, but whatever.

At least it meant there was hope for the rest of them.

Although, it might have been a refreshing change of pace to give in to despair. They'd been in the Void long enough for it to be warranted. But the others were gloomy enough. If Nix gave in too, who would bring up the vibes? Certainly not Kai, if he returned— he acted like they were all the banes of his existence. And their nightmare demon was a bit too creepy to be the life of the party. And sweet Chaos was slowly losing his marbles out of boredom.

So it was up to Nix to be his usual charming self.

"Why don't you take a nap?" he suggested. Just because they didn't need to sleep in the Void didn't mean it wasn't the easiest way to pass the time.

So much time.

Chaos's gold eyes flashed at him petulantly, the flames reflecting in them there and gone in an instant. "I'm tired of naps."

"Maybe if you ask nicely, Nightmare will give you bad dreams."

Chaos's dour expression took on a hopeful cast. "You think?" He didn't wait for an answer, hopping off his rock, presumably to find their fourth.

A very suggestible thing, wasn't he?

Nix debated taking a nap himself but ultimately stayed right where he was. He'd stare at the portal a little while longer.

Not many demons in their original set of one hundred had watched the human world all that often. But humans were Nix's bread and fucking butter—why wouldn't he watch them every chance he got? One needed to understand someone to seduce them, and Nix understood humans. They were glorious, really— weak and greedy and flawed.

Just the way Nix liked them.

The others treated their contracts like chores, but Nix was happy to be bound to the Book. Happy to be bound to the human realm. Happy to be at a human's service again and again and again.

He slid his hands down his body slowly, imagining it was some human's touch. It didn't matter who—man, woman, neither of the above.

All lust was equally delicious.

And yet.

Nix dropped his hands and sat up quickly, glancing around to make sure Chaos hadn't crept back in during the last minute. Once assured of his privacy, he waved a hand, turning the portal's gaze to follow one human in particular.

Nix had begun watching Kai as soon as he'd realized Kai had been summoned, unable to resist his curiosity. He'd seen the little cutie pie who'd called their warrior demon out of the Void. He'd listened in on a phone call with a harsh, cold, commanding voice. *Mm.*

Nix had followed the voice to its origin—New York City and an office building the owner of said voice rarely seemed to leave.

The summoner's brother. Ivan.

In the past few days, Nix had gotten addicted to watching him. There was something about him, beyond just his mighty fine good looks. A tight air of control Nix would have loved to mess with given the chance.

And maybe he should have felt bad for spying on one particular human—it was more of an invasion of privacy than his normal haphazard viewings—but they'd never meet, so what did it hurt?

And if it gave Nix ideas—images of specific hands on his body, a cold voice murmuring filth in his ear—so what? He was trapped for the time being. Who could fault him for making the most of it?

He let out a happy sigh as the portal focused in on a familiar light-haired head bent over what appeared to be paperwork. It wasn't the most stimulating of activities to spy on, but it would do for now.

Anything to pass the time.

1

Ivan

Ivan blew through the front doors of his office building, ignoring the security guard's desperate greeting, and stalked to the elevators, where he slapped the button hard enough to sting his palm.

The prize he had tucked into his suit jacket burned—was the heat real or imagined? Ivan didn't know. He didn't care. What mattered was that he needed to make use of it before others came searching for it.

Before his *brothers* came searching for it.

Ivan's brothers.

His betrayers, more like. Ivan scoffed as he stepped into the elevator, hitting the button for the top floor, this time with a gentler touch. Everywhere he turned—betrayal. He'd been raised to lead, they'd been raised to follow, and yet they kept fucking. It. Up.

A radiating pain alerted Ivan to the fact that he was clenching his jaw hard enough to grind his teeth down to nubs. He released the pressure with a concentrated effort, wincing as he stretched the tense muscle out.

This was what family did to people.

He stepped out of the elevator and walked quickly into the only office on the floor. *His* office. Because *he* was the leader of this business their father had built from the ground up with blood and determination, even if his brothers liked to pretend otherwise.

Once in the safety of his domain, the double doors closed and locked, Ivan threw his prize on his desk. It looked simple enough on the outside: an aged, leather-bound book. But if Ivan's baby brother was to be believed, it was a Book with a capital *B*, one that could summon a demon.

And why wouldn't Ivan believe Sascha? He'd seen Sascha's demon with his own eyes just a few hours before. Seven feet of pure muscle, with horns and wings and an air about him that said he wouldn't mind killing whoever—or whatever—dared get in his way.

Ivan had known something was going on with Sascha—he'd started acting strangely a few days ago, two months into his hiding out in Maine. And not strange as in his usual ditzy forgetfulness, but...cagey. When he hadn't responded to Ivan's texts and calls for a whole two days, Ivan had gone to investigate in person.

And had promptly discovered his brother with a giant, horned, *winged* demon he'd summoned "accidentally." Even more alarming, their other brother, Alexei—who had cost Ivan millions in a botched deal and fled the state two years ago—was there in the company of his own pet monster, a vampire he claimed to love.

But was it love, or was it a power grab?

Because as far as Ivan could tell, everyone had a monster but Ivan.

He tapped his fingers on the leather cover of the Book. All he could hear—other than the ringing in his ears—was his father's voice in his head.

If they don't fear you, you're dead. And you'll deserve it, won't you? For being weak. For being unworthy.

How could Ivan's brothers fear him when they each had a supernatural entity at their disposal? How could *anyone* fear him when he was losing control of the only people in the world who were supposed to have been conditioned from birth to follow his orders?

Unless...

Unless Ivan had a supernatural entity of his own.

Ivan flipped open the Book. It was filled with strange symbols, each accompanied by stanzas of writing in a language he'd never seen before. Each symbol representing a demon.

But how to choose? Sascha had shown him the symbol that had summoned his demon, Kai. It was a swirling blue number that took up most of the page.

So Ivan should choose an even bigger one, yes? Ivan had greater power and strength of will than either of his brothers, as he'd proven time and time again. He needed a demon to match.

Especially if he was to have any hope of keeping his empire from crumbling.

He flipped through the pages, stopping after a mere moment on one that caught his eye. It was a stark red symbol made up of harsh lines taking up the entire page. Ivan could even swear that page was hotter than the rest, the paper nearly burning his fingers.

This was it. Ivan could feel it.

This was *his* demon.

Now all he had to do was summon it.

He remembered exactly what Sascha had told him (although Sascha had meant it as explanation, not instruction)—copy the symbol, say the words, spill the blood.

Spill the blood.

Ivan didn't have a knife on him. A gun, yes, but that would no doubt be overkill for his purposes.

He hit the intercom button on his desk phone.

"Yes, Mr. Kozlov?" his secretary answered.

"I need a knife. A sharp one."

There was a brief pause, but Tara knew better than to question his demand. *Some* people knew how to treat the leader of a Bratva family. Some people knew the meaning of respect.

"I'll bring it right away, sir."

Ivan waited, impatience thrumming through his veins. Her desk was on the floor beneath his. Ivan hadn't wanted anyone on his floor, not since Alexei had left. Definitely no simpering receptionist to greet him each day. He'd wanted to be able to press a button and be taken to his sanctuary without seeing a soul.

While he waited, he stared at the symbol. The more he looked at it, the more Ivan felt how *right* it was. Some of the tension left his body, his jaw unclenching again.

Yes, his brothers had betrayed him. Yes, Ivan had a mole in his organization, one who'd conspired to cause Sascha harm in this very building. But here was a solution. A way out. A way to secure his hold in New York. His hold on his men.

As if to mock him, Ivan's cell buzzed, Sergei's name coming up on the screen. He ignored the call from his supposed right-hand man. Did Sergei know Ivan had gone to Maine? Ivan had driven himself, had ducked out without even alerting his driver.

Sergei couldn't know.

Either way, now wasn't the time.

There was the ding of the elevator and the telltale sound of Tara's heels on the floor. She appeared a moment later, sharply dressed as always, her dark hair slicked back in a bun. She approached the desk carefully and set a steak knife in front of him, the handle pointed toward him, the blade wisely pointed toward herself.

"It's from the break room. It was all I could find."

"Fine." Ivan grabbed the knife, testing its sharpness. "That'll be all."

She left quickly. She wasn't a timid woman by any means, but it was possible Ivan was even less...welcoming than usual, at the moment.

Unhinged, perhaps? a wry voice in his head that sounded suspiciously like Sascha suggested.

Ivan waved the thought away. It was fine. It was all going to be fine.

His new demon would make sure of it.

He sat in his office chair, a cushy thing he'd gotten when he'd refurbished the office. (*Weak*, his father's voice told him every time he sat in it. *Pampered and weak*.) He took out a paper and pen from his desk drawer, painstakingly copying the symbol from the Book. He studied the words a few times over before reciting them as best he could as he cut the tip of his finger with the knife, a few drops of blood falling on the copy he'd made.

He waited.

And waited.

For a long moment, there was nothing. Ivan tapped his finger on the desk. Had he failed in his task? A new pressure built in his chest at the thought. He couldn't afford to fail. Not here, not now.

But gradually, so low he thought at first he was imagining it, a hissing filled the air. It grew steadily in volume until it was all Ivan could hear.

And then red smoke was billowing into the room, collecting into a column three feet around and nearly ten feet tall.

Massive. Just as Ivan had thought.

A deep, raspy voice rang out. "You called for me, human?"

For the first time in he didn't know how long, Ivan smiled.

———

DESPITE ALL HIS EARLIER HURRY, Ivan hesitated, taking a moment to appreciate the size of the smoke column, the deep sound of that voice. He'd been right to choose the red symbol—this demon was going to be huge. A goddamn monster. It was going to put Sascha's warrior demon to shame.

As it should.

Ivan *should* have the most powerful weapon available, not his brothers. They didn't know the cost of the family business, the dangers that lurked at every corner. But Ivan knew. It was what he'd been raised for.

The only thing.

Their father had come to this country a minor player in the Russian Mafia, barely making enough to keep his family above water. He'd carved his place into the American branch by taking the dirtiest jobs offered, stabbing as many backs as he could along the way.

He'd taken his power by way of blood, until his name was as feared and respected as any other in the area.

And then he'd died suddenly, of a fucking aneurysm of all things, leaving Ivan in charge decades sooner than they'd expected. Which would have been fine, maybe. Alexei had been there as his enforcer, Sergei at his side to help smooth over the transitions, Sascha safely tucked away on the sidelines.

And then Alexei had fucked Ivan over, and all Ivan's grief and rage and pent-up aggression had led to a few...poor decisions. Enemies made where he couldn't afford them, the Carusos chief among them. If he didn't handle it correctly, he'd have a mob war on his hands. And the odds of himself and both brothers making it out alive?

Slim to none.

A rumbling from the smoke column reminded Ivan he'd yet to reply. "I wish to summon a demon," he said.

"And here I am. Fully summoned." There was a subtle hint of

amusement in the demon's voice. Was it *laughing* at Ivan? Unacceptable.

Ivan rose from his seat, straightening his spine. There was no time for awe. No time for hesitancy. No time for reflections on his past.

They needed to start things on the right foot. This demon was to be at his beck and call. To serve him and him alone.

"I wish to form a contract," he said firmly. "I need a weapon at my disposal."

There was a long pause. Ivan barely dared to breathe. Would the demon refuse?

But the demon spoke again, and relief flooded through him. "And your terms, human?"

This part Ivan had thought through on the drive from his brother's hideout in Maine back to his own office in the city. Ivan's problems right now were threefold.

One: A rival family from the Italians, the Carusos, were making trouble.

Two: There was a mole in Ivan's organization, leaking information to them.

And three: Ivan's control over his empire was becoming...slippery, as evidenced by the prior two issues and the actions of his wayward brethren.

The Carusos Ivan had given to Sascha and his demon to deal with, assuming they took the bait he'd so generously laid out. Which left him with his mole and the bigger problem of the state of his business.

So his terms...

"A piece of my soul," he began.

The heat in the room increased noticeably.

"Yes," purred the demon from its smoky hiding place.

The spicy scent in the smoke tickled Ivan's throat. He cleared it. "And in exchange, you aid me in strengthening my hold in New York."

"Done," the demon said quickly.

"And the contract isn't complete until…" Ivan paused. He didn't want to say this part. Hated the weakness it revealed. But he didn't have a choice, did he? "Until myself and my family are safe."

"That's two demands," the demon pointed out, nothing in its voice giving away how it felt about that.

"The two are intertwined."

A husky laugh rang out. "All right, then. I, Nix of the Demon Realm, will aid Ivan Kozlov"—Ivan startled, although he kept his reaction from showing. He'd never told the demon his last name —"in strengthening his hold in New York *and* ensure his and his family's continued safety, in exchange for a piece of his immortal soul." The column of smoke shifted and swirled, still revealing nothing. "Place your hand inside the smoke, Ivan."

Ivan walked around his desk with careful steps and stuck his arm into the column. He hissed at a sharp pinch of his wrist.

Had he just been *bitten*?

Sascha had skipped that part of his explanation.

Whatever monster lay inside the smoke held Ivan's wrist a moment longer, its thumb brushing against his skin. Ivan suppressed a shiver, wondering if another bite was coming.

And then he was released.

Ivan stepped back, trying to keep his composure as the smoke finally began to dissipate. But it was surprisingly difficult to contain the giddiness that was bubbling up inside him. What other Mafia boss in New York could claim to hold a demon under their thumb?

Not one.

Ivan would finally be allowed a moment to recoup. To act instead of react. To *breathe*. To—

Ivan blinked as the last of the smoke cleared. He stared at the demon it revealed.

What in the ever-loving *fuck*?

This demon wasn't any bigger than Sascha's seven-foot monstrosity—he wasn't even any bigger than Ivan. He'd be shorter, in fact, if not for the red horns curving out of his head.

It was...wrong. All wrong. This demon didn't look like a warrior. He looked like...like...

He looked like a *stripper*.

Or whatever the demon equivalent was. All cheekbones and plush lips and miles of leg. His skin was lavender, his eyes a glowing purple. He was wearing leather pants and a sheer shirt that revealed a chest tattoo and what were clearly barbells in his nipples. He had the longest, lushest hair Ivan had ever seen on a man, wavy and red and pulled into a high ponytail, revealing pointed ears.

And was that a *tail* swishing out from behind his legs?

The demon grinned, flashing sharp teeth, the only appropriately vicious thing about him. "Hello, Vanya," he purred, using the diminutive of Ivan's name.

And why the fuck was the demon's voice higher? What had happened to the deep rumble in the smoke?

At Ivan's continued silence, the demon's grin grew even wider. "Cat got your tongue?" He sashayed closer, and that strange spicy scent enveloped Ivan again. "Want me to loosen it for you?"

2

Nix

Dear Ivan was staring at Nix, his mouth gaping open like a fish. Poor baby. Had he really thought he was summoning a warrior demon like Kai?

That was hilarious.

And maybe it had been a little naughty of Nix to let him continue thinking that. Nix hadn't *intended* to trick him, at least not initially. He always kept the smoke column up because he needed time to assess which form to take to appeal most to his bargains. But then Ivan had requested a weapon, and Nix had realized his form didn't matter—Ivan wasn't summoning him for incubus purposes.

More was the pity, as the brother Nix had been spying on was even more appealing up close, with coloring as cold and icy as his voice. Pale-blue eyes, pale lashes, white-blond hair he kept shorter on the sides and combed neatly on top. His features were surprisingly pretty for a man who must be nearing his forties, though he filled out his suit in a way that suggested he was hiding some muscle underneath it.

And, judging by the little hitch of breath and dilation of his pupils when Nix had appeared, Ivan liked Nix's true form just fine.

For all that he only wanted Nix as a weapon.

And while Nix had been a bit naughty, so had Ivan. Really, shame on him for asking for such deliberately vague terms in his contract. Secure his empire, keep his family safe? If one read it by the letter, Ivan could keep a contracted demon at his side for a long, long time. After all, when was the family of a mafioso ever truly safe?

Any demon would have been a fool to take it.

Any demon that actually wanted to *complete* their contract, that was.

Nix, however, was in no hurry. It was positively delicious to be back in the human realm. And how enticing to have been summoned by this human in particular. How—

Oops, there he went.

Nix darted behind the desk and steered the cushy desk chair under Ivan right as the human collapsed, his pretty eyes rolling back in his head, clearly hanging on to consciousness by a thread.

Poor baby indeed. Initiating a contract did tend to take it out of a human. It was actually quite impressive that Ivan was managing to stay conscious at all. He must have a particularly strong force of will.

But Nix already knew that. He could feel it in the soul piece lodged in his chest, given to him by their bargain. And what a soul piece it was. Absolutely scrumptious, this little tidbit. Full of complex, conflicting emotions.

All soul pieces tasted slightly different—some were sweet, some were salty, some were so bitter they were hard to stomach. But this one was like a big, juicy hamburger with all the fixings.

(Not that Nix had ever *had* a hamburger. But the human commercials made them look awfully tasty.)

Ivan let out a weak gasp, and Nix focused back on the human the delicious soul piece had come from. Ivan's head was rolling on his shoulders, his chin brushing against his chest. He seemed to be having a hard time looking up, so Nix dropped onto his knees, placing his elbows on Ivan's legs and resting his chin on his folded hands.

"You're not—" Ivan began.

"A big, bad warrior demon?" Nix finished for him. "Afraid not, sweetums."

"Your voice..."

"Oh." Nix hid his grin, clearing his throat with a weak (fake) cough. "Must have been the smoke." He blinked guilelessly. "Sorry if you got the wrong impression."

"You're *small*."

Nix pinched Ivan's thigh. "I beg your fucking pardon." They were practically the same height, both of them reaching six feet at least. And if Ivan was talking about other things...well, Nix wasn't small there either.

Ivan didn't react to the pinch, just kept staring. "You —you're—"

Nix threw him a bone. "I'm an incubus."

Ivan's brow furrowed adorably. "Isn't that a type of sex demon?"

"Some would say that." Nix's lips curled into a catlike grin, and his pinching gave way to a soothing stroke. "Why, Vanyechka, you have need of one?"

Now Ivan stiffened under his touch. "I don't fuck men," he said coldly, gathering his composure from who knew where.

"Good thing I'm not a man." But Nix put his hands back under his chin. No more petting for the repressed mafioso.

"I don't fuck male demons either."

Nix pushed his lower lip out into an exaggerated pout. "More's the pity."

Was now a good time to tell Ivan he could smell desire? Probably not. Poor thing was shell-shocked enough as it was. He was just...blinking at Nix now. He seemed to do that a lot.

"Do you need water?" Nix asked him. "Or maybe some smelling salts?" It had been a while since Nix had catered to a human, and he'd never had the pleasure of one of these newer, modern models. He was a bit embarrassed to realize he was out of practice. "A massage, perhaps?" he asked hopefully.

Ivan ran a hand through his hair, mussing those perfectly coiffed strands. "How am I going to fix anything with this? With *you*?" A muscle in his jaw clenched. "We'll break the contract. I'll send you back and try again."

Nix's tail flicked with irritation, even as he tried his best not to be offended. His new bargain didn't *mean* to be hurtful. But still. "No can do, handsome," he said, clicking his tongue. "A contract is binding."

"Then I'll summon another."

Nix narrowed his eyes. *Rude.* "Only one at a time, sugar pie. Only one, full stop, actually. One summoning per lifetime."

"God*damn it.*"

Goodness. Poor Ivan was a real high-strung piece of work, wasn't he?

"Hey," Nix soothed, choosing to be the bigger and better person, despite Ivan trying to throw him out like yesterday's trash. "So I'm not a warrior. I can still help you. I'm stronger and faster than any human you'd find. And I'm impervious to human weapons. And I can do *this*." Nix shifted forms, choosing Ivan's secretary, plucking her image perfectly from Ivan's memories.

Nix couldn't read minds, exactly, but he could take certain images. Glimpses. It helped him when it came to giving a contract exactly what they desired. Exactly *who* they desired.

"Oh." Nix had expected a bit of shock, but Ivan's stunned gaze grew immediately calculating as it roamed over Nix's new, familiar form. "That's a very neat trick."

Nix preened, trying to flip his hair before he realized the secretary kept it in a high and tight bun. "Isn't it, though?"

He switched back to himself, not missing the flash of appreciation before Ivan caught himself.

Not interested in male demons? *Tell me another one, Vanya baby.*

"Now, Ivanushka." Nix settled his chin more firmly in his hands, batting his lashes up at Ivan. "Tell Nixie here all your troubles."

"That would take an eternity."

"Even better." Nix was in no rush. The more time in the human realm, the better. If he was lucky, he could milk this contract until the end of Ivan's (hopefully) very long life.

Ivan stared off at a point somewhere above Nix's head. "My father was a Mafia man."

Starting right off with the father. Nix *knew* it. He could smell daddy issues a mile away.

"He came from Russia. Built his business in New York from the ground up. Raised me to take over. My younger brother Alexei was supposed to be my second." Ooh, those were some real bitter emotions coming up with the brother. Nix jotted that down in his imaginary Ivan notebook. "My youngest brother, Sascha, was meant to...stay out of it. Stay safe. Protected."

Sascha. That was the brother who'd summoned Kai. Well, he was certainly protected now, with a warrior demon at his side.

"My father died five years ago," Ivan continued, his voice not giving away how he felt about that at all. "And I took over. Two years ago Alexei botched a deal on purpose. He ran off, leaving me out of millions of dollars and on bad terms with another family. I lost my temper. I was...harsher with our business associates than maybe I should have been."

Ivan's fingers reached out absentmindedly, and for a moment, it seemed he was going to toy with the ends of Nix's ponytail. But after a pregnant moment, he seemed to realize what he was doing and drew his hand back like he'd touched fire.

He cleared his throat. "One particular family, the Carusos, sent someone after Sascha. They stabbed him. He recovered, but...they had to have inside help—the attacker confirmed it." A twinge of real hurt and despair resonated in Ivan's soul piece, there and gone. "The Carusos will be dealt with. I expect my brother and his demon at any moment. It's the rest..." Ivan hesitated. "I don't know who to trust. How to hold on to my men."

"And letting it all go?" Nix asked because honestly, all this Mafia mess sounded like more trouble than it was worth.

"Isn't an option," Ivan answered quickly.

His voice was firm, but there was something there. Some deep pain. Nix was tempted to poke at it, but he let it go.

At least for the moment.

"Then we'll fix it," Nix said brightly. "I'm yours to use, Ivan."

Lust pulsed through the air, sharp and heady, even as Ivan's face remained completely impassive. Well, wasn't that interesting? But just as quickly, it was gone. Ivan's eyes began to droop.

He really had been staying awake out of sheer force of will, hadn't he?

Ivan slumped forward, eyes shutting completely as he lost the battle with consciousness. Nix pushed him gently back into the chair, wheeling it over behind the desk.

He hit the intercom button, modulating his voice to fit Ivan's. "No interruptions for the rest of the day."

"Yes, Mr. Kozlov," the secretary responded promptly.

And now all Nix had to do was wait.

———

IT DIDN'T TAKE NEARLY AS LONG as Nix had expected for Ivan to stir.

Strong force of will indeed.

Or such a lack of trust in his surroundings his subconscious was unwilling to remain unconscious for any extended period of time.

Or maybe a little of both.

In the meantime, Nix had explored the office. Or the whole floor, really. The office he'd been summoned in was high-ceilinged and expensive-looking with its hardwood floors and big windows, but it was...empty, for lack of a better word. There was the massive desk, sure. Ivan's chair and a few on the other side. An uncomfortable-looking leather couch. And that was mostly it. No decorations. No plants. Not a throw pillow to be found.

Like Ivan was allergic to comfort. To beauty.

There was also a fat stack of ledgers on the desk Nix had peeked through. Ivan seemed to be in charge of a number of businesses, varying in their levels of legal legitimacy. Nightclubs with gambling in the basement and drugs passing through them. Laundromats used for laundering more than just clothing. Property on the docks that gave him some serious leverage with other families wanting him to look the other way on their suspicious shipments.

A busy man indeed.

Besides the main entrance off the elevator hallway, Ivan's office had two other doors. One led to a smaller inner office with a large conference table, and another led to living quarters of sorts, containing a bathroom that was surprisingly luxurious given the austerity of the other rooms and an inner bedroom with a spare bed, some extra sets of suits, and an absurd number of locks on the door.

Clearly Ivan spent the majority of his time here. There was no one else on the floor, not even the secretary Nix had spoken to. Perhaps she was on the level below?

Nix had been tempted to go down and see her—he did so love meeting new people—but he hadn't wanted to leave Ivan unattended.

And it seemed that had been wise, as the human was rousing already. Nix hopped onto the desk in front of the chair Ivan was passed out in, crossing his legs and waiting to be noticed.

Ivan blinked blearily for a moment—looking awfully cute as he did so, like a disgruntled owl—before his features settled into their usual cool mask, distrust practically radiating off him. "What did you do to me?"

"Moi?" Nix pressed an innocent hand to his chest. "Not a thing, my dove. The contract takes it out of a person. Your body needed to recharge." At Ivan's continued suspicion, Nix gave in to the urge to roll his eyes. "I *can't* harm you, even if I wished to. The contract doesn't allow it. I can only ever act in your best interests."

There was an almost imperceptible release of tension in Ivan's body. "Right," he murmured. "And Sascha hasn't come looking for his Book yet?"

"I told your secretary not to disturb you." At Ivan's sharp look, Nix shrugged. "I didn't think you'd want anyone else to see you incapacitated. Was I wrong?"

There was a brief flash of surprise across Ivan's face, there and gone in an instant. Was it so foreign to him, to have someone else watching his back? It must have been, the touchy creature.

Nix scooted a little closer on the desk so his knee was mere breaths away from brushing into Ivan. "So what now?"

"We wait. I need Sascha and his demon for my next move."

Nix nodded seriously because that seemed to be the right thing to do. "I see."

They stared at each other for a bit. Ivan didn't seem to blink much, other than the times when he was clearly processing some sort of shock. It could have been creepy, but Nix enjoyed the intensity, especially paired with the little curlings of desire Ivan had no idea he was giving off.

How long would it take him to break? To acknowledge his attraction to Nix's form? With how much Ivan seemed to value self-control, Nix was a little worried it could be a very, very long time.

But then again, time was something Nix had an awful lot of.

Eventually Ivan spoke again. "Tell me. Why did you accept the contract if you're an incubus?"

Nix smiled guilelessly, swinging his top leg so it tapped Ivan's chair. "I like to be useful."

Ivan's hand darted out, clamping tightly around Nix's ankle, halting his movement. "Is it in my best interest to lie to me?"

Oh, he was sharp. Nix's grin grew slightly less guileless. "White lies don't count, handsome."

Ivan only stared back at him, all cold and expressionless, his fingers digging into Nix's skin. He was probably amazing at poker, as long as he didn't touch the other players.

Nix sighed, kicking his foot to break Ivan's hold and stretching out on his side on the desk, facing Ivan, placing his own head on his palm. "Maybe I was bored," he offered. "We're stuck between contracts, you know. In a place called the Void. There's nothing to do. Nothing to see." Unless spying on the human world counted as a hobby. "No one to fuck," he added pointedly.

Ivan quirked a brow. "You think we'll be fucking?" he asked, his tone suggesting it was the most preposterous concept he'd ever heard of. Like Nix had suggested they ride an ostrich straight to the moon.

Just as an example.

Nix arched his own brow. "A demon can dream, right?"

Ivan's fingers flexed. "You're lying on my ledgers."

"So I am." Nix bolted upright, just to be obliging. Maybe also to see if Ivan would flinch.

He didn't.

"Why do you have all these, anyway?" Nix asked, pushing at one of the ledgers. "Shouldn't everything be digital now?"

"They're left over from my father's time. I've been...modernizing since he passed. Though, it's a slow-as-fuck process. I'm going to have Cooper digitize them."

"Who's Cooper?" Nix asked quickly, much more interested in the people in Ivan's world than the business. "Is he hot?"

He didn't miss the flash of annoyance on Ivan's face, there and gone as quickly as his surprise had been.

Ooh, was Nix's mafioso feeling possessive?

"My cousin," Ivan said coldly. "Also my employee. He takes care of the...digital side of things."

"And is he h—"

"Did you miss the part where he's my *cousin*," Ivan snapped, finally letting some of that temper out in his voice.

Nix grinned at him. "Testy, testy." And no wonder, with those massive bags under Ivan's eyes. Nix wagged a finger. "You need real sleep."

Ivan ignored him.

"I saw a bedroom," Nix pressed. "Sleep while we wait for Sascha. We can tell your people to let us know if he arrives."

Ivan leaned back in his chair, pinching at the bridge of his nose. "And how am I going to explain you?"

"Tell them I'm your new personal assistant," Nix said, placing a good amount of emphasis on the *personal* part of things.

"You?" Ivan's gaze roamed over Nix, hot as a brand. "Looking like that?"

Nix glanced down at himself. "And what's wrong with the way I look?"

Ivan's eyes flicked to Nix's shirt, then back down to his leather pants. "Flamboyance doesn't play well with the Bratva."

Nix narrowed his eyes at him. Sure, he could shift forms at will, if it was really an issue. But he didn't want to—not for any extended period of time. Ivan had accepted the contract with Nix as he was (and yes, Nix had tricked him, but so what?), and Nix couldn't remember the last time he'd had a contract where he'd gotten to be himself. Ivan couldn't take that away from him already. "Lucky you're the boss, then, isn't it? What you say goes, isn't that right?"

Ivan's fingers flexed again. "That's right."

The lust tendrils in the air thickened, as did the tension in the room. *Oh, Ivan. Babycakes. Boss man. You're too easy.*

Nix licked his lips exaggeratedly. "We're all just here to serve you, aren't we?" he crooned, leaning closer. Close enough to smell Ivan's cologne, some intriguing scent with a peppery finish.

And just like that, the lust in the air dissipated. Ivan's expression shuttered, all the heat leaving his gaze. "You're toying with me," he accused flatly.

Nix fought the urge to pout. Grumpy much?

Definitely in need of a nap.

"I'm an incubus," he said easily. He wasn't going to be scared off by a little mood swing. "We like to tease. You can handle that, can't you? Handle little ol' me?"

"You're laying it on a bit thick."

"I *like* it thick."

Ivan's lips twitched.

Holy crap. Had Nix almost gotten a smile?

Ivan stood from his chair, not even giving Nix a moment to appreciate his victory. "I'll sleep. You'll keep watch."

Nix tossed him a salute. "Sir, yes, sir."

"And if Sascha comes, you'll wake me immediately."

Nix hopped off the desk, trailing after him. "How shall I wake you? With a kiss?"

Ivan stopped abruptly, so much so that Nix bumped into his back. He turned and offered Nix an impressive glare. "May I remind you, you're here to help me, not seduce me."

Nix grinned at him. "Why not both?"

Honestly, Nix had no idea what he was doing at this point. He was pushing too hard, and he knew it. And as a master of seduction, he knew better. But Ivan's reactions were so varied and strange—hot one moment, cold the next—it was like Nix couldn't help poking at him.

Bad incubus, he chided himself. *Very naughty.*

Ivan stepped away from him and stripped off his suit jacket, tossing it onto the leather couch. Yes, those were definitely some muscles lurking under that button-down. Nix resisted the urge to lick his lips again, this time for real.

"It's you who couldn't handle me," Ivan told Nix coolly, loosening his tie.

He strode across the office to the door to the inner bedroom, Nix hot on his tail.

Then Ivan shut the door right in Nix's face.

See? Hot and cold. A poor demon could get a serious case of whiplash.

Still, Nix grinned at the wood in his face. "I've handled worse," he told the door. "And I managed just fine."

3

Ivan

Ivan woke up where he almost always woke up—the spare bedroom in his office building. He was as familiar with the bare wall in front of his eyes as he was the back of his hand. And it might not have been a five-star hotel, but it was much preferable to his father's old habit of napping on a cot in his warehouse.

Maybe sleeping poorly had been part of why the old man had been such a miserable son of a bitch. Maybe not.

It was best not to try to figure it out. Nothing good came from going down that road.

What had woken Ivan up? Not his alarm.

Ivan turned away from the wall he was facing and was met with glowing purple eyes. Only years of "training" as a child not to flinch—not to show any sign of weakness—kept Ivan from shooting up in bed.

Right, he'd summoned a demon yesterday. An incubus, as if he had any use for one of those. An incubus who was staring at him, very, very close.

Weren't incubi the demons that preyed on sleeping humans?

Ivan let himself blink once. Twice. His heart rate was elevated, but that wasn't something another person would be able to tell. "What are you doing, exactly?" he asked, pleased with how measured and calm his voice came out.

Nix was kneeling at his bedside, arms folded over the side of the bed with his chin resting on top. Ivan turning over had placed their faces only a hair's breadth apart.

Nix's slow grin emphasized his plush lips, but Ivan kept his gaze determinedly on his eyes. "Watching you sleep, my liege."

"Why?"

If the smile was dangerous, the pout was lethal. "Because I got bored."

"Sascha should be here soon." Ivan did sit up now. Careful. Controlled. "And I need to freshen up."

What he needed was to get away from those lips. That face. That spiced scent.

He rose from the bed and strode to the bathroom, busying himself with becoming human again. He brushed his teeth, splashed water on his face, put his hair to rights.

He returned to the bedroom with his heart rate under control and his sense of self securely back in place. Incubi were designed to be tempting, weren't they? But that didn't mean Ivan needed to be tempted. He was stronger than that.

Nix was sitting on the bed now, long legs crossed, his tail flicking back and forth. It looked almost like a lion's tail, long and lightly furred, with a tuft of soft-looking hair at the end. Except unlike a lion's tail, it was red.

It was...distracting.

As were the legs.

Jesus fucking Christ, what was wrong with Ivan's brain? He didn't fuck men. Not once, not ever.

But he'd never met a man who looked like Nix.

It was...confusing him. The long hair. The pretty face. The *tail*. The strange mix of it all was messing with Ivan's brain; that was all it was. It had been too long since Ivan had taken someone.

He clearly needed to fuck something.

Isn't fucking an incubus's specialty?

Ivan dashed the thought from his mind. He had enough trouble holding on to his organization without adding men to his repertoire. There was already Alexei and Sascha, and Ivan knew how his men spoke about them when they thought he couldn't hear.

More so about Sascha, since Alexei would have been able to beat them all into the ground, the massive fuck.

Still, straight was simpler. Straight was...well, straight was just what Ivan *was*. He liked fucking women. He always had.

He ignored the incubus and his legs and tail, making his way to the freestanding clothing rack that held his suits. He flicked through his shirts, loosening his tie and unbuttoning his top two buttons as he did so.

Nix stayed right where he was.

Ivan finally shot him a glance. "*Well?*"

"Yes, Vanya?" Nix asked, all innocence. He did that a lot for someone who was supposed to be on Ivan's side. Lied through false affect. Or omission. Or just directly to Ivan's face.

"I'm changing," Ivan told him.

"Mm." Nix's tail flicked out again. Once. Twice.

"Do you *mind*?"

"Not at all." Nix rose from the bed and sauntered—had Ivan ever met anyone before who actually sauntered?—Ivan's way, that fucking tail swishing behind him. Ivan expected him to continue past and through the door, but Nix stopped right in front of him. Close.

Too close.

Before Ivan could tell him off, strong hands were delving into Ivan's hair and scratching at his scalp with a gentle, soothing touch. The incubus had sharp talons at the ends of his fingers—it shouldn't have felt good. It should have hurt.

It didn't.

It took all Ivan's self-control not to close his eyes and groan. How long had it been since someone had touched him like this? It wasn't a kind of familiarity he allowed his random fucks.

But just as quickly as they'd surprised him, the hands were gone.

"There," Nix said with satisfaction.

Ivan blinked dazedly at him. Had Nix only been...messing up his hair?

What the fuck was this creature's game?

"Listen, demon," he started harshly.

"Listen, *Nix*," the incubus had the gall to correct.

"Listen, Nix." Nix had a long, elegant neck, and Ivan wanted nothing more than to wrap his hands around it and squeeze. Would he listen then, with Ivan's tight grip around his throat? "You are here to serve me, aren't you? Mine to summon. Mine to command. *My* demon." Ivan wasn't sure the point of that last part, but it felt right coming out of his mouth.

Nix didn't look chastised. He looked...intrigued. He trailed his finger down Ivan's chest. "Mm, tell me more about how I'm yours, baby."

"I—that's—"

The intercom at Ivan's desk went off, loud enough to be heard in the bedroom. "Sascha's on his way up," the security guard at the front desk reported.

Ivan would deal with this—this *insubordination* later. "Stay here," he told Nix before making his way into his main office, taking a seat behind his desk.

Sascha arrived a moment later, dressed in a way that was clearly meant to be a "fuck off" to Ivan's old constraints. Instead of his old black suits, he was wearing white and baby blue, and gold fucking jewelry.

He looked so similar to Ivan—the same pale coloring, with similar refined features—only younger and smaller. Softer. Was it the softness in him that had made their father choose to protect rather than torment for the first time, when it came to his children? Or had it just been the unlucky happenstance of the order of their birth?

Close behind Sascha came the demon brute, his horns and blue skin nowhere to be found.

He was still a huge fucker though.

"Sascha," Ivan greeted. "I expected you ages ago."

Sascha, predictable as ever, immediately started with demands. "We need the Book, Ivan."

Anger flared, hot and bitter in Ivan's veins. It was so like his baby brother, to have a weapon at his disposal and not think to share it with Ivan. To not think their family might need every bit of protection it could get. He was selfish, just like Alexei.

"Why?" Ivan asked. "To summon more demons, perhaps? Maybe give one to Alexei? Then the two of you can really fuck me over."

Sascha threw his hands up like the spoiled brat he was. "God, Ivan, what the fuck? You really think we're conspiring against you? When have I *ever* wanted even a piece of your empire? You're such a lunatic."

"Am I? I had two brothers who were supposed to be at my side. Now I have none."

"Well, maybe you should take a long, hard look at the way you *treat* people."

Ivan sighed. It was always like this with his brothers. As if feelings trumped safety. As if they hadn't been raised in the same dangerous world Ivan had. (Never mind that Sascha hadn't, really. Had been sent away to school for most of it. He still knew enough to know better.)

Sascha thought Ivan power-hungry without ever considering that Ivan's *power* was all that kept him from being shot down in the street.

Their father's rise to the top hadn't come without its costs, and one of those was a host of enemies that would be eager to bring any one of the Kozlov children down.

"I don't have time for this," Ivan told him.

"You never do!" Sascha yelled. Predictably, he began chastising Ivan for being the way he was. The way he'd always been. "What would it take for you to just chill out for a few seconds and act like a real brother and not a controlling asshole?"

Ivan didn't have an answer for that. He might be controlling, but he'd been that way for a long, long time. It was too late for him to change, and Sascha should know that by now.

And then there was Nix's voice, sultry as ever. "Personally I think he needs to get laid, but that's just me. I could be biased."

So much for staying in the inner bedroom.

Nix was...human-appearing now. Like Kai. Except Nix didn't look like a brute in his human form. He looked like sin incarnate. And he was wearing sunglasses indoors, for some reason.

Kai growled at his appearance. "Incubus."

Ivan was distracted, not at all himself, as Kai and Nix bickered (apparently the demons knew each other), Sascha wide-eyed and flustered by Nix, mentioning something about a bond.

All of it was white noise until Ivan saw Kai's hand around Nix's throat.

Rage, swift and sure, had him rising to his feet and snapping out, "Get your hands off my demon."

Just because *he* wanted to wring Nix's neck didn't mean anyone else was allowed to.

But apparently Nix didn't need his protection. He slid out of Kai's hold like nothing but his own will had kept him there in the first place. And then Sascha was suggesting privacy, and Nix and Kai were heading to the inner office, Nix agreeable to Sascha's request in a way he had yet to be with Ivan.

Leaving Ivan with Sascha.

———

"You know I love you, right?"

Ivan clenched his jaw, taking his eyes off the door to the room Nix had disappeared into.

Of course that was the first thing Sascha told Ivan. Of course he thought the emotion behind it all would trump the rest. That love would fix what was broken.

Love is a weakness, his father's voice taunted. *And you know what happens to weak men?*

It wasn't Sascha's fault, exactly. Their father had raised him differently—the pampered baby, exempt from the life that ruled the rest of them. It was something Ivan still didn't understand, with his father's disdain of softer emotions. But maybe in the end he was nothing more than a hypocrite. Maybe he really had loved Sascha more than his two older sons, had wanted something better for him than the painful, jagged lessons in brutality he'd given them all their lives.

"It's okay if you can't say it back," Sascha told him with a sad smile. "But I didn't summon Kai to hurt you."

"I'm aware."

"Then why did you steal the Book and summon your own demon ten seconds after discovering him?"

Why did Ivan even need to explain this? "I have a mole in my organization," he said evenly. "A mob war on the horizon, a loose cannon of a middle brother, and an oblivious younger one."

Did that make it clear enough?

But Sascha focused on the wrong words, as usual. "I'm not oblivious," he argued. Ivan gave him a pointed look, and Sascha conceded, "Okay, sometimes. But that's the way you and Papa molded me. I have a business degree, you know. I could be an asset, if you'd let me."

Except Sascha still didn't get the *point*. Whether the summoning was intentional or not, Sascha had kept it from Ivan. Even knowing there were men after their family, men who had ordered Sascha stabbed and would no doubt like to do worse.

It was just another reminder Ivan was doing it all alone.

And yet Sascha claimed he wasn't oblivious? That he could handle being an asset to Ivan's business? That suddenly—out of nowhere—he wanted to be useful?

Sascha let out a big sigh, like Ivan was the problem. "I know our family messed you up. Papa...being Papa. Mom leaving."

Ivan looked away. He knew better than to touch that lie. He knew what it would do to Sascha. And still he found himself saying, "Our mother didn't leave." He couldn't help but laugh at Sascha's clueless expression. "I thought Alexei would have told you by now," Ivan said bitterly. Those two had always been thick as thieves, hadn't they? "Our mother didn't leave," he said again. "Our father had her killed."

Sascha's continued confusion only stoked Ivan's sudden rage. Had Alexei really not known? Had their father kept him in the dark?

Why had Ivan been the only one to bear this fucking burden?

Why was it always only him?

"She intended to leave," Ivan explained coolly, keeping his anger contained, letting it burn at his insides rather than show on his face. "She was going to take you and Alexei with her." Another bitter laugh escaped him. "Not me. I suppose she thought at eleven years old, I was already a lost cause. And while our father might have been willing to let *her* go, he wasn't willing to lose his sons. He ordered a hit."

He could still remember his father showing him the body, Sergei's hand heavy on Ivan's shoulder. *"This is what happens to those who run, Vanya."*

Across from him, Sascha's breathing turned jagged. He was panicking, not as adept at controlling his reactions as Ivan had always been forced to be.

Ivan sat still through it, watching his youngest brother gasp and choke. He remained still and calm. Nonreactive. That was the only way to be.

Eventually Sascha seemed to get a hold of his breathing. "And Alexei knows this?"

"I always assumed he did." Ivan shrugged. He'd never discussed it with Alexei point-blank. Nothing good would have come of it. "Maybe I assumed wrong."

Sascha cried some more, and Ivan waited it out.

"Okay," Sascha finally said, meeting Ivan's eyes. "Okay. So I guess the question is, How like our father are you going to be, Ivan?"

You need to be exactly like me, Ivan, if you want to survive. If you want those brothers of yours to survive with you.

Ivan didn't answer him.

But apparently Sascha didn't need an answer, and Ivan forced himself to focus as Sascha began to list his demands. He wanted to stay in Maine—wanted to get away from Ivan, more like. He wanted to run one of the legitimate businesses—not get his hands dirty with the rest, of course. And he wanted Ivan to visit only if he acted like someone other than himself. Human. Caring. Brotherly.

Finally, they got to the point of it all. To the Carusos and the meeting Ivan had scheduled that would allow Sascha's demon to do away with key members of the family.

When Sascha realized Ivan had anticipated his arrival, he gave Ivan an accusatory look. "You planned this, didn't you? For me to bring Kai and fix it for you."

At least Sascha was finally paying attention to the game.

"Maybe I've grown tired of cleaning up our family's messes all on my own," Ivan told him.

"*Your* messes."

"Alexei started it," Ivan pointed out. It had been Alexei running like a coward that had been the turning point here. How exactly was that Ivan's mess?

"Alexei just wanted out," Sascha told him, defending their middle brother like he always did. "That's all he ever wanted. To have his own life."

Who the fuck didn't want that? And why did his brothers think wanting something meant it could be a reality—without consequence, without bloodshed? "Some of us don't have that luxury," Ivan told Sascha.

Maybe it was the residual fatigue from having summoned a demon, but the rest of it was hazy. Ivan gave Sascha the Book so he could bond with his demon, whatever that meant. Kai burst in from the inner room and acted as if Sascha were a helpless, wounded puppy Ivan had kicked.

And then they were gone.

Nix turned around from where he'd been yelling after Kai. Teasing him about their time in the Void together. "Leaving without a goodbye? Does this mean you don't want to spend another eternity together? I'm hurt, Kai!"

He really did tease everyone, then.

But Nix's grin dropped quickly when he caught sight of Ivan's face. Which was funny because Ivan's face was a blank fucking slate. "What's wrong?"

Ivan tapped his fingers on his desk. "Why would anything be wrong?"

Nix narrowed those striking purple eyes. "I have a piece of your soul in my chest, Ivan. I can feel when you're hurting."

Ivan grimaced. That was...inconvenient.

Or was it? The demon was obligated to help him, bound by the contract between them. For once, maybe it didn't matter if Ivan showed his cards a bit.

What a novel thought.

"I told him our father murdered our mother."

Nix cocked his head. "And was that the truth?"

It was a good question. Ivan couldn't help but smile. At least the incubus was no fool. "It was the truth. She was going to take my brothers and run."

Again, Nix heard what was unspoken. "Not you?" he asked immediately.

"Not me."

"Mommy issues," Nix murmured, tapping his finger against his lips.

Ivan almost laughed. "My father murdered my mother in cold blood and you're calling it 'mommy issues'?"

"Yeah," Nix said with a shrug. "Your walls are miiiiiles high, and now I know why."

"The walls were there before she was killed," Ivan found himself saying.

Nix nodded knowingly. "Mommy *and* daddy issues. Called it."

Who the fuck was this creature? Was it a demon thing, that Ivan could tell Nix one of the worst things in his past and Nix could take it in stride? *Tease* him about it?

Ivan refused to be charmed by it. "I regret summoning you," he said.

Nix gave a bright, high laugh. "No, you don't. You're just in a foul mood."

"I'm always in a foul mood."

Nix cocked his hip, giving Ivan a once-over. "Even when you fuck?"

"Especially then," Ivan snapped.

His words didn't even make sense, but Nix grinned and gave an exaggerated shiver, as if Ivan had said something delightful. "Then, Vanya, baby, you've been fucking the wrong people."

Silence was the only acceptable answer. Ivan kept his mouth shut.

Nix's inspection of him grew appraising. "You're drooping like a wilted flower. When did you last eat? Don't humans need food to survive?"

Ivan grabbed his phone off his desk, losing interest in the conversation. He'd been distracted for days now, and there was real work to do. Calls to make, at the very least. "We can have Tara order something," he said absently.

"Mm, no."

Ivan looked up from his phone. "No?" he repeated.

"You have a home, yes?" Nix asked. "Somewhere that isn't this depressingly bare office?"

Ivan almost gave him another smile for the audacity. *Almost.* "This office cost quite a bit of money to renovate, you know."

Nix waved a hand at the walls. "And you couldn't have sprung for a painting or two? A vase of flowers, perhaps? Either way, I don't want to be here anymore." He clasped his hands to his chest, fluttering his lashes. "Take me home, big boy?"

Ivan should refuse, if only to show Nix he couldn't be pushed around. But he was...tired. Still foggy. And he should make an appearance at the apartment every now and again, if only to remind the building staff who paid their bills. "I'll need to work still."

Why was he even telling Nix that? It made it sound like he was asking permission.

"Perfect." Nix clapped once and then began walking out of the office, clearly expecting Ivan to follow. "You can show me the ropes."

Ivan had a feeling he'd lost his way somewhere. That their roles had been switched somehow. Nix certainly wasn't acting subservient, not in the least. Ivan should put a stop to this, yes? Remind Nix who was in charge?

He really should.

Ivan stood from his desk and followed the demon.

4

Nix

As Nix slid into the town car, Ivan's driver's eyes widened comically in the rearview mirror.

Nix flicked his ponytail over his shoulder, treating the man to a sultry smile as Ivan joined him in the back seat. The driver was somewhere in his late sixties, perhaps, with deep lines etched into his sun-weathered skin. "Well, hello, handsome," Nix purred. "What's your name?"

Ivan's hand shot out, settling tightly on Nix's thigh.

A warning? Nix raised a brow. "I can't say hello?"

Mr. Grumpy Pants didn't answer him, addressing the driver instead. "Oleg. Eyes forward."

"Yes, sir." The driver—Oleg, apparently—dutifully shifted his gaze back to the road, gliding the car onto the busy street.

The slightly acrid scent of fear wafted back from the front and settled on the leather seats. Nix leaned in close to Ivan, murmuring in his ear, "What an intimidating master you are."

Ivan's grip on his thigh tightened. It might have been painful, if

Nix were human. He might have been into it even if it were. Ivan seemed to think he was cowing Nix into submission, but the silly beast was just turning Nix on.

"This is my new assistant, Oleg," Ivan said coolly, as if he wasn't practically clawing into Nix. "You'll be seeing him around."

Nix leaned forward as far as Ivan's restricting grip would allow. "His new *personal* assistant," he amended. "Pleasure to meet you. Don't worry, I don't bite. Not like our boss man here."

Ivan pressed the button to raise the partition, separating them from the driver.

Nix turned to toss him a pout, only to pause as Ivan dropped his head back against the seat, his eyes closing with a deep sigh. It was a surprisingly vulnerable position, his neck stretched and bare. Nix had a feeling not many people saw him this way.

He wondered why he was allowed.

The answer came to him immediately. *Because the contract keeps you from hurting him. He has a guarantee you're safe.*

Ivan was clearly someone who'd been raised since birth to believe the other shoe would drop at any moment, and it would guide a knife into his back when it did. Nix had overheard enough of Ivan's conversation with his brother to know things were fraught there. What had Sascha called him? A controlling asshole. A lunatic.

But of course, if Ivan really *did* have a mole, then he'd only been proven right in his paranoia.

And then there was the whole mother thing. Murdered by the father? Big yikes. The whole situation made Nix happy to be a demon. Demon parents—if you could call them that—procreated, birthed, and scattered to the winds once their youngling was self-sufficient. Mated pairs would stay together, but they didn't keep their spawn with them.

So Nix didn't have any fraught family politics to mess with his head. Which made him the perfect person to help dear Vanya—he had no baggage of his own to get in the way.

He studied Ivan's face, cool and composed even at rest. The bruising under his eyes was still there. It wasn't dark enough to be wholly unattractive, but it definitely betrayed some fatigue. He had a few lines too, although not as deeply etched as Oleg's. Frown lines on his forehead. Not the telltale crow's-feet of the happy and well adjusted.

Ivy-poo wasn't doing much smiling, was he?

"How old are you?" Nix asked.

"I turned forty in January," Ivan answered without opening his eyes. He hadn't removed his hand from Nix's thigh, though his grip had loosened.

Did Ivan even notice it was still there?

Touch-starved. Majorly. Nix didn't need to be an incubus to diagnose that much.

Nix twisted to face him fully, careful to keep his leg where it was (he didn't want to risk dislodging that poor, searching hand), propping an elbow on the leather interior and resting his head on his fist. "And what did you do to celebrate?"

"Got very, very drunk."

Ivan would have done it alone, Nix realized immediately. He wouldn't have wanted to let himself be that undone in front of any other people.

And since Ivan was being so forthcoming...

"Why do you care if I flirt with your driver?"

Ivan's hand clenched. "You're supposed to be my assistant. Your actions reflect on me."

Nix clucked his tongue. "You're the boss. What do you care what your driver thinks about you?"

"Appearances are important," Ivan answered immediately, with the rehearsed tone of one repeating someone else's words.

"True power lies in not caring what anyone else thinks," Nix countered.

Ivan's eyes opened the tiniest crack. "Did you see that embroidered on a throw pillow somewhere?"

"No throw pillows in the Void." Nix pursed his lips in mock disappointment. "Or in your dreary office, for that matter. Is your apartment equally dreary?"

Ivan's eyes closed again. "Yes."

"Mm. Can't wait."

There it was again. At the very corner of Ivan's lips. A little twitch. Nix knew it—there was definitely a sense of humor hiding in there somewhere.

Deep, *deep* in there.

Traffic kept them in the town car for quite a while, even though they didn't seem to be covering much distance, but Nix let Ivan rest peacefully for the remainder of it. No doubt he was going to get straight to work once they got to their destination. He'd said as much, and Ivan didn't seem the type to make idle threats.

Nix was a bit sad to leave the car when they got to their destination, as it meant Ivan's hand finally slid off his leg. It wasn't like Ivan had even been doing anything fun with it, but the weight of it had been...nice.

Maybe Ivan wasn't the only one touch-starved.

They waltzed into the apartment building like they owned the place. (Ivan might actually own the place, for that matter.) The doorman nodded at Ivan respectfully, and Nix didn't miss the bulge of the gun holster under his jacket.

Ivan's gaze slid over to the man. "My assistant will be coming in and out," he said, presumably talking about Nix. "Don't give him any trouble."

"Yes, sir."

Nix gave the man a salute for good measure and was rewarded by Ivan grabbing his upper arm tightly, tugging him deeper inside.

Nix grinned at him. "You're very grabby, did you know that?"

Ivan dropped Nix's arm like it had burned him.

"I like it." Nix sidled up close, grabbing Ivan's arm instead. He was given a mighty glare, but if glares were enough to subdue him, Kai would have managed it centuries ago.

Ivan pressed the button for the top floor in the elevator. The penthouse. Of course. It was probably the only apartment on that level, wasn't it? Just like his lonely office.

Ivan's phone buzzed, and he slid it out of his suit jacket pocket, replacing it immediately without answering, but not before Nix saw the name.

"Who's Sergei?" he asked, shaking Ivan's arm lightly. "Is he ho—"

"My father's right-hand man," Ivan snapped. "Mine now."

There was that surge of bitterness again, strong enough to fill the entire elevator.

"You know who your mole is, don't you?" Nix asked softly.

"You're very perceptive," Ivan said coolly, his tone controlled once more. "Is that a sex worker thing?"

"You're awfully mean when you're cornered," Nix countered as the elevator dinged, announcing they'd reached the top. He shifted back into his demon form, arching a brow at Ivan. "Is that a trauma thing?"

Ivan shook Nix's arm off and stepped out of the elevator. Sure enough, it opened directly into a large apartment.

The place reminded Nix of Ivan's office. High ceilings, big windows, steel beams and concrete, and not a piece of unnecessary decoration to be found.

"I don't know," Ivan said after a moment, and it took Nix longer than it should have to realize he was answering Nix's earlier question. "I suspect it is."

Ivan was already turning away before Nix could say anything

in response. "Explore as you like. I'll be in my office. Don't interrupt."

———

ONCE AGAIN NIX found himself exploring a large, luxurious, *empty* space.

Seriously, what did Ivan have against a little decor here and there? Had his father used an interior decorator as the hit man when he'd had the mother killed? Had her bludgeoned with a painting? Ordered her suffocated with a throw pillow?

Okay, well, those were dark musings. But that was Ivan's fault. If he'd had some fresh-cut flowers to lighten the place up, maybe Nix wouldn't be quite so affected by the doom and gloom of it all.

The apartment was spacious but all one level. The living room housed a large pure-white couch—and there was no greater sign that someone didn't *use* their couch than making it such an unforgiving color—across from a TV Nix couldn't figure out the remote to. The kitchen was a chrome nightmare with all the modern appliances but no ingredients to use them for. The larger of the two bedrooms had a king-size bed that clearly hadn't been slept in in days. And the presumed guest bedroom was perfectly made up, with guest toiletries that had never been opened.

It was like Ivan had paid top dollar for the best of the best and then never used any of it.

Nix could already guess the office Ivan had shut himself into was the most frequented room in the house.

Nix did have slightly better luck with the en suite bathroom attached to the larger bedroom. There was a shiny tub that had clearly rarely—if ever—been frequented, but the shower was where Nix found the source of Ivan's scent. It wasn't cologne, after all, but soap. A bar of soap with some Russian-sounding name and a peppery finish.

Nix sniffed at it, getting lost in a little fantasy of his handsome Vanya naked and soaped up in the shower.

But alas, Ivan was too hard at work for such things.

Nix returned the soap and wandered back over to the closed door of Ivan's office, walking back and forth in front of it while he waited for his contract to get over his hissy fit.

The human hadn't eaten any food, either, though he'd promised to. Naughty man.

Actually, Nix was feeling a bit peckish himself. The soul piece in his chest technically sustained him, but it had been an awfully long time since he'd had a proper dose of lust. Ivan's little repressed tendrils hardly cut it, tasty as they were.

Nix needed some full-blown desire to sate his appetite.

Or maybe not needed but wanted.

Po-tay-to, po-tah-to.

His pacing in front of Ivan's office door was interrupted by Ivan's voice ringing out, clear even through the heavy wood. "Stop that."

Nix stuck his tongue out at the door. "I'm not doing anything."

"I can see the shadow of your feet moving in front of my door."

"Oh, I'm sorry, are my 'foot shadows' bothering you?" Nix asked, as bitchy as could be.

But Ivan, impervious to sarcasm as well as hunger, only answered, in all apparent seriousness, "Yes."

"Then can I come in?"

There was a pause, then a terse, "Fine."

Nix didn't wait for a retraction. He threw open the door and sauntered in, finding Ivan seated at an exact replica of his desk in the office, right down to the office chair he was seated in. The only difference was a lack of big old ledgers in front of him.

Nix cocked a hip against the desk. "What are you doing in here anyway?"

Ivan leaned back in his chair, pinching at the bridge of his nose. "Getting things in order for Sascha and Kai's rush on the Carusos tonight. I want men in place in case the remnants of the family try to retaliate. But my men can't know *why* they're in place yet."

"Because of your pesky mole," Nix surmised.

"Precisely."

It sounded like Ivan had things under control, so Nix changed the subject to where he wanted it. He gave Ivan an alluring pout. "I'm feeling peckish, master."

Ivan didn't react to Nix's "master." Maybe he was becoming immune to the teasing. "There's surely something in the kitchen."

Nix shook his head. "One: There surely *isn't*. And two: I don't eat human food."

A glint of real curiosity shone through Ivan's fatigue, there and gone in a flash. "What do you survive on, then?"

Nix leaned in closer. "Think about it, Vanya, baby," he purred. "I'm an incubus."

"You survive off sex?" Ivan asked, sounding skeptical.

"Desire," Nix corrected.

"And you need that," Ivan said flatly. "To live."

Always so suspicious. He was acting like Nix was lying.

Which Nix sort of was.

"Okay, technically your soul piece keeps me *alive*," Nix told him with an eye roll. "But it's not the same. And I get terribly grumpy if I'm not satisfied." He widened his eyes. "You wouldn't want to leave me unsatisfied, would you?"

Ivan tapped his fingers on the desk. "What are you proposing?"

"Where do you go to get your rocks off?"

Since Nix was waiting for it, he caught the images right away. Dark clubs. Dingy gambling basements. Bleached blonde hair and tight, short dresses. And an especially intriguing little flash of Ivan in his town car, his hand up someone's skirt while the driver kept his eyes straight ahead.

Nix cocked a brow, fighting a smile. "Really, Ivan? Bottle blonde divorcées? Isn't that a bit cliché?"

The images shut off in an instant. "It's easy," Ivan said simply.

It was incredibly hard not to smirk. "I'm sure it is," Nix murmured. He straightened from the desk. "Take me to one of your clubs, then."

"No."

The refusal didn't exactly surprise Nix, but the speed of it did. "Why not?"

"You're *my* demon, aren't you?" Ivan asked, his voice possessive even as his expression stayed flat, giving nothing away. "So you stay with me. At my side. You're not fucking anyone else during our contract, no matter how...peckish you may get."

"Jealous, Vanyechka?"

Ivan's eyes narrowed. "Don't be dense."

Dense, was he?

"Fine," Nix snapped, losing a bit of his own temper. "Then I'll use *you*."

He darted around the desk and slid onto Ivan's lap, straddling his thighs.

"What are you doing?" Ivan's surprise didn't show outwardly, but Nix could hear his heart rate pick up. It had been the same when Nix had surprised Ivan awake the day before—the human's raised heartbeat the only sign of his surprise. That was some iron-clad self-control Ivan had going on.

Nix wanted to shatter it.

He put on his most plaintive voice, gazing into Ivan's icy eyes. "I'm hungry, master."

The slightest shudder went through Ivan's body. *There*, Nix thought with satisfaction. *Not so immune after all.*

"I'm not fucking you," Ivan told him, though he made no move to push Nix off his lap.

"I told you. It's about desire. It doesn't have to be sex." Nix leaned in close, whispering into Ivan's ear, "Think about your blondes."

"I can't think about them when you're on top of me."

Oh, Ivan. Baby. Did he even know how that sounded?

Nix's lips curled into a catlike grin. "Then think of me. Or think of nothing. Just feel, hm? Close your eyes. Let your demon do the heavy lifting."

He half expected to be tossed off—and not in the fun way—but Ivan surprised him, closing his eyes. Nix closed his as well—reluctant as he was to take his eyes off Ivan's handsome face—leaning back and focusing in on those little tendrils of desire pulsing from Ivan's core. A few more than usual had appeared when Ivan had been remembering his past dalliances, but they'd multiplied considerably when Nix had climbed on top of him.

Nix fed them with his own energy.

"What are you doing?" Ivan asked, his voice rough and low.

"Shh." Nix shifted in place, enough to feel that Ivan was hardening underneath him. It would have been *so* delicious to grind down on that bulge. But even Nix knew that would be pressing his luck. He'd be good.

Sort of.

Nix leaned in close again, breathing in the desire he'd stoked. Now that he'd coaxed a little more out, strengthened what was there, it was all feeding on itself, arousal begetting more arousal.

And fuck, did arousal smell good on Ivan.

Nix hummed, running his nose along Ivan's neck, drinking it all in. Ivan's hands landed on his hips, locking him in place.

Nix grinned at the touch. "Tell me, master, how long has it been since you've fucked?"

Ivan's answer was husky. "Too long."

"Poor baby." Nix nosed along Ivan's chin. "I bet you're vicious in bed."

Ivan's eyes shot open, narrowing. "I'm not a monster. I don't hurt my partners."

Nix hummed. "You could hurt me a little. I wouldn't mind."

Nix's human definitely needed a healthier outlet for all that pent-up aggression, and Nix wasn't opposed to being the recipient.

Ivan's hands tightened on his hips, and Nix purred, "Just like that. As hard as you like. I won't break."

Images flashed at Nix again, but they weren't of the blondes this time. There was Ivan, fucking Nix over that horrid white couch in the living room. Nix on his knees, sucking Ivan off under his desk. Nix in Ivan's bed, stretched out on his stomach, ass tilted upward.

Nix breathed in deep, practically intoxicated by the rush of desire. He nuzzled even closer, until his lips were on Ivan's neck, his hands buried deep in Ivan's hair.

Ivan groaned.

Nix rocked gently in his lap, testing, beyond thrilled when Ivan rocked back up against him. That was it. That was *it*.

He moaned, latching onto Ivan's neck and sucking hard. Nix wanted to get in there. Inside Ivan's mind, inside his skin. To bathe in all the complex deliciousness of his soul. Forget subsisting on a mere little piece—Nix would take the whole fucking thing.

Ivan was growing even harder underneath him, forming a bulge that promised all kinds of goodness. Would he let Nix take him in hand, stroke him to completion right at this very desk? Ivan could use the release, and Nix wouldn't even ask for an orgasm of his own. He'd be good. He'd be so very, very good.

A buzzing sound broke through his fog.

Nix froze. Ivan froze.

There it was again. Ivan's phone.

Nix's tasty mouthful jerked away, Ivan leaning back and away from his touch. But Nix wasn't pushed off just yet. Ivan held him there, on his lap, staring at him while his chest heaved with haggard breaths. His pale hair was mussed, and a dark bruise was already forming on his neck.

Nix wanted to kiss him. He couldn't, could he?

Fuck. *Fuck.* He'd been so *close* to a real meal.

Still, it was a lot further than he would have expected. He'd need to take his victories where he could get them.

Ivan's breaths steadied faster than Nix would have liked. "I need to take this," he said, his hands finally releasing Nix's hips.

"Of course," Nix agreed, his voice throaty and low.

He shifted off Ivan's lap slowly, and Ivan's gaze dropped immediately to Nix's bulge—impressive in its own right, and incredibly obvious in his tight leather pants.

Nix grinned widely, patting Ivan's shoulder before he sauntered toward the door. "Thanks for the snack, boss. It was very, *very* tasty."

5

Ivan

Ivan slammed his phone down on his desk, hanging up the thousandth call in however many hours. It was an insufferable task he shouldn't have been bothering with in the first place. It should have been someone else in charge of all the moving parts. Someone well below Ivan in the organization. At the very least, it should have been Sergei.

But Sergei wasn't an option right now, so it was up to Ivan to organize all the brutes, wasn't it?

And now he had a headache forming between his brows, sharp and merciless.

Maybe he should have eaten like the incubus had suggested.

The incubus. The *fucking* incubus.

That incorrigible demon was the reason Ivan was hard at work with an intermittent erection, suddenly turned on by every stiff fucking breeze, like he was going through a second adolescence (not that he'd been allowed to be distracted by hormones during his actual adolescence).

Ivan had been tempted, after that display earlier—Nix's firm weight on his lap, his mouth hot and searching on Ivan's neck—to take his cock out and jerk off right there. To cover his desk with his cum the way he wanted to cover that demon's stupidly pretty mouth with it.

But Ivan knew, somehow, that Nix would know he'd done it. And then Nix would think he'd won, that he'd beaten Ivan.

He hadn't. Ivan didn't lose, at least not in the long run. Maybe he had to concede in the occasional battle, but never the war.

He was only pent up; that was all. And Nix had whatever sex magic an incubus held on his side, messing with Ivan's head.

So, yes, Ivan's cock was full and heavy every time he pictured Nix's absurdly attractive face, every time his mind wandered to the expanse of skin visible under Nix's sheer fucking shirt. What of it?

So, yes, Ivan wanted nothing more than to slide his dick between those ridiculously full lips, to pluck at those nipple piercings, to order the incubus to suck, order him to *behave*, until he swallowed down every bit of Ivan's reluctant arousal. It didn't mean anything. It couldn't.

Ivan didn't fuck men.

So Ivan would wait and jerk off in the shower tonight, like it was any other night, and if the demon dared to make any remarks, Ivan would blame it on the regular bodily functions of a healthy male human.

And he'd lock his bedroom door.

The matter decided, Ivan adjusted himself in his slacks and turned on his laptop, busying himself with work for a few more hours as he waited to hear from Sascha that the deed was done. Ivan's brother and his demon were meeting with the Carusos tonight, ostensibly to discuss Ivan's willingness to allow his ports to be used for the Carusos' new shipments of human cargo, but in reality to allow Kai an opportunity to do away with Luca Caruso—

the head of the family—and any men he brought with him, cutting their organization off at the knees.

It would have been a tricky maneuver with only mortal subordinates to rely on, but Kai was a warrior demon more than capable of slaughtering the lot of them without allowing any of Ivan's men —his brother—to come to harm.

If Sascha had the gall to summon a demon behind Ivan's back, the least he could do was to put the demon to good use.

But even after the sky had gone dark, hours after Sascha should have confirmed the meeting was over, Ivan didn't hear anything from his brother. He didn't hear anything from anyone. Not until his phone rang, the apartment's security guard on the other line.

"Sergei's here."

Every muscle in Ivan's body tensed at the announcement. He forced them to relax one by one before he spoke. "Send him up."

Nix appeared in the doorway after a mere moment, having obviously eavesdropped on the last (and probably every other) phone call. He leaned his lithe figure against the doorjamb, cocking his head. "Is that wise?" he asked, presumably referring to Sergei's imminent arrival.

(And now Ivan had to be grateful that, at the very least, his unexpected visitor served as a distraction from his own stubborn arousal.)

Ivan gave the demon a blank look. "Why wouldn't it be?" At Nix's unimpressed stare, he waved a hand in the direction of the hallway. "Go. Stay in the guest room until he leaves."

For whatever reason, Nix listened to him, straightening with a sigh and disappearing on quiet feet, the snick of the guest bedroom door shutting gunshot loud in the otherwise silent apartment.

Ivan waited in his seat, breathing evenly, fingers wrapped around a pen so he wouldn't tap at his desk in the meantime.

Sergei had known him too long, was too aware of Ivan's tells, for Ivan to allow himself free rein to fidget.

He remained in his desk chair even as he heard the elevator door open into the apartment, and a moment later, there was Sergei in the office doorway, a sight as familiar to Ivan as his own father had been. Maybe even more so. He was no artist, but Ivan was sure he could draw from memory Sergei's stocky form, his dark hair now peppered with more than a bit of gray, his nose that had been broken more than once.

The man who'd been in charge of Ivan's education. And, with that, his discipline.

How many beatings had Ivan endured under Sergei's hands?

That was before, of course. Back when Sergei had answered to Ivan's father. Now Sergei answered to Ivan. Loyal to the end; that was Sergei.

What a fucking joke.

He was carrying a white cardboard box, spots of it almost transparent with grease. He set it down on the desk, lifting the lid. The enticing smell of spiced meat wafted to Ivan's nose.

"Piroshki," Ivan murmured.

Sergei nodded. "From the bakery in my neighborhood," he said, his Russian accent subtle but never fully gone, even after all his years in New York. "The good one."

Ivan eyed the little meat-filled pastries, his stomach tightening to the point of cramping. "I haven't eaten yet."

Sergei scoffed in a way that managed to sound fond. "Of course you haven't."

Ivan didn't take one yet, but he did meet Sergei's eye. "Thank you."

"My pleasure, boss."

Boss. It was what Sergei had called Ivan's father. What he now called Ivan, ever since Ivan's father's last breath.

Ivan had never considered it an ironic title, but apparently that only showed how little he'd known.

He sat back in his chair, folding his hands over his midsection. "To what do I owe this visit?"

Sergei took the seat across from him, thumping down with his usual lack of grace. "I've heard whispers," he said as soon as he was seated, cutting to the chase already. "The Carusos were taken down tonight. A major hit."

"You don't say?" Ivan said lightly. "About time."

Sergei didn't so much as twitch, but his dark eyes bore into Ivan's. "There's talk that Sascha was involved."

"Our Sascha?" Ivan's lips quirked into an almost smile. "How unlikely."

"They're saying Luca is dead," Sergei persisted, his tone giving away nothing as to how he felt about that development. "And eight other men, all higher-ups. His stepson, Matteo, is missing, presumed dead as well. And the rest are scrambling."

"We should make sure they don't scramble into any trouble, then," Ivan said. "Tag and Jace are close to the Carusos' main warehouse. Have them clean up any stragglers."

Sergei's eyes narrowed, and he leaned forward as far as the desk would allow. "What are Tag and Jace doing close to Caruso territory?"

"Carrying out my orders," Ivan told him firmly, allowing some of his irritation to creep into his voice. "Is that a problem, Sergei?"

Sergei sat back, seeming to realize the fine line he was walking. In an instant, he was the picture of ease. "No," he said with a smile. "Of course not."

He tucked a hand into his breast pocket. Was he about to draw a gun? Maybe Ivan would end the night with a bullet to the head.

What would the incubus do then?

It was a stupid fucking thought to be his last one, but Ivan couldn't come up with anything else. He was too tired, maybe. From the summoning. From life. From Sergei's stupid games.

But Sergei only pulled out a handkerchief, blowing his nose loudly before speaking again. "You know, a deal with the Carusos would have benefited us."

Ivan resisted the urge to scoff. He knew exactly who a deal with the Carusos would have benefited, and it sure as fuck wasn't him. "Would it really?"

"Your father would have taken it."

"My father's dead," Ivan said flatly.

Sergei tucked his handkerchief back in his pocket, making a quick sign of the cross. "May he rest in peace."

"I'm sure the fires of hell are keeping him nice and toasty."

Unsurprisingly, Sergei was unamused. He gave Ivan a heavy, knowing look and heaved a sigh. "I'm worried about you, Vanya."

Somewhere underneath the ever-present rage, Ivan was curious. Where was Sergei going to try to steer him now? Did he already have a backup plan now the Carusos were a dead end? He must have. He was a traitor but not a fool.

"You should take a wife," Sergei told him, with all apparent sincerity.

Ivan was so genuinely surprised by the suggestion he couldn't contain his startled laugh. "I should?"

"Mm." Sergei smiled at him, the picture of a caring older relative. "A good woman, Ivan. A few babies. It'll settle you."

Like it settled my psychopath of a father?

It was the most preposterous suggestion Ivan had ever heard, but he only nodded. "I'll take that into consideration."

Sergei grunted, apparently satisfied with that response.

For a moment, it felt like old times. A few months ago, Ivan would have broken out the vodka for them, settled in and talked with Sergei deep into the night. They would have planned for the future, reminisced about old times (always glossing over the brutality, always painting Ivan's father as a calculated leader rather than an unhinged sadist). Sergei would have played the role Ivan had once thought Alexei would fill. The loyal second-in-command.

Was it on one of those nights that Sergei had decided to betray him? Had Ivan let something slip, some tell that had made Sergei decide he wasn't worth following any longer? Shown some weakness he wasn't aware of?

Even knowing what Ivan did, he was still tempted to take out two glasses. It wasn't like he had anyone else to drink with these days.

But Sergei stood abruptly before he had a chance. "I'll see to the men, then. Make sure no stragglers are left to cause trouble, hm?"

He would too. Sergei's play with the Carusos had failed, and he was smart enough to know a losing hand when he saw one. It would take time for him to regroup, if usurping Ivan was still on his agenda.

If that had even been the point of all this.

Sergei pushed the box of pastries closer to Ivan. "Eat. Get some sleep. And think on what I said."

Ivan tipped his chin. "I always do."

He watched Sergei leave. He took the vodka out of his desk drawer, followed by a single glass.

———

NIX APPEARED in the doorway of Ivan's office sometime later, catching Ivan in the act of biting into one of the piroshki. He rested a hip against the doorframe. "You sure you should eat that?"

Ivan finished chewing. Swallowed. Washed it down with vodka. He sneered, or at least he tried to. His facial expressions weren't cooperating quite the way they should. "Sergei wouldn't poison me. He'd shoot me point-blank, like a real man."

Nix laughed, low and throaty. "Oh, Vanya. There's so much wrong with that statement I can't even begin."

Ivan shut his eyes. Opened them again. "You sound like Sascha," he accused. "Sascha on one of his rants about toxic masculinity."

Ivan's youngest brother didn't contradict him often—or at least, he didn't used to—but when he did, he always liked to do it with gusto and sass.

"Good." Nix grinned, flashing sharp teeth, his tail flicking out from behind him. "I liked him."

Ivan scowled down at his glass, which was empty again. He wondered if Nix controlled the tail's movements or if they were involuntary. "You only met him for a moment."

"I saw enough." Nix's expression turned thoughtful. "He'll be good for Kai, I think. He's...sweet."

"He was allowed to be."

"So bitter, Vanya."

Nix straightened from the doorway and prowled closer, circumventing the desk to come up behind Ivan's chair. Normally Ivan wouldn't allow someone in that position—letting someone into his blind spot was asking for a bullet to the back of the head —but he was feeling...heavy tonight. Who cared if the incubus snapped his neck?

Then again, Nix couldn't. He wasn't allowed to hurt Ivan, so he wouldn't. It was a simple equation, and he was the only person in the world Ivan could say that about.

If only everyone was held to such constraints.

Ivan picked up another piroshki.

Nix's voice was quiet behind him. "You're softer with him."

"Sascha?" Ivan asked, almost laughing at the thought. Sascha would surely have something to say about such an accusation. To say he would disagree was putting it lightly.

"Sergei."

Ivan paused, the piroshki held to his lips. "He raised me," he said eventually.

"And now he's betrayed you. How tragic." The words could have been sarcastic, but Nix didn't sound taunting. That spiced, smoked scent he carried around with him drifted to Ivan's nose.

Ivan suddenly wished he could see his face.

Fingers carded through Ivan's hair, and he dropped the piroshki in an instant, uncaring where it landed, closing his eyes and leaning back into the touch. He didn't exactly groan, but it was close.

"Is this part of the contract?" he asked, his voice strangely hoarse. "Tending to me?"

The fingers in his hair stilled, then started up again. "Sure. You can say that, if you want."

What Ivan wanted was too difficult a question for the moment.

For now, Ivan needed a moment. Just...a moment, being touched by someone who wasn't cruel, or conniving, or indifferent.

So he let Nix play with his hair, the touch eventually evolving into more of a scalp massage, Nix's fingers firm and confident and perfect. Ivan wasn't sure how long it lasted. Minutes. Hours. Centuries. Nix didn't make it sexual, even when Ivan finally groaned at a particularly firm bit of pressure. When he was done, Nix only patted Ivan's head, then walked around the desk, plopping into the chair across from him, his tail hanging over the side.

Ivan blinked blearily at him, then poured himself another glass. "It took me longer than it should have, to realize who my mole was," he said, even though Nix hadn't asked him.

Maybe it was the visit from Sergei, the reminder of old times, that was making Ivan chatty.

Or maybe it was just the vodka.

"I hadn't been able to fathom it. He's known Sascha since he was a baby."

Nix leaned his chin on one hand, his pretty eyes fixed on Ivan. "Why did he do it?"

"I don't know." Ivan let out a bitter laugh. "I haven't asked. But he was the only one who knew where Sascha would be and when. He thought to frame the driver, but Sascha had sent his driver away the night before without telling us. He'd bribed him to keep quiet about it."

"And does Sergei know you know?"

"Not yet."

"And how long are you going to keep him at your side?" There was no judgment in Nix's gaze, no sign that he thought Ivan was an idiot for not acting sooner. Only consideration.

"Not much longer." Despite his occasionally maudlin thoughts, Ivan didn't have a death wish. Keeping Sergei at his side indefinitely would be beyond foolish. His current hesitation was risky enough.

Nix studied him in that way of his. Like he was seeing through every bit of Ivan, right down to the core. "You don't want to hurt him," he surmised.

"I want to kill him," Ivan corrected.

"Those two things aren't necessarily mutually exclusive."

Ivan didn't want to think about that. He didn't want to think about Sergei at all. Why had Nix even brought him up? "My brother spoke of using the Book to bond," he said, changing the course of the conversation. "What does that mean?"

Nix shrugged. "Kind of what it sounds like. They're going to bond their souls together. It allows Kai to stay here, even without a contract. Think of it as a marriage."

"My baby brother's getting married?"

Ivan wanted to feel something about that, but everything was numb. At least if Sascha was really foolish enough to love some-one, it was someone who could protect him.

"I'd say he's already done it," Nix said lightly. "I don't think Kai could bear to wait."

Ivan stared at Nix. It wasn't fair that he looked so pretty sitting there, even with his usual spark of mischief dimmed. "You're not teasing me tonight," Ivan pointed out.

Nix hummed. "You're much too sad."

Ivan didn't bother protesting. But really, that showed how much Nix knew about human emotion. Ivan wasn't sad. He was never sad. He was just...numb.

"I'm going to lock my door tonight." Ivan tried to raise a brow, but he wasn't sure if he managed it. Or maybe he was raising both of them. "So no watching me sleep."

"Whatever you need to do to feel safe."

Ivan frowned at him. "I'm not scared of you."

Nix flashed him a small grin. "My mistake."

"You made a mark," Ivan told him, suddenly remembering. He touched the tender spot on his neck. Sergei must have seen it.

"Oopsie." But Nix didn't sound very sincere.

They sat there in silence for a while as Ivan ate half the box of piroshki, washing each down with a gulp of vodka. Nix's purple eyes never left him. He barely seemed to blink.

Normally Ivan didn't like people watching him eat—the act was too human, too vulnerable—but he couldn't find it in himself to care tonight. And Nix's eyes were so pretty. Ivan liked having them on him. Liked having his demon at hand.

When he finished eating, he stood from his desk, taking a moment to find his sea legs before he crossed over to where Nix sat. The demon stared up at him, his face for once unreadable.

And then Ivan did what he'd been wanting to do since Nix had knelt at his feet when Ivan was only half-conscious, right after their contract had been made.

He reached out a hand and raked it through that fiery hair, loosening Nix's ponytail and letting the whole wavy mass fall down around Nix's face.

Nix didn't protest. He didn't even blink, his eyes seeming to glow in the lamplight.

Ivan would have liked to say the long, loose hair made Nix look like a woman, but it didn't. The angles of his face were too harsh, maybe, or the line of his chin too strong, even with those damned plush lips.

Or maybe Nix had dug himself too deep under Ivan's skin for Ivan to pretend.

Ivan wound the hair around his fist, tugging Nix's head back. "You'll behave tonight," he ordered, his voice strangely husky.

Nix peered up at him with hooded eyes. "Yes, master."

Whether mocking or sincere, the words were what Ivan wanted to hear. He leaned forward, pressed a firm kiss to that stupid, taunting mouth, tugged Nix's hair once more for good measure, and walked out of the room.

6

Nix

The days and nights were boring when someone's mean (and sad—oh so very sad) contract didn't allow for any fucking. Especially the nights.

So. Very. Boring.

Dawn creeping up through the apartment's windows was the most glorious thing Nix had ever seen, and even then Ivan didn't come out of his room for another hour.

His *locked* room.

True to his word, that Ivan. Even after his little display at the desk the other night, he'd been locking his door every single night when he went to bed, like Nix was the boogeyman and Ivan needed protection from him.

Nix could have broken the lock, of course, but if dear Vanya felt the need to guard himself against little ol' Nix, then so be it.

The human had still cracked, with or without Nix's help.

He'd *kissed* Nix.

And true, there hadn't been any tongue or groping or any of the fun extras Nix so very much enjoyed, but it had still been mouth to mouth. Nix hadn't expected such an advance for another week or two, at least.

Thank the Book for vodka.

Although, Nix had a feeling it had been less about the alcohol and more about the way Sergei's visit had split a fissure in Ivan's defenses. There had been real vulnerability there, after the stocky Russian had left.

But clearly Ivan hadn't been feeling as open in the aftermath. It had been almost two weeks now, and Ivan had kept Nix firmly at arm's length. He spent almost all his waking hours at the office, his crew of brutes coming in and out, and apparently Nix wasn't allowed.

Ivan claimed he needed to capitalize on the Carusos' downfall before other families swooped in and beat him to it, but it felt to Nix like he was stalling.

Ivan hadn't mentioned Sergei since that night, and Nix hadn't seen the betraying bastard around. He'd almost have liked to invite him over, if it meant Ivan would crack again. If it meant Ivan would *touch* him again.

Speak of the handsome devil.

Ivan clearly wasn't feeling any more open this morning. He came out of his room fully dressed, in another black suit that could have used a bit more tailoring. Did he have something against showing off that firm ass of his? *Probably*, Nix thought, on his back on the ugly white couch, one knee crossed over the other. Most likely Ivan thought firm asses weren't good for *appearances*.

"I'm heading to the office," Ivan said tersely the moment he entered the living room, knotting his tie without looking at Nix.

"And me?" Nix asked, already guessing the answer.

"You'll stay here." Ivan gazed coolly down at him, still

somehow avoiding Nix's eyes. "I don't need any distractions today."

Nix made a face, but he was ignored. He sensed the Book on Ivan's person, the demonic energy radiating out from his suit jacket. Ivan had taken to transporting it back and forth between his office and the apartment ever since Sascha had brought it back to him.

"Why were you so intent on getting that back, anyway?" Nix asked, nodding to where Ivan was concealing the tome. "Sascha wouldn't have been able to summon another demon, you know."

"Alexei could." Ivan scowled at his own words, bitter as always at even the mention of his middle brother. "He already has a vampire, I don't need him adding another supernatural creature to his arsenal."

Nix sat up, tucking his legs under him. "Your brother has a vampire?" he asked eagerly.

He half expected Ivan to tell him to mind his own business, but Ivan answered, "He does. A strange excuse for one though. He was...small." Ivan rubbed at his neck, on the opposite side from where Nix's lovely hickey had been before it had faded. "But still strong."

"What a fascinating family you have."

Ivan's only answer was a sneer of disgust.

Touchy, touchy.

"And what do I do while you're gone?" Nix asked, already bored with whatever answer Ivan was going to give him.

Ivan's cool blue gaze finally met his. "You'll behave."

He really liked that word, didn't he? Nix narrowed his eyes at him. "And how am I supposed to complete our contract when you leave me behind at every opportunity?"

But Ivan was already heading to the elevator. One silly little kiss and he was fleeing like Nix was some sort of toxic waste.

Humans were so *fragile*.

Nix waited until that firm ass was shut behind elevator doors before he decided to amuse himself with a more thorough search of Ivan's bedroom. He'd been mostly entertaining himself with human television, but he was beyond bored with that now.

In his second go-around, he hit pay dirt, pressed against the back of Ivan's bedside table drawer. A photo of an older man—pale-blond hair buzzed short, tattoos peeking out from under his sleeves—with what was undoubtedly a teenaged Ivan, looking painfully young and painfully miserable.

This must be the father, then. Nix studied him, but not much could be revealed by a photo. He was looking straight at the camera, as expressionless as adult Ivan could be. His mouth was pressed in an unforgiving line, and he had a tight hand clenched on young Ivan's shoulder.

Nix was tempted to tear the photo in half, to separate the two of them before the father's damage could take. But it was only a photo—what good would that do?

Instead he sneered at it, as haughty as he could manage. "I'm going to fix what you broke," he whispered, low and mean.

He froze, cross-legged on the floor by Ivan's bed, stopped short by his own words. Why was he so determined to help Ivan? Nix could easily coast here, allow the contract to keep him in the human realm without going to any extra lengths for his so-called master. He didn't *have* to listen to all Ivan's orders, as long as Nix's actions weren't directly harmful and didn't actively work against the goals of their contract.

Nix could have gone out any of these past nights and immersed himself in lust, if he'd really wanted. Could have fucked any human he wished.

But he *hadn't* wanted, not after that kiss. For all that it had been dry and brief, it had still been...real.

Nix was never allowed real. It was all about illusion, about veils upon veils of fantasy and want. Nix used different clothes, different forms, different personalities, even, shifting each to fit what the contract needed. Sometimes it wasn't even about any form Nix took at all—sometimes he was aiding in building desire between two humans, or aiding a human in finding any spark of desire inside themselves at all.

And Nix had always liked that fine—he didn't need it to be about him, not when it all still allowed him to feast on a hearty meal.

But it was different here. Nix hadn't used any illusions with Ivan, and Ivan still wanted Nix. He didn't *want* to want him, maybe, but he did. And that was a whole new level of interesting.

And then there was the way Nix could feel Ivan's soul piece in his chest, somehow heavier and more intoxicating than any soul piece he'd had before. He could feel all the hurt and bitter pockets of regret weighing it down, even as he could taste the sharp tang of Ivan's essence, delicious as anything Nix had ever tasted before.

There was so much potential there, with Ivan's inner strength, his self-control, his air of command. He could be great, even, if tended to properly.

And what does one human's potential matter to you?

The answer should have been nothing. And yet...

What would Ivan's soul taste like if Nix could heal even a fraction of those hurts?

Nix pictured the stretch of Ivan's neck in the town car, taut and vulnerable. His bleary blinking and shaky legs, stinking of vodka and regret after Sergei's visit. The tug of his hand in Nix's hair and the dry press of his lips.

It was all...enticing. Too enticing for a demon like Nix to even hope to resist.

It would be nice to have someone to discuss it with though.

Repression might have been Ivan's bread and butter, but it wasn't Nix's. This was the best gossip about himself he'd had in centuries, and he had only his own hollow head to repeat it in. He didn't have a way to reach Kai, even if Kai were willing to talk with him about such things. He didn't have a way to reach Ivan, either, for that matter.

He needed one of those pocket phone things.

In the meantime...

Nix placed the photo back carefully, speaking to the only person who might be paying attention. "Are you watching, Chaos?" he asked, aiming his question at the wall across from him. "I would be, if I were you." Nix let out a long breath. "I think you'd like it here. I think you'd like it a whole lot."

He'd been thinking that, as he and Ivan had ridden in the town car that first time. The claustrophobic crush of traffic, the din of angry honking, the swarming mass of humans on the sidewalk. Chaos would have loved it all.

Nix rested his head on his raised knees. "We need to find someone to summon you."

He'd never tried to coordinate someone else's summoning before, but Nix wanted his friend back. They'd spent too long in the Void together to never see each other again. And maybe he also wanted to see what would happen. Chaos was sweet but... feral. Unhinged, even for a demon. Contract or no contract, he wouldn't have followed silly commands like Ivan's "wait for me while I go to the office" nonsense.

Nix flicked his tail, thumping it against the hardwood. And why should *he* follow silly commands either? It wasn't like he was of any use hanging around here.

He stood, changing back into his human form as he did so. He changed his outfit while he was at it, switching out his current sheer shirt for something soft and silky.

Ivan was a tactile man, after all.

Nix took the elevator down to the ground floor, finding the same doorman he usually did in the mornings. He waltzed up to him. "Hello, there," he said, grinning when the doorman's eyes widened at his approach. "What's your name?"

"Carl, sir."

"Mm. And how do you like working for Mr. Kozlov, Carl?" Nix was taking a stab that the man was employed by Ivan directly and not the building. Or the more likely case, which was that Ivan owned the building altogether.

"I enjoy it very much, sir."

That was a lie. But Nix didn't sense anything nefarious underneath it. No twisted plots or conflicting loyalties. Most likely the guy just thought Ivan was a bit of a dick. Or he hated his job in the normal way most people did, without wanting their boss literally dead.

Neither a rat nor a mole. See? Nix was useful as hell. Ivan didn't even know just how useful Nix could be.

Ivan didn't know who to trust? Nix could tell him. Being an incubus was about understanding people, after all. Nix didn't have to read minds to know when someone was lying.

This doorman was in the clear. Although, he couldn't possibly be working twenty-four hours a day. Nix cocked his head. "How many others share your position?"

"Um. Two, sir."

"And when do you change shifts?"

"Seven, three, and eleven."

Nix would have to investigate the other two at a later date, then. He patted Carl's chest, straightening the man's lapel while he was at it. "Very good. Call me a car, Carl. I'm headed to the office."

———

NIX WAS a little surprised to see the same driver as the day before pull up. He would have thought the man was assigned to Ivan alone.

He slid into the back seat anyway, immediately leaning in close to stick his head practically through the partition. "Hey, Oleg darling! Why aren't you with the big bad boss?"

"Orders. If you need driving, I take call," Oleg told him, his Russian accent obvious now that he was speaking more than two words at a time.

"Oh my. Ivan designated a driver for little ol' me?" Nix fluttered his lashes. "He's a sweetheart, isn't he?"

Oleg coughed, then cleared his throat, steering the car into the flow of traffic. "As you say."

Nix grinned, opening his senses and cocking his head to study the driver. "And how long have you been driving for him?"

"Since he was little boy." Oleg gave a small smile. "Car was not as nice then."

"And what did you think of the father?"

A sharp tongue of fear licked out from Oleg, as well as the teeniest, tiniest tendril of hate, even as his expression gave nothing away. "He was...firm leader."

A man who knew how to keep his mouth shut. But Nix wasn't above a little prodding. "Not very nice to his sons, though, huh?"

There was a long silence before Oleg spoke, his voice flat. "No. Not very nice."

Nix sat back, satisfied for the moment. Whatever his feelings for the father, there was no treachery in Oleg's veins. There was even the advantage of the little bit of sympathy he clearly still held for young Ivan.

Nix smiled to himself. That was two people accounted for, at least, among however many. Nix really needed a more efficient method though. He crossed his legs, tapping a finger against his mouth. He needed Ivan to call a meeting, perhaps. To gather a large host of his men all at once.

What Nix needed, really, was for Ivan to use him properly.

Nix's brain immediately flashed back to the images he'd seen in Ivan's head before. The naughty, naughty images, all of Nix.

He smirked to himself, rubbing his hands against the soft leather of the town car's seats. Ohhh yes. What he wouldn't give for Ivan to use him properly.

Nix blew Oleg a kiss as he hopped out of the car in front of Ivan's office building. He waved to the security guard as he walked on through. He'd need to investigate the man on the way out, but he didn't want to give him a chance to warn Ivan of Nix's arrival and get Nix barred from entry, in case Ivan was still feeling testy.

There was already someone waiting at the elevator, a young man a few inches shorter than Nix, made even more so by his hunched posture. His tawny mop of hair was clearly in need of a cut, and he was fiddling with the strings of the worn hoodie he was wearing, strings that were already frayed, looking like they'd been chewed on more than once.

Nix sidled up next to him. "Going up?"

The young man shot a startled glance toward Nix, his glasses glinting under the fluorescents.

It was Nix's turn to startle—the human's eyes were two different colors. One brown, one green. It was striking, even behind the layer of his glasses.

Nix was quick to compose himself. It was rude to stare, even if it was for nice reasons. He gave the stranger a smile instead. "Well, aren't you lovely?"

He would be too, if he was polished up a bit. He'd be, at the very least, a very fine cutie.

The young man immediately looked down at his feet again. "Uh—"

The elevator arrived, saving him from coming up with a reply.

Nix shot him a wink as they stepped in together. He wanted to ask the man's name, but the anxiety rolling off him would have been palpable even if Nix hadn't been a demon.

He was shy, to say the least. Shy to the point of real apprehension.

And he'd hit the button for the top floor, so they were both heading for Ivan's office. Nix would find out who he was soon enough anyway.

Nix gave a little bow when the elevator stopped. "After you."

The man shuffled in front of him, shooting him a glance every now and then over his shoulder. He was acting stiffly enough that Nix might have thought him a threat, but there was no malice coming off him. He was just a naturally nervous little creature.

Cute butt though.

Nix darted in front of him right when they got to Ivan's door, waltzing through so he was the first thing Ivan saw.

He was at his desk, predictably, his tie gone and his top buttons unbuttoned. Nix could immediately sense the Book in the room. The demonic energy was now radiating out from one of Ivan's desk drawers.

Ivan looked up with a scowl, though he didn't seem too surprised to see Nix. "What are you doing here—"

"You have a visitor," Nix interrupted. He stepped aside with a flourish to reveal his new friend behind him.

Ivan's scowl dropped, his expression neutral once more. "Cooper," he greeted, not seeming surprised to see his new guest either.

Ah. The cousin. Nix turned to Cooper with new interest. It was hard to see any family resemblance, and the darker coloring was only part of it. Ivan closely resembled his father—maybe Cooper was connected to the mother's family?

Cooper stared down at his own feet, even as he addressed Ivan.

The anxiety radiating off him thickened. "You needed me?" he asked, barely above a mumble.

Ivan tapped at his desk with one finger. "We have two people who need identification."

"Fake IDs?"

"Not enough. We need thorough documentation of their existence. Enough for travel, residency...whatever they might require. And it needs to come from nothing."

Cooper looked up from his feet then, apparent interest breaking through his reserve. "Social security cards, even?"

Ivan nodded. "Can you do it?"

"Uh, sure." Cooper tugged at the strings of his hoodie, biting his lip in thought. "I need approximate ages. Photos."

"I can get you those." Ivan pushed the pile of ledgers on his desk toward them. "And I need these digitized."

Nix came closer, stepping between them and watching as Cooper gathered the ledgers. He knocked his hip against the desk drawers, catching Cooper's attention. "You missed one."

"Oh. Um, thank you." Cooper grabbed blindly, adding the last of it to his pile and hugging them against his chest.

Ivan cleared his throat. "This is Nix, my new assistant. He's one of the ones needing ID."

Cooper met Nix's eyes fully for the first time for the briefest instant before he looked away again. "You, um, have a preference for your birthday?"

What a sweetheart. Nix winked at him. "Whatever you think best, Cooper, darling."

Ivan gave Nix's hip a smack. "Don't flirt with Coop. He can't handle your teasing."

Nix simpered at him. "Not like you, Vanya."

Cooper's eyes widened, his gaze flashing between them. Ivan only grunted, as if in annoyance, but his arm darted out, tugging Nix away from Cooper and into his side.

Nix leaned into the touch easily, sitting halfway on the arm of Ivan's chair, happy to play along with any little show of dominance Ivan might desire.

Ivan tilted his head to the door. "That'll be all, Coop."

Nix waggled his fingers. "Bye, Coop. So lovely to make your acquaintance."

Cooper ducked his head back into his hoodie and walked out the door without another word.

Nix clucked his tongue. "Poor baby. He's terrified of you."

"Coop's scared of everyone. Social anxiety or some bullshit. He prefers his screens to people."

"That's a shame." Nix brushed Ivan's pale hair back from his face. "He's a cutie."

Ivan grabbed his hand and held it still. "Behave."

"Why should I?" Nix asked, tugging his hand back and leaning in closer instead. If he slid over just a smidge, he'd be on Ivan's lap.

Ivan still had an arm wrapped around Nix's middle, his fingers toying with the hem of Nix's shirt, even as he frowned up at him. "What are you doing here, anyway?"

"I missed you."

"Likely story."

"Your doorman and your driver are loyal," Nix told him, deciding to be helpful even if Ivan was being difficult again. "Same with Coop there."

Ivan's eyes gleamed with interest. "You can tell?"

"I can tell. I read people. I'm useful, Ivan." Nix smirked. "So use me."

"Mm." Ivan dropped hold of Nix's shirt, and his thumb began stroking against Nix's hip instead.

Nix cocked his head. Something had cracked again, at some point during their brief time apart this morning. Nix's human was open in a way he hadn't been earlier.

Really, a person could get whiplash from the back-and-forth.

Or he could take advantage, and wedge himself into every little opening offered.

That sounded like more fun.

Nix lowered his head until his mouth was a hair's breadth from Ivan's. "Did I do good, boss?" he murmured. "How about a reward for behaving so well?" He licked his lips, fighting back a giggle when Ivan's thumb immediately paused its stroking, Ivan's gaze fixed on his mouth. "Perhaps another kiss?"

7

Ivan

Ivan stared into the incubus's strange violet eyes. He smelled of spice and oddly sweet smoke, as he always did. Even in his human form, Nix was otherworldly. Too alluring by half, and he knew it.

Ivan should have kicked him out the moment he'd arrived.

But something about Nix waltzing into his office, despite Ivan's strict instructions to remain at the apartment, had thrown Ivan for a loop. He was used to being feared, even by those who claimed to love him. And yet Nix hadn't so much as allowed Ivan to chastise him.

So Ivan had let Nix stay, and now the demon was asking for a fucking kiss.

Give him an inch and he'd take a mile.

Ivan had been drunk that other night when he'd pressed their lips together—not anywhere near a right state of mind. He'd been compelled against reason and unable to stop himself. But today? Now?

He'd been doing so well too. There had been enough loose ends after Sascha and Kai had taken down the Carusos that Ivan had been able to bury himself in work, keeping the incubus at arm's length. If Ivan didn't look at him, or touch him, or smell him, he could manage.

He should have known it wouldn't last.

When Sascha had come by and dropped off the Book two weeks ago, he'd told Ivan he seemed to be coming apart at the seams.

And, hell, maybe Sascha was right.

Because, in spite of all his better judgment, Ivan found himself tugging Nix's head down and claiming his mouth, forcing his own tongue in the moment they made contact. There would be no chaste press of lips this time. Ivan was going to lick all the mocking words right out of Nix's mouth, suck the sass off his tongue, until he was as mindless as he'd made Ivan.

But Nix only moaned, sliding off the arm of the seat and onto Ivan's lap, his hands delving into Ivan's hair as he deepened the kiss. With that single touch, all the blood rushed to Ivan's dick, and he was hard faster than he'd ever been in his life.

It was some sort of demon magic. It had to be. Sex wasn't like this for Ivan. Sex was a release. An occasionally inconvenient necessity. It was never all-consuming. No attraction had ever haunted Ivan's mind the way his attraction to this demon did.

How did one exorcise a demon like this? Ivan had only one idea—as Nix battled him for dominance, exploring Ivan's mouth like he owned it—and Ivan knew it was a bad one.

He jerked Nix back by his ponytail, breaking the kiss, ignoring Nix's frustrated whine. "Are you still hungry?" he asked, hating how raspy his voice came out.

The demon had claimed he fed on lust and desire. It could have been bullshit, but if it wasn't...

Nix's eyes lit with some inner fire as his tongue swept over his lower lip. "Famished."

"Suck me off," Ivan ordered. The damning words were out of his mouth before he could stop them, and Nix's answering grin was smug enough to torment.

"Yes, master," he purred.

Such a little shit. But even if the words were taunting, Nix's actions weren't. He slid off Ivan's lap onto the floor in one graceful movement, eager fingers unbuckling Ivan's belt in an instant.

Ivan leaned back, his hands clenching on the arms of his chair. He had the crazed thought that if he let go, even for a moment, he might do something unforgivably stupid—like tug the incubus back onto his lap and rip off all his clothes, press himself into that lithe body, and never come up for air.

Nix would let him too. He'd let Ivan fuck him for days on end if he wanted to.

It was possible Nix would let Ivan do anything he desired.

It was a fucking dangerous thought.

So Ivan kept his hands where they were, his gaze burning into the incubus's absurdly beautiful face.

There was a man kneeling at Ivan's feet. A man about to suck his cock.

Except it wasn't a man at all—it was Nix, the infuriating demon seemingly sent from hell to torment Ivan. Like he was a test Ivan was destined to fail.

Ivan's hands clenched tighter on their armrests as Nix pulled him out of his slacks. Ivan's cock was fully hard, his foreskin retracted back far enough to reveal the angry red tip.

"Oh my." Nix peered up at him with heavy-lidded eyes, his hands sliding up Ivan's thighs. "Haven't we been blessed?"

Ivan's lower belly clenched. How fucking stupid, to fall prey to idle flattery. "None of your teasing," he growled. "I want your mouth. Now."

"Who's teasing?" Nix countered, but he lowered his mouth and sucked gently on the head of Ivan's cock, licking all around the tip like he was feasting on an ice cream cone. Even with that taunting touch, his mouth was an inferno, hotter than any Ivan had ever had before. It should have burned—should have *hurt*—but it only made heat lick up Ivan's spine.

Nix raised his head and grinned up at Ivan. "Like this, master?"

Ivan gritted his teeth. "Deeper."

"Oops." Nix stroked along the inside of Ivan's thighs, as if in apology. As if he wasn't tormenting Ivan on purpose. "My mistake."

He lowered his head again, swallowing down more than half of Ivan's cock, but he didn't use any suction. He only held Ivan in his mouth, raising his brows. Ivan could hear the question without it being asked: *Like this?*

"*Suck*," Ivan ordered, the command coming out like a curse.

Nix hollowed his cheeks immediately, impudent and merciless. *Holy fucking shit.* Ivan groaned, his eyes slamming shut and his head thumping against the back of his chair.

That heavenly suction stopped.

Ivan opened his eyes to find Nix staring up at him again, those plush lips stretched around Ivan's cock, completely motionless. His ears were rounded in his human form. Ivan found himself missing the strange pointed shape. He cursed, grabbing Nix's hair and winding it around his fist. He tugged. Hard. "Keep going."

He wanted it to be an order, but it came out like a plea.

Either way, Nix popped off his cock instead, grinning up at him. "Show me." He placed his hand over Ivan's fist in his hair, encouraging. "Show me how you want it."

Ivan wondered if this was Nix's way of keeping him present. So Ivan wouldn't be able to close his eyes and pretend it was some woman kneeling on his office floor, sucking him into oblivion.

As if Ivan could. The incubus was all he could picture every time he closed his eyes. Every night since he'd summoned him, images of him had danced through Ivan's brain, taunting and tormenting.

Maybe that was the price of giving up a piece of his soul.

Maybe he should have read the fine print before making that bargain.

He tugged once more on Nix's hair, and Nix's eyes grew hooded again. Ivan remembered Nix claiming Ivan would be vicious in bed.

"You want me to hurt you?" he asked.

Nix tutted at him, his hands sliding down to Ivan's knees. "You can't hurt me, Ivan."

Just as the incubus couldn't harm Ivan under the contract. So it went both ways, then. Neither of them could hurt the other. But... no. That was a dangerous thought to give in to. Ivan knew better, didn't he?

Either way, it wasn't the time. If the demon wanted him to let go, Ivan would let go.

Ivan tugged Nix again by the hair, reveling in the sharp gasp Nix let out, pulling him up onto his dick. Nix moaned around his cock, hollowing his cheeks again and sucking like his life depended on it, like he was rewarding Ivan for losing control.

His hands landed on Ivan's hips, encouraging.

He wanted Ivan to fuck his mouth.

As if Ivan had the strength left to refuse. "Tap my hip if you need to breathe."

Nix popped off him again, ignoring Ivan's responding glare. "Oh, Vanya, baby," he crooned. "You think I need a silly little thing like oxygen?"

Ivan's balls tightened. *Fuck.* This demon was going to be the death of him, wasn't he?

He tugged Nix back down, thrusting his hips up at the same time. It was unlike anything he'd felt before—that damned heat, the tight constriction of Nix's throat. Nix didn't gag, only moaned again, the sound muffled by Ivan's dick.

Ivan meant to close his eyes, to focus on the feel of it. But he couldn't look away as he fucked Nix's mouth.

Nix didn't gag, but he *was* sloppy.

The demon was a slutty mess, moaning and licking and sucking with no shame, or at least as best he could around Ivan's sharp tugs of his hair and ruthless thrusts of his hips. He looked turned on beyond belief, his hands tight on Ivan's hips, his eyes both hazy and hot.

He looked like *he* was the one getting sucked off.

Ivan was used to blow jobs being perfunctory. The women he fucked wanted a taste of power, maybe, or a chance to say they'd sucked off a mob boss. They'd never acted like getting a mouthful of Ivan's cock was the key to all their desires.

They'd never given Ivan permission to be brutal. To be harsh. To lose himself in them.

"Stop," Ivan ordered hoarsely when Nix had him too close to the edge.

Nix stopped, his cheeks still hollowed, and somehow Ivan could feel his pout.

"I want to come on your face." Ivan was beyond the point of caring how much he may have been admitting. The depths of his obsession he might be revealing.

Nix pulled off slowly—so fucking slowly—and his puffy, abused lips curled into a grin. "Of course you do," he purred, his voice throaty and hoarse. "You want my hands, baby?"

Jesus. "No." Ivan shut his eyes. Cleared his throat. Opened them again. "Just...sit still."

Nix sat back on his knees obediently, although his hands slid from Ivan's hips back onto his thighs, petting lightly over Ivan's slacks.

Ivan stroked himself furiously, his balls already high and tight from the aching pleasure of Nix's mouth. Nix watched him. Or, more accurately, Nix watched Ivan's dick, gazing at it longingly, like he already wanted it back in his mouth.

"Look at *me*," Ivan ordered, wishing he had his hands in Nix's hair again, to control his movements the way he wanted.

But apparently he didn't need it. Purple eyes met his in an instant, and Nix's lips curled up again. "That's it, Vanya, baby," he crooned. "Give it me, hm? Cover me with it. I've been so good for you, haven't I? I deserve a taste."

"*Fuck.*" Ivan groaned through his release, his thighs trembling and his vision going dark at the edges as he fought to keep his eyes open, to watch his hot cum spurting onto Nix's face, covering his cheeks, his lashes, his wicked fucking mouth.

Ivan's demon. Claimed by him. Marked as his property.

Fuck.

What was *wrong* with him?

Nix licked at his lips immediately, his eyes still on Ivan's. He hummed, like he was savoring the flavor. His sweet, smoky scent was everywhere, fogging Ivan's brain.

Ivan slumped back into his chair, panting hard. "Fuck. *Fuck.*"

He sat there, limp and boneless, as Nix scooped every bit of Ivan's cum off his face, sucking his fingers clean lazily, watching Ivan all the while. When he was done, he laid his cheek on Ivan's knee, peering up at him. "Are you going to freak out on me now?" he asked softly, nonjudgmental, as if either answer would be acceptable.

Ivan rubbed a hand down his face. "Why would I?" he asked, grateful his voice had returned to some sort of normalcy. "You were hungry. I was..."

"Horny?" Nix supplied.

Ivan narrowed his eyes. "In need of release."

"And do you feel better now?"

Ivan did. And he didn't. It had been the fiercest orgasm of his life, and it still hadn't been enough. Ivan could already tell what he'd see when he closed his eyes tonight. Nix. Always Nix.

Was Ivan going to have to fuck this demon to get him out of his system?

Nix's face softened into a look of deep understanding. "Poor baby," he crooned sympathetically.

He rose slowly from the floor before sliding his knees onto Ivan's chair, allowing ample time for Ivan to push him away.

Ivan didn't. He let Nix back onto his lap. He let Nix kiss him, let him bite into Ivan's lower lip. Ivan deepened the kiss and licked the taste of his own cum out of Nix's mouth.

An eternity later, Nix leaned back, his gaze assessing.

Ivan stared back at him. "You're filthy," he told him, wanting it to come out as an admonishment, but only too aware he sounded fond and indulgent.

"I am." Nix grinned at him. He was clearly hard in his leather pants, but he made no move to address it. "It drives you crazy, doesn't it, darling?"

Ivan didn't even know what they were talking about anymore —the blow job, the filth, Nix himself. But he gave the only answer he could. "Yes."

———

IVAN WORKED for a few hours more, Nix curled up—suspiciously docile—on his office couch. Ivan had promised Sascha a job managing one of his less nefarious clubs, so he was taking the steps necessary to facilitate that change.

He needed to find a new Sergei soon. This was too much grunt work for the head of the organization to be indulging in.

For his part, Nix seemed happy enough to watch Ivan, only asking occasional questions about the business. He had the sleepy, contented air of a cat who'd just had his cream. It sent a strange, warm thrill through Ivan. He'd fed his incubus—had given Nix exactly what he'd been craving—and he hadn't even needed to touch him to do it.

Except Ivan *wanted* to touch him.

He sighed, leaning back in his chair. Surely such thoughts were a sign of an overworked brain.

Nix perked up immediately at the change, prowling over and setting himself on the arm of Ivan's chair again. It felt too right to have him there—like that was his place, at Ivan's side. Within arm's reach.

Ivan glanced up at him blankly, determined to focus on business. "You sussed out the intentions of a few of my men," he began.

"I did."

"You could get a read on the rest?"

"I could," Nix told him, sounding approving, like Ivan was a student who was finally following along.

Ivan let out a long breath. That was a powerful skill in a world as treacherous as his. "Maybe you are a boon, then," he mused. "Maybe you weren't just sent here to curse me."

Nix's lips twitched with amusement. "Why not both?"

It was the fatigue that made Ivan grin.

Nix latched onto his weakness immediately, as if one little smile was a sign that Ivan would indulge him. "Why are you so determined not to fuck men?" he asked, like that was an appropriate change of subject.

"It's not a matter of being determined. It's never been an issue before."

It hadn't. Ivan didn't look at the men who worked for him and ache to bend them over his desk. He'd never been tempted by the clubs Sascha and Alexei frequented. He supposed, if he thought hard about it...maybe there'd been a pretty face now and then. Those effeminate men who'd mastered a particular sort of allure.

Although, Sascha would probably tell him his phrasing was offensive.

But Ivan had always liked fucking women. Maybe none of them had compared to Nix's mouth on his cock, but Ivan had desired them at the time. He liked their soft bodies and sweet smell. The warm, wet feel of them on his cock.

None of them as warm as Nix.

Nix pinched Ivan's shoulder, his eyes narrowed. "Trying to make me jealous, Vanyechka?"

Ivan cocked his head, suspicious. "Tell me truthfully—do you read minds?" It was a horrifying prospect.

"No," Nix admitted with a pout. "But I catch glimpses sometimes. Images. Especially if they have to do with desire."

"But you can read intent. As you did with my men."

"To an extent."

Ivan was tempted to ask what Nix read in him, but he already knew he wouldn't want to hear the answer. He'd worked hard his whole life to be unreadable—to not let his father see any cracks in his armor, to not let the men under him see the strain in his leadership. It had been the only way to survive.

And now he'd let in the one creature his defenses didn't work on.

Sascha had been right—Ivan *was* coming apart at the seams.

Out of nowhere, Nix hopped off his chair, beckoning with one hand. "Come. You're not spending the night in the office."

Ivan glanced at his watch. "It's only five p.m."

"That's when normal humans stop working, isn't it? There's a whole song about it. Something about nine to five."

"Why would you possibly know about that?"

"The Void was very boring."

The Void. Where Nix had come from and where he would return when their contract was done. Ivan ignored the ice-cold rush of panic in his gut. It wasn't about Nix, not really. Ivan just didn't like it when the things promised him were taken away.

But no matter. Ivan's terms had been vague. He wasn't sure if the contract would ever be complete.

The thought almost made him smile again.

"All right. Take me home, demon." Ivan got on the intercom, instructing Tara to have Oleg pull to the front.

Nix cocked a hip in his ridiculous leather pants, a sly grin on his lips. "You sure you don't want me on my knees again before we go?"

Ivan scowled as he stood from his chair. "That was a one-time event."

Nix gaped at him, looking genuinely put out. "Are you serious right now?"

Ivan sighed. "I don't—"

"Fuck men. Yes, yes." Nix rolled his eyes. "Sing me a new one, *master*."

He turned on his heel, giving Ivan his back and striding toward the elevator, seeming not to care whether Ivan followed or not.

Apparently even an incubus had his limits with rejection.

Not that Ivan cared. So what if he'd hurt the demon's feelings? There were worse things in the world than a bruised ego. It was best to remember that.

They went down the elevator together, and Nix stayed silent, his gaze focused straight ahead.

They approached the front desk. There was the security guard with a deliveryman leaning over his desk, a package next to his hand.

Ivan had only a moment to sense something was off.

The security guard cried out, and Ivan was already reaching for his gun when the deliveryman raised his, firing two shots straight at Ivan.

Ivan prepared himself for the bite of a bullet, hoping against the odds he'd be hit in the shoulder and not the chest.

He knew better.

Would Alexei and Sascha mourn him? Or would they rejoice that their wicked, wayward brother finally met the end he deserved?

A flash of red, and there was Nix in front of Ivan, taking the bullet meant for him. He grunted on impact, falling back against Ivan.

Ivan caught him with an arm around his middle and fired his gun with his other hand, but his aim was impaired by the demon in his hold. The fake deliveryman was out the door in an instant.

Ivan should chase after him. He shouldn't let him get away.

But how could he, when Nix was bleeding in his arms?

Whoever the man had been, he wouldn't be able to stay hidden for long. It didn't matter how long it took, how many heads Ivan had to crack. Ivan would find him.

He'd shot Ivan's demon.

His life was already forfeit.

8

Nix

Nix had blood on his shirt.

It wasn't his sartorial ideal, but there were worse things, seeing as he could change his clothing at will. He should change it right now, in fact.

But he was kind of enjoying the way Ivan was pawing at him so frantically.

"Let me see," he was growling, turning Nix to face him and tugging at Nix's shirt as if he would tear it in two with his bare hands.

It would have been kind of hot, in a different context. But there wasn't time to enjoy it—they weren't safe staying where they were, and another bullet hitting Ivan instead of Nix was obviously unacceptable.

Nix had already fucked up beyond belief. He should have caught the man who'd shot him—he was fast enough, so that was no excuse. Kai would have gotten hold of him in an instant. But

Nix wasn't used to being hit by human weapons. He was an incubus, not a warrior demon. He was strong, but he wasn't skilled in combat.

Maybe he wasn't the right demon for Ivan after all.

Well, too fucking bad, he thought petulantly. *I'm keeping him anyway.*

Nix grabbed Ivan's hand, stilling it with a gentle squeeze. "I'm fine, Ivan. We need to go. It's not safe. And won't the police be showing up?"

Ivan scoffed. "No one in this building would dare call the police."

He still had a hand on Nix's chest, but with the other, he raised his gun. Apparently the security guard had dared to move.

"Not an inch," Ivan growled, the darkness in his voice stirring up something hot in Nix's insides. "Or you get a bullet to the head. You let him in."

The fear coming off the man was positively rank. "W-We were expecting a shipment of office supplies. As soon as he was in… He had a gun on me, boss. I—I tried to warn you."

Ivan met Nix's eyes, and Nix nodded. The guard was being truthful, as far as he could tell. He reeked of fear, obviously, but not guilt, and certainly no cunning.

And he *had* cried out.

Ivan lowered his gun, but he didn't holster it. "Send all the security footage to me. Jace will be coming by to double-check it."

With that, he was herding Nix out the door, but at the last minute, he turned back. "And don't let Tara leave the building."

"She knew we were heading out now," Nix mused as they approached the waiting town car.

"Yes."

"What will you do if she's guilty?"

Ivan gave him a look.

"How vicious," Nix murmured.

She'd deserve it, though, in Nix's opinion. Ivan had come much, much too close to getting a bullet in the chest. Ice water flooded Nix's veins at the thought. It was a strange sensation. Was this what real fear felt like? Nix had smelled it on others, but he'd never had cause to feel it so intensely himself.

Ivan steered him into the town car with a firm hand on his back. Oleg was waiting in the front seat. If he'd heard the gunshots, he didn't give any sign of it.

"Drive," Ivan ordered, slamming the car door shut behind them. Oleg obeyed, eyes straight ahead, by all appearances unfazed by the blood staining Nix's shirt.

"Hospital?" Ivan asked harshly.

Nix looked to him. Was that question directed at Nix? Ivan was radiating disquiet, his eyes locked onto Nix's bloody chest. Had he forgotten what Nix was? "Ivan," Nix reminded him gently. "I'm a demon."

"Right." Ivan turned to Oleg again. "My apartment. No— Andresen's Hotel."

Nix raised a brow, and Ivan answered his unspoken question.

"Sergei knows I know. It's the only reason he'd try something so desperate. We need a moment to regroup."

The hotel was closer than Ivan's apartment, and they arrived quickly. Ivan threw Nix his suit jacket, and Nix put it on to cover up his bloody shirt, deciding not to mention the fact that he could summon his own jacket at will.

The jacket smelled like Ivan, after all, and there was just something so classic about wearing one's lover's clothes, wasn't there?

They stepped out of the car, and then Ivan was ducking his head back in to threaten his driver. "If anyone finds me here, your life is forfeit."

Nix tossed in a quick, "Bye, Oleg!" and threw him a kiss for good measure, hoping to offset Ivan's panicked harshness. So touchy after one little bullet.

Then again, when Nix thought about *Ivan* getting hit...

That fake deliveryman should pray to all his gods that Nix didn't get his hands on him first.

They were given a room quickly enough after Ivan intimidated the poor woman at the front desk, pushing past any questions of a reservation with cold indifference and a heavy credit card. Ivan was on his phone in the elevator, presumably talking to Jace, instructing him to pick up the security footage and to detain Tara until Ivan and Nix had a chance to speak with her, then to stand guard at the hotel and shoot Sergei on sight if he should appear.

Nix eavesdropped shamelessly and with great interest. How exciting it all was.

As soon as they were in the room, the door bolted behind them, Ivan turned to Nix.

"Strip."

Nix placed a hand on his chest in faux surprise. "Why, Ivan."

Ivan gave him a frustrated look. "I don't care that you say you're fine. I want to see."

Far be it for Nix to refuse to get naked when his master commanded. Nix snapped his fingers, the jacket sliding off and his bloody shirt disappearing. (He didn't actually need the snapping, but it added an extra bit of fun, and he figured they could use the levity.)

The bastard had gotten him squarely in the chest. Twice. Ivan stared hard at the blood that remained, then wiped his finger through it, revealing the unmarked skin below.

The hand he brought up to his face so he could eye the blood was shaking, but his voice was firm with his next command. "Change back into your demon form."

Nix cocked his head, then widened his eyes in surprise as he realized Ivan's reasoning. "You think this might be an illusion?"

It was laughable, that Nix would only be pretending to be unharmed, but he shifted anyway. The blood smearing his chest turned a dark purple, but his skin stayed unmarked beneath it.

Nix hadn't realized quite how tightly wound Ivan had become until the tension in his frame eased. "Good," he said with a harsh breath. "Good."

He eyed Nix's nipple piercings for a long moment before his gaze tracked down the rest of Nix's torso, as if Nix might be hiding more bullet wounds from him. His assessment stopped abruptly at the waistband of Nix's low-waisted leather pants, where a bit of red lace was peeking out provocatively.

Ivan's gaze shot back up to Nix's. "What the fuck is that?"

Nix grinned at him, all sharp teeth. "My panties, of course."

He thought for a moment that Ivan would turn away, perhaps begin to strategize revenge or something equally appropriate, but his human surprised him. "Show me," he ordered.

Nix wouldn't make him ask twice. He snapped his fingers, and his leather pants went the way of his shirt.

Ivan was close enough that the long breath he let out cooled Nix's skin. "Jesus."

Nix preened. He was awfully fond of this conjured pair of red lacy underwear. He liked the way it framed his bulge in particular. He hadn't been sure if Ivan would feel the same, given his silly ideas about appropriate appearances and whatnot, but the budding tendrils of desire cutting through Ivan's panic said otherwise.

And yet Ivan's gaze was roaming over Nix again, like his brain hadn't caught up to the evidence before him. Nix grabbed his chin, forcing Ivan to meet his eyes. "Ivan Kozlov," he said firmly. "I am a *demon*. A gun isn't going to be the end of me."

"I'm going to kill him," Ivan swore.

It was Ivan's scent more than his words that made Nix take notice of the fact that he was trembling not in fear but in rage. It was thick in the air, spicy and hot, a rich, heady sauce blanketing whatever arousal Nix's naughty panties had inspired. "I'm sure you will," Nix murmured.

They stood there, breathing each other's air, and Nix soaked up that rage, letting it run through him in turn. Anger wasn't usually his food of choice, but it was still a strong human emotion, and those were hard to resist for a demon.

Ivan's gaze kept dropping back to Nix's panties, where Nix's cock was beginning to strain against the lace.

He couldn't help it—Ivan was acting all fierce and angry and ordering people to strip willy-nilly. How was Nix meant *not* to get turned on?

He'd been very good in Ivan's office earlier. He'd feasted on Ivan's desire and had asked for nothing else for himself in return. But he wanted more now. He wanted that thick cock inside him. Wanted Ivan to paint his insides the way he'd painted his face. Wanted to drain Ivan of all he had, then coax him back to hardness and do it all again, until Ivan was begging Nix for a reprieve.

"I can take these off too," he offered, his voice low and sultry.

Ivan's hand drifted to Nix's waist, fingering the lacy band of his panties, and then dipped just below, his light touch sending tingles along Nix's skin. But he stayed silent.

Of course. In all the hubbub, Nix had let himself forget Ivan's preposterous "one time only" assertion and his own annoyance with it.

Nix didn't want one time. He wanted all the times. It had been the hottest thing in the world, to have Ivan's harsh grip in his hair and his full cock in Nix's mouth, his hips thrusting hard enough to bruise Nix's throat (if he were human, that was). To have him lose control of that tight restraint of his, all at Nix's hands.

No illusions. No tricks. Just Ivan wanting Nix exactly as he was, so fiercely he'd been mad with it.

"What will happen if you fuck me, Ivan?" Nix asked softly,

running his hands along Ivan's broad shoulders. "Will the world collapse?"

Ivan snapped Nix's waistband against his skin. "Bratva men... they're old-fashioned. Toxic, Sascha would say. It was challenge enough with Alexei and Sascha preferring men. But all three of us? The leader of the family? I'd be shot in my sleep."

Nix scoffed. "I'm not sure if you noticed, baby, but you were just shot at in broad daylight."

"That's different." Ivan shook his head. "I've spent my entire adult life trying to protect Sascha from the wrath of men too bigoted to—"

Nix cut in, impatient, "Then replace your men."

Ivan stopped short, his fingers twitching against Nix's skin. "What?"

"We're already tidying things up around here, aren't we?" Nix continued, eager to have Ivan finally listening. "Then let's switch it *all* up, hm? Why shouldn't you be able to do whatever you want? *Fuck* whoever you want? You're the one in charge."

Ivan's gaze snapped to his. "And the men who won't follow?"

"What happens to Mafia men who disobey the boss?"

"Vicious," Ivan murmured, repeating Nix's assertion from earlier. His pupils were taking over his pale eyes, and the desire in the air was thickening.

Nix lowered his voice, letting himself sway into him. "They all knew what they were getting into, didn't they? You can still have your empire. But it will be one of *your* making, not this mess your father left you."

Ivan's hand had dipped lower into Nix's panties, his fingers practically brushing at the base of Nix's cock. Nix stepped even closer, running his nose along the line of Ivan's neck. "Does that turn you on, Vanya?" he murmured, already knowing the answer. "The thought of taking charge so absolutely?"

Ivan's laugh had a bitter edge to it, even as he continued to stroke Nix's skin. "It's why my brothers hate me. The fact that I want it so badly. They think I should reject it all, not covet it." He wrapped his free hand around Nix's throat, stilling his movements and catching his eye. "Does that disgust you too?"

Disgust him? How could Nix be disgusted by Ivan? By a little thing like Ivan wanting a bit of power in a world that had proven to be harsh and terrifying?

Nix wouldn't want to be powerless here either.

And Ivan seemed to keep forgetting that Nix had tasted his very soul—he knew all its sour and bitter pockets already. There wasn't anything Ivan could say or do that would surprise Nix into hating him.

Nix had been around humans for many, many years. Ivan was hardly the worst of them.

"You think I care about human morals, Vanya?" Nix laughed, low and throaty. "I like that you're vicious, baby. That you want to keep your crooked little kingdom. And if you go too far, I'll be here to rein you in."

There was another charged moment, the air between them electric, and then Ivan was tugging at the waistband of Nix's panties. "Take these off. *Now.*"

Nix arched a brow. "No more one-time thing?"

"Fuck one time. You're *my* demon," Ivan growled, tightening his hand around Nix's throat as he lowered his mouth to his. "I'll have you whenever the fuck I want you."

As Ivan claimed his mouth, Nix had to backtrack and give a bit of credit to their fake deliveryman. Because if Nix had known getting shot was the key to breaking down a few more of Ivan's barriers, he'd have managed it day one.

"Off," Ivan growled, repeating his demand and breaking the kiss to stare daggers at Nix's offending panties.

Nix could have disappeared his underwear the same way he'd disappeared the rest, but he chose to slide them down instead, enjoying the way Ivan's gaze was locked onto everything he revealed. Locked onto Nix's dick, in fact.

It was a nice dick, if Nix did say so himself. Slimmer than Ivan's, but long enough, and with such pretty colors, a dark red at the base lightening to a pale lavender at the narrowed head.

"No hair," Ivan murmured, petting the skin at the base of Nix's cock. He brushed his finger along the length, circling the tip, and Nix shuddered at the touch. He'd basically been edged for days now. If Ivan wrapped a full hand around his cock, he might just explode.

But Ivan raised his hand, rubbing the precum between his fingers thoughtfully. "Thick," he mused.

"Mm," Nix answered mindlessly. He didn't need foreplay, no matter how much he was relishing Ivan's interest in all his bits. What he needed was Ivan's cock inside him that very instant.

Ivan's hand slid around, grabbing at Nix's ass. It slid steadily upward from there, palming at the base of his tail. Nix hissed at the touch.

Ivan smirked at him. "Sensitive here?"

"Very."

Ivan looked down to where the bulk of Nix's tail had crept around his leg. If he was put off by having a demon's tail wrapped around his calf, he didn't show it. "And the rest of it?"

Nix blinked innocently. "Has a mind of its own sometimes."

Ivan hummed, his fingers sliding down to Nix's crease, dipping in without hesitation. Apparently having made up his mind, he wasn't going to be shy about it.

Thank the fucking Book for that.

But Ivan stopped short once his fingers brushed against Nix's hole.

Oh, right. That.

Ivan stared at him. "What— Are you *wet?*"

"How many times do I need to tell you?" Nix placed a hand on Ivan's chest, pushing him up against the wall. He'd mount the human himself if he had to. "I'm a demon, baby. An incubus." He grinned at Ivan, snapping sharp teeth. "Did you think I wouldn't be self-lubricating?"

9

Ivan

There was some sort of slick substance between Ivan's fingers. A tail wrapped around his leg, twisting and pulsing against his skin. And a cock pressed against his hip, leaking strangely thick precum onto his slacks.

Any one of those things should have been enough to turn Ivan off. To remind him to put a stop to this before he did something that would change the course of his life irrevocably.

But he couldn't stop. If he didn't fuck this demon sometime in the next sixty seconds, it was entirely possible Ivan was going to lose his mind.

It wasn't a want anymore. Not some idle thought or wayward fantasy. It was a fucking *need*. Ivan needed to get his cock into this infernal creature before the last of his control fractured beyond repair. One more minute without that inhuman warmth clenching around him and he'd become a mindless fucking beast.

More than he was already.

Ivan knew he was being brainless. He knew Nix getting shot

had been a nonissue. Nix wasn't fucking human, and the wounds had closed seemingly as quickly as they'd been created. But something about the gunshots, and Nix's warm body falling against him, had set off a storm within Ivan.

What if Nix's human form had turned out to be vulnerable after all? What if he'd been taken from Ivan? What if Ivan had never gotten a chance to take what Nix had offered him over and over again, kept back by his own stubborn resistance to letting himself want something his father had made very clear was never, ever allowed?

The very thought of it was enough to make Ivan want to burn his office to the ground.

And then there were the red fucking panties. Sheer and lacy and absolutely obscene stretched around Nix's demon cock. Ivan had wanted to take them off with his teeth, to bite into Nix through the lace until he made a mark on the demon's skin that actually *took*.

Those panties were intolerable. They should be burned. Disintegrated.

Too late now. Instead, Ivan flipped Nix around, pressing his front against the door. "Self-lubricating," he repeated, kicking Nix's legs apart. He didn't know much about fucking men, but he knew something about fucking. "That's convenient."

"Isn't it?" Nix peered back at him, wiggling his ass enticingly. As if Ivan needed any further fucking enticement. "No face-to-face? Trying to close your eyes and pretend I'm someone else, Vanya?"

More like Ivan was afraid that if he looked into Nix's purple eyes while he fucked him for the first time, he might do something unforgivably stupid. Like order him to never leave. Forbid him from getting hurt. Beg him to fix everything in Ivan's life that was so irrevocably fucked.

Ivan lowered his forehead to Nix's shoulder, a mirthless

chuckle leaving his lips. He unbuckled his belt, unzipping himself with shaking fingers and tugging his cock out. "Your *tail* is wrapped around my leg right now. Who am I pretending you are? I just—I need—"

"Ah," Nix said, like he understood. Like he realized Ivan was too turned on and desperate to make this anything but rough and ugly. And maybe he did understand. He seemed to understand too much, always. Blasting through Ivan's defenses like they were made of tissue paper.

Ivan couldn't afford to fuck men? Apparently Nix would rearrange his entire empire for him, help him take a firm enough command that he could parade Nix around naked with a collar and no one would dare question it.

Nix groaned, arching his back so Ivan's already rock-hard cock slid against his crease. "Oh my," he murmured. "Now there's a naughty thought."

Ivan tugged at the base of Nix's tail, committing to memory the soft, velvety feel of the skin there. "Stop reading my mind," he scolded.

Nix gave a throaty chuckle. "Stop wanting me so badly."

"I *can't.*"

"I know." Nix sounded smug. Satisfied that he'd finally driven Ivan to the edge, maybe.

"Do I need to...stretch you open?" It wasn't Ivan's first time with anal—some of the divorcées had been more adventurous than others—but it was his first time with a self-lubricating sex demon.

"If I were human. As it is..." Nix spread his palms flat against the door, creating an arch in his back that would put a porn star to shame.

Ivan tugged once again at the base of Nix's tail, moving it out of the way. The rest of the tail whipped off of Ivan's leg, wrapping around Nix's instead, leaving his ass exposed to Ivan's gaze.

Ivan spread Nix's cheeks, staring intently at his hole. It was a darker purple than the rest of Nix's skin, hairless like the front of him had been. And wet, just as Ivan had felt. He could see some sort of clear, slick substance leaking out of him.

Ivan wanted to touch. He wanted to lick. He'd never thought he'd want to taste another man's hole, but he sure as fuck wanted to taste Nix.

But there wasn't time now. Ivan needed to fuck Nix more than he'd ever needed anything.

He notched the blunt head of his cock against him, using a hand on Nix's shoulder for leverage as he pressed in.

Holy fuck.

Maybe Ivan shouldn't have listened to Nix. Demon or not, it was still a tight fit. And hot. So fucking hot. But Ivan persisted, pressing into Nix like he belonged there, as Nix whispered filthy encouragements ("Yes, Ivan. Deeper. Give it to me. Give it all to me."), peppered with little breathy moans at each new inch.

Like he was just as desperate as Ivan.

By the time Ivan bottomed out, he was gasping for air, the hot clench of Nix's channel around his cock somehow both infernal and divine.

He was going to be ruined for anyone else after this, wasn't he?

"Why the fuck do you feel so good?" he asked, pressing a bite into Nix's shoulder, mouthing at the soft skin there while he tried to get his bearings.

It wasn't just the feel of Nix around Ivan's cock, although that was enticing enough to drive a man mad. It was like there was a fog in the air. Something heady and smoky that had Ivan feeling almost drugged with arousal.

There was some measure of relief when Nix sounded almost as wrecked as Ivan when he answered. "I'm an incubus. Desire feeds more desire. You'll be—" He moaned, clenching tightly around Ivan's cock when Ivan bit at his shoulder again. "—be a puddle when I'm done with you."

Ivan didn't doubt it. He wrapped one arm around Nix's middle, the other coming over his shoulder to cover Nix's hand against the door with his own. They were close enough in height for it to have been awkward, if not for the way Nix was bending himself, canting his hips for Ivan's pleasure.

Ivan withdrew slowly, reluctant to leave the warmth he'd found, then rocked his hips, groaning as he drove in.

He stuck with short, shallow movements, wanting to stay as deep within Nix as he possibly could. He put all his weight behind it, and the hotel door thudded with each thrust.

Nix wasn't exactly quiet, either, keening and moaning and hissing at Ivan to go harder. He pressed back into each of Ivan's thrusts, barely letting Ivan withdraw, as if he couldn't bear the distance any more than Ivan could.

They were going to get security called on them at this rate.

Ivan couldn't find it in himself to care. All he could focus on was Nix—his firm body pressed against Ivan's, the smoky scent of his skin, the throaty sound of his moans.

Sweat dripped off Ivan, sticking his dress shirt to his skin. Nix had been right, of course. Ivan was melting. But he couldn't stop, couldn't pause. Not even long enough to strip off his damned shirt.

Ivan wasn't much for dirty talk. He wasn't much for words, period. But an endless chant began to leave his lips without permission, timed with each thrust of his hips. "Fuck. Fuck. *Fuck.*"

His orgasm began building too fast, the feel of Nix around him too much to bear.

"You better not pull out," Nix whined, seeming to sense Ivan was close. "You better fill me up. I want it all. Every fucking drop, Ivan."

Ivan wrapped that mane of hair around his fist, baring Nix's slender neck to his gaze. "Such a needy fucking slut," he growled.

"Yes, baby," Nix moaned, like Ivan had just whispered the sweetest of endearments into his pointed ear. "Yes, yes, yes."

Ivan's orgasm was merciless, a tsunami crash where all he could do was hold on, wrapped around the demon, his hips shuddering as he emptied every bit of himself inside him.

He bit into Nix's neck at the end of it, pressing his teeth in as hard as he could and wrapping his hand around Nix's cock. Ivan didn't know what he was doing there, but he jerked Nix the way he himself liked it—fast, furious, and just this side of brutal.

It seemed to do the trick. It didn't take long until Nix was keening once more, spurting that absurdly thick cum over Ivan's fist.

Good. *Good.*

They stayed there, standing against the door, Ivan's panting breaths loud in the quiet room. The mark he'd made on Nix's neck was already fading.

He had a beautiful neck, Ivan's demon. He had a beautiful everything—his face, his hair, the lines of his body. As if every part of him was specifically designed to tempt Ivan. Ivan was barely human at this point, drained to the point of exhaustion, and already he wanted him again.

He sighed, rubbing his forehead into Nix's shoulder. "This isn't the end of it, is it?"

"No, baby." Nix turned, and Ivan hissed as the movement forced his softening cock to withdraw from that overwhelming heat. Nix laid a hand on Ivan's cheek before bringing Ivan's cum-covered fingers to his mouth with a catlike grin. "This is just the beginning."

———

IVAN DIDN'T KNOW exactly what dazed state he was in—or what demon magic Nix had worked—that he found himself sometime later completely nude in the hotel bed with the incubus draped over him.

Ivan was half-hard again already, but he was determined to ignore it. If he started fucking the incubus every time he wanted him, it would set a dangerous precedent.

They'd never leave the bed again.

As it was, Ivan was on his back, the crisp white sheet pulled up low on his hips, while Nix was sprawled on his side, half on Ivan's chest, toying with Ivan's chest hair while Ivan idly worried one of Nix's nipple piercings.

He'd neglected them during their frantic fuck against the door. It was an awful waste, considering Ivan had been wondering how Nix would react to have them pulled almost since he'd first laid eyes on them.

He sighed. "I'm afraid that wasn't my best effort just now."

"Really?" Nix said, scratching his talons lightly across Ivan's chest with a small smirk. "I found it quite satisfying."

"Not much finesse," Ivan mused.

That was putting it lightly. He'd been like an animal, really, driving into Nix over and over again without a single thought toward technique.

Nix slid his leg against Ivan's over the hotel sheet. "Well, there's a time for finesse and a time for passion, wouldn't you say?"

Ivan scoffed. "Is that would you'd call it? Passion?"

Nix cocked his head, purple eyes gleaming. "What would you call it?"

"A very specific type of insanity."

Nix grinned, flopping onto his back with a laugh. "You flatter me, Vanya."

Flattery hadn't been Ivan's intention, but so be it. He let go of Nix's nipple piercing, trailing his fingers lightly over his chest instead, as Nix had done with his. He paused in the center. "Your tattoo moves when I touch it."

The red symbol was swirling around the point of contact with Ivan's finger, like if it could escape Nix's skin, it would be wrapped around it, much in the same way Nix's tail was once again wrapped around Ivan's calf.

"Mm," Nix hummed. "It's magic."

Ivan eyed Nix—the lavender skin, the purple eyes that had been glowing ever since they'd fucked, the curling horns he was somehow avoiding poking Ivan's eyes out with. "Magic. Of course."

"We get them when we enter into the Book."

"Why did you?" Ivan couldn't imagine willingly subjecting himself to such a thing. But then again, there was much about Nix that was incomprehensible.

"Oh, I've always wanted to be in the human realm." Nix stretched his arms out over his head, looking very feline in his movements. "There are some incubi who feed on our own kind, but I've never found it satisfying. I prefer mortals."

Ivan's fingers drifted to one of Nix's piercings again. "Have you fucked women?"

"I've fucked all kinds."

Ivan tugged the piercing, not quite as harshly as he wanted. "You liked it?" he asked, the question coming out gruff.

"Of course." One of Nix's hands trailed to his other piercing, tugging it in time with Ivan's teasing. "Women are divine."

"I always liked them."

"I'm sure you did." Nix flicked his gaze to Ivan. "You know bisexuality is a thing, don't you, Ivan?"

"I was raised by a vicious mobster, not under a rock."

Ivan might not be ready to say the words out loud but wasn't completely dense—he was becoming increasingly aware he wasn't the straight arrow he'd believed himself to be. As evidenced by the purple cock he was currently staring at—as Nix hardened under their combined touch—one he was seriously considering putting his mouth on at some point.

"Of course, darling." Nix turned onto his side again, completely uncaring of his nudity or his erect state, propping his head up on his hand. "And how did your vicious mobster father reconcile his backward beliefs with your brothers' predilections?"

"Alexei I think he genuinely didn't know. Sascha..." Ivan shrugged. "Denial, I suppose. He was always softer with him anyway."

"Do you wish he'd been softer with you?"

"What good would wishing for that do? He's dead."

It was probably the wrong thing to say, when they were sharing truths—he was probably fucking all this up—but Ivan was new to pillow talk. Normally it was just a hurried fuck and then calling his driver.

But if Nix minded Ivan's bluntness, he didn't show it. His hand was drifting under the sheet, his aim unmistakable.

Ivan caught his wrist. "No touching my cock while you discuss my father, if you please."

Nix flashed him a taunting grin, but he didn't fight Ivan's hold. "Then we'll change the subject." His grin dropped, a thoughtful look taking over. "I think we should be staying with Sascha and Kai in Maine."

Ivan was caught off guard by the suggestion. "Why?"

"Kai's better at protection than me. He's an actual warrior—the kind of demon you intended to summon." Nix managed to sound both sheepish and pouty at the thought. "And I think we'll want backup if we intend to shake up your men, and sweet Sascha might need some in-person convincing. He doesn't seem very fond of your business."

"He hates me," Ivan admitted.

"Ah, ah." Nix raised his free hand and wagged his finger in Ivan's face. "He can hate how you act without hating *you*. He loves you, silly. Humans are very complex that way. Also—" Nix's voice lowered into a seductive purr. Taking advantage of Ivan's loosened grip, he dipped his hand under the sheet, tracing Ivan's cock in the idle way he'd been tracing his chest earlier. "I need a vacation. You've been working me to the very bone."

"You interviewed a total of two of my employees." Ivan kept his voice cool, even as blood rushed to his dick with each dancing touch of Nix's fingers.

"And got shot," Nix added, thumbing at Ivan's cockhead. "*And* was railed quite aggressively against a hotel room door, I might add."

"Is getting fucked by me one of your duties, then?" It should have been insulting, but heat pooled in Ivan's belly at the thought: Nix under his command, taking everything Ivan had to give him.

"It is," Nix told him, pushing Ivan once more onto his back and looming over him. "And I'm afraid it's going to be quite a constant demand on my faculties."

He swung his leg over Ivan, settling over Ivan's thighs, holding himself above him like a taunt.

He was stunning. Tall and strong and most likely completely out of Ivan's league, if Ivan wanted to care about such things.

Ivan ran his hands up Nix's silken thighs. "Why isn't my cum leaking out of you right now?" he asked, not sure if he was curious or disappointed.

Disappointed, surely. He'd wanted to see it, the evidence of his claim.

Nix blinked at him, his lips twitching as if he was holding back a smile. "Heavens." He wrapped a hand around Ivan's cock, stroking him firmly. "What a thing to say."

Ivan arched up into the touch even as he frowned. "Tell me."

"I absorbed it." Nix winked at him. "Incubus things, don't you know."

It was Ivan's turn to pause, even as Nix continued to jerk him off. "You can't mean... Can I—?" He cleared his throat. "Absorbed *where*?"

Nix threw his head back and laughed. "Oh my god, you silly goose! I can't get pregnant, if that's what you're thinking." His laughter stopped abruptly, and he cocked his head, his hand stilling. "But isn't that what Sergei suggested the other night? A wife and a couple of tots?"

There was something dangerous about Nix's tone, and Ivan was suddenly alert to the fact that sharp talons were wrapped around his dick.

He met Nix's eyes squarely. "I'm not bringing children into this world," he said firmly. "I'm not that cruel. And I don't want a wife."

"Good." Nix softened again, as abruptly as he'd transformed in the first place. "I'd hate to have to bully the competition."

It was a preposterous statement. As if Nix were really in competition to be Ivan's...wife? Companion?

But Ivan didn't argue the point, because Nix was holding Ivan's cock steady, lowering himself down onto Ivan in one smooth glide.

Ivan cursed, biting down on his lip hard enough to taste copper.

"Mm." Nix rolled his hips in a way that should have been illegal, smirking down at Ivan. "Now what was it you were saying about finesse, darling?"

10

Nix

The first slow roll had Ivan's hands shooting up to Nix's hips, grasping hard, as if to stop Nix from moving.

Nix paused, cocking a brow, but Ivan didn't try to hold him back—he simply held on, his fingers digging into Nix's skin, his eyes dark and heavy-lidded.

So Nix moved again, taking special pleasure in the way it made Ivan's jaw clench. "How's that, master?" he purred.

Ivan didn't answer, except for a grunt. Nix grinned anyway, taking a moment to find his rhythm. It didn't take him long, now that he knew the intimate feel of Ivan's cock inside him.

Nix had meant what he'd said before—he didn't always need finesse. He hadn't even noticed the lack of it earlier. He'd been too busy being swept away by the force of Ivan's desire, so potent once he'd finally let go of that tight hold on his control. Slamming Nix against the door, biting into him, giving him that thick cock over and over.

It had been everything Nix had wanted from him and more.

But there was something to be said for this way too. For Nix being able to angle himself so Ivan's cock rubbed against him just right, the coarse hair on Ivan's thighs brushing against the soft skin of Nix's ass.

And Nix got to look at him, his beautiful human.

Nix liked Ivan like this—rumpled and sex-addled, bare and open, his eyes locked onto Nix with burning intensity. Nix was already well sated—by Ivan's desire, by his cum inside him—but he couldn't help taking more. He was greedy by nature, and Ivan was bringing out the worst of it.

Ivan's gaze lowered and locked onto Nix's nipples. Nix raised his hands—with the next roll of his hips, Nix flicked his piercings, moaning at the little zing that went through him.

He laughed when Ivan's hold on his hips tightened even further. "You're so easy, Vanya," he teased.

"You're the first to ever say so."

"Mm." Another languid roll, another laugh as he watched Ivan try to bite back his moan. "They just never knew what buttons to press, did they?"

It was Nix's turn to moan as Ivan punched his hips up at just the right moment, sending sparks along Nix's spine as his cock angled perfectly within him.

Nix tossed his hair over his shoulder, leaning down over him. "You're a quick learner, aren't you?"

Ivan's hands swept up his sides. "I've never had any complaints."

Nix narrowed his eyes. "I bet you haven't."

He could admit to himself he'd gotten a bit jealous before, as he'd been reminded of Sergei's silly assertion that Ivan needed a wife and babies.

Nix's Ivan? Please. As if a human companion could ever do for him what Nix could.

It had been funny before, but now that Nix had gotten a taste of what Ivan had to offer him, he wasn't feeling up for sharing.

Not now. Not ever.

Nix had been serving humanity for centuries—offering up their wants on a silver platter in exchange for tiny morsels of their souls—and now it was his turn to get what he desired.

He was keeping this mess of a human for himself.

Nix gasped as Ivan's hand sneaked up to twist his nipple. He was glaring up at Nix. "What are you thinking so hard about?"

Nix's tail whipped around Ivan's wrist, and he leaned down even closer to hover his mouth over Ivan's. "I was wondering if you could make me come just from playing with my piercings," he whispered.

Ivan's breath was hot against Nix's lips. "Liar."

Nix smirked.

But Ivan had a point. That was more than enough thinking. Nix was full of gorgeous human cock, the desire in the room a thick, heady fog, and it was time for another meal.

He set a steady pace, his hands on Ivan's chest to balance himself, gasping encouragements every time Ivan's hips met him halfway.

Eventually Ivan seemed to tire of toying with Nix's piercings by hand alone. He lunged up, tugging Nix's nipple into his mouth, flicking his tongue around the barbell.

Nix leaned back, clasping Ivan's head to him, his talons digging into his hair. He moaned. "Oh. Oh *yes*."

The hand not constrained by Nix's tail snaked to his lower back, encouraging Nix's movements as Ivan sucked and licked.

Nix rocked furiously in Ivan's lap, chasing the buildup of that desire. He could feel it in his own belly, could sense it lighting up Ivan's form. It was intoxicating. It was everywhere.

Nix wanted all of it. Wanted every bit of Ivan's pleasure. Wanted to be filled by him once more.

"Again, Ivan," he ordered, clenching down. "Again."

Ivan bit down on Nix's nipple and thrust up into him hard, locking him in place with the arm around his hips, his muscles trembling as he came.

Nix tossed his head back, absorbing the rush, letting it light up all his nerve endings. He was grateful when Ivan sneaked a hand around his cock as he had before, taking Nix over the edge with him. Nix wouldn't have been able to do it himself—he couldn't move, frozen by the intensity of the wave taking over them both.

He stayed in Ivan's lap for a long time, holding Ivan to him, both of them trembling. The back of Ivan's neck was damp with sweat. Nix loved it. It was such a human thing, proof of how hard Ivan had worked to please them both. Just like the way Ivan was panting, struggling to catch his breath.

Nix stroked his hair soothingly. "How was that? Did I perform my duties well?"

Ivan's forehead dropped back to Nix's chest. "*Fuck.*"

Nix would go ahead and take that as a rave review.

———

NIX WOKE up alone in bed.

He'd actually fallen asleep, hadn't he? He hadn't been able to help it, really. He'd been absolutely stuffed, sated with Ivan's desire.

After riding his human until he'd been a trembling mess, Nix had taken him into the shower and teased him until Ivan had let him suck his cock again.

Ivan had glared at him afterward. "I'm forty years old," he'd said, aiming for cold dismissal but missing the mark a bit with his kiss-bitten lips and numerous hickeys. "I can't be fucking you every second of every day."

But then he'd jerked Nix off aggressively in the shower, kissing him all the while like he was going to devour him right there and then, so Nix didn't take his words too personally.

Plus, Nix was figuring him out a little, his Vanya. Talking about his feelings had clearly been trained out of Ivan by the toxic men in his life, but physical connection was where he kept meeting Nix again and again.

If Nix needed to be fucking Ivan "every second of every day" to keep those walls even a minute bit lowered, then so be it.

Oh dear. He grinned to himself. *What a burden to bear.*

Nix had taken Ivan to bed because his human had needed the rest, but then it had been Nix who'd fallen asleep first, all warm and cozy with Ivan toying with the nipple piercings he seemed to be becoming quickly obsessed with.

That was what Nix got for overeating.

But he hadn't been able to help gorging—Ivan's desire was so potent, and all of it was for Nix alone. The way he'd fucked Nix against that door, desperate and a little brutal? Not to mention the way he'd let Nix ride him just the way he'd wanted, holding Nix's hips tightly enough to bruise but letting him lead the pace anyway.

Nix rose from the bed, fishing Ivan's button-down off the floor and slipping it on because he'd seen it in the movies and always wanted to try it. (Or, more accurately, he'd seen it while watching *humans* watch movies.)

But he and Ivan were about the same height, so the shirt didn't actually hang tantalizingly at Nix's thighs. Instead, his bare ass and cock hung out, more silly than sexy.

So Nix threw on another pair of lace panties for good measure.

He left the bedroom portion of their suite to find Ivan at the hotel desk, one of the hotel's white robes covering his nudity. He looked softer than Nix was used to seeing, his hair still mussed from sleeping on it wet, his neck displaying the numerous love bites Nix had left on him.

Nix strode over and settled sideways on Ivan's lap.

Ivan's hand immediately moved to toy with the hem of Nix's panties. "I hate these," he grumbled.

"No, you don't," Nix told him with confidence. Ivan could frown at them all he liked, but just the sight of them had increased the desire in the room by a third at the very least. "What are you doing out here?"

"Thinking about your proposal."

"It's a good one, isn't it?" Nix liked it very much, if he did say so himself. Ivan's hesitation around Nix had been cute and all at first, but if he was going to be the leader he had the potential to be, he needed to be able to embrace himself completely.

And that included, as far as Nix was concerned, having Nix at his side. And in his bed.

"We'll need a show of force," Ivan mused, his fingers stroking against Nix's hip. "I don't want to leave any room for thoughts of retaliation."

"Well, Kai's huge," Nix pointed out. He really was, especially in his demon form. Seven feet tall before one included the horns. Plus, he had a mighty pair of leathery wings, when he felt inclined to display them. Which wasn't often enough, in Nix's opinion. If *Nix* had giant bat wings, he'd be rocking them on every occasion. Building themed outfits around them, even.

"We'll need more than just one intimidating demon," Ivan told him, bringing Nix out of his sartorial musings.

"You said your other brother has a vampire."

"That's not an option."

"Why not? Isn't it a family business, this whole grand thing your father built for you?"

"Alexei left," Ivan said, bitter as always. "Both me and the business. After blowing a deal and costing me millions. A little 'fuck you' to remember him by." A frisson of hurt made its way through the bitterness. "He was supposed to be my right-hand man."

Poor Ivan. Nix patted his shoulder. "Well, now you have me." At the look Ivan gave him, Nix bristled. "What?"

Nix would be amazing right-hand man material. And if Ivan said otherwise, he was getting a kick to the shin.

"I had my cock in you just a few hours ago," Ivan told him, like that was somehow pertinent to their conversation.

Nix frowned at him, trying to understand. "You're not allowed to fuck your right-hand man?"

Ivan's lips twitched. "Historically, no."

"How boring," Nix mused. And completely irrelevant human nonsense, which he would ignore as such. He tossed his hair over his shoulder. "Anyway, you should ask."

"Ask what?" Ivan asked absently, his searching hand beginning to move rather enticingly closer to Nix's package.

"Ask Alexei," Nix reminded him instead of thrusting up into Ivan's touch. See? He was completely focused, despite Ivan's wandering hand. Nix could be an amazing right-hand man *and* bed partner. "And Sascha too. Ask your brothers for help, Vanya."

That was what Nix would do in a pinch—ask Kai or Chaos. Hell, he'd even take his chances with Nightmare, if he was completely desperate.

Ivan stiffened under him—and not in the fun way. "My brothers never help," he said coldly. "Alexei's too selfish. Sascha's too scattered."

"Have you ever *asked* though?"

Ivan stared at him for a moment, then took out his phone. He hit a few buttons, and Alexei's name popped up on the screen.

They waited.

No answer.

Ivan cocked a brow at him.

Nix huffed. "Try again."

Ivan tried again. And once more.

On the third attempt, there was, instead of an answer, a request for FaceTime. Ivan accepted it, his expression unreadable. He had the phone angled so Nix was off-screen but able to see well enough. Which was good because Nix was curious about this middle brother.

But the man who appeared on the other end didn't look like Ivan at all. And he certainly didn't look any older than Sascha. He looked young and...small, with dainty features and a mess of dark hair.

"Where's Alexei?" Ivan asked immediately.

Ah. So this wasn't the middle brother at all.

Nix studied the screen. Was this the vampire, then? He looked more like a little doll than a creature of the night. But then again, Chaos was proof enough that deadly force could come in small packages.

The vampire scowled at Ivan fiercely. "Alexei's not here."

"I can see him behind you."

Ivan had a point. There wasn't another face on the screen, but there was clearly a broad body behind the vampire. It looked like he and Alexei were sitting on a couch together.

The vampire sniffed. "He doesn't want to talk to you."

"Why did you pick up, then?"

"You kept calling."

"You could have put the phone on silent," Ivan said, exasperation breaking through the ice in his voice.

The vampire's scowl deepened. "I was trying to show him videos of *cats*." He said it like an accusation. "I hit the button on *accident*."

Well, this was cute and all, but the argument was becoming both ridiculous and fruitless. Nix leaned into frame, waggling his fingers. "Hello, there. We haven't met. I'm Nix."

The scowl dropped from the little vampire's face immediately, his gray eyes widening. "Oh, hello. I'm Jay. You're very beautiful."

Nix liked him already. "Well, thank you, sweetness. You're adorable yourself."

There was some muffled grumbling on the other end, but Jay didn't seem to pay it any mind. He put his face closer to the phone's camera. "Are those horns on your head? You're a demon, aren't you? Do you have wings?"

Nix grinned at his eagerness. "No, but I do have a tail."

"Amazing," Jay breathed. He cocked his head. "What are you doing with Ivan? He's awful."

Nix ignored Ivan's scoff, leaning sideways across his lap to hide him from view. "I'm helping him turn over a new leaf."

"But...why?"

"Because I like the mean ones."

"Well, that's..." Jay seemed too polite to tell Nix that was crazy, but he seemed to be thinking of it.

"We could really use your help as well."

"Well, the thing is... So Alexei's not a big fan of Ivan right now." Jay lowered voice conspiratorially. "Ivan shot Alexei last time, you know."

"Ivan did?" Nix asked, fighting back a laugh. How like his human to leave out that little detail. "How naughty."

"Very naughty, yes." Jay nodded sagely. "So I'm not sure Alexei's going to want to help."

"If he could think about it, Ivan's very sorry," Nix added, ever the diplomat.

Ivan pinched his side. "I'm *not*," he growled.

Jay narrowed his eyes, clearly having caught the denial. "He doesn't sound sorry."

"If you two come to help, I'll show you my tail."

There was a long, thoughtful pause on Jay's end, and then he cleared his throat delicately. "I'll...discuss it with Alexei."

A large hand covered the screen, hiding Jay from view. Clearly

Alexei had had enough of the conversation. There was only a moment for Jay's frantic, "Bye, Nix!" before the call ended.

Nix leaned back, peering at Ivan. "Well, he was just adorable, wasn't he?" He realized Ivan was glaring at him, and he raised his brows. "What? Would it kill you to at least *pretend* to be sorry, to aid your plea? Isn't that what humans do? Lie to get what they want?"

Ivan pinched at the bridge of his nose. "I must be losing my mind listening to you at all." He flicked his fingers at the edge of Nix's panties. "Or thinking with my dick."

Nix preened. Maybe Ivan had meant it as an insult, but all Nix had heard was Ivan admitting to liking Nix's panties. "I think with my dick all the time," he reassured Ivan. "I highly recommend it. It's a wonderful way to live."

Ivan's answer was to push Nix off his lap. "Come. Get dressed. We need to stop at the office before we head to Maine."

"To interrogate Tara?" Nix would have a choice word or two for her if she'd been the reason Ivan had been placed in danger.

But Ivan shook his head. "She's been cleared. The video shows the deliveryman outside well before we called for the car. He entered the building when he saw Oleg pull up. He didn't receive a call from anyone we could see."

"Then why the office?" Nix pouted, following Ivan into the bedroom. "Not more *work*."

"I need to grab the Book." Ivan slipped off his robe, and Nix was so busy admiring the display of lean muscles and the thick, tempting vision of Ivan's half-hard cock that it took him a minute to catch up with what Ivan was saying. "I don't want Sergei storming in and taking it by accident."

Oh. That.

Nix cleared his throat, stripping off Ivan's shirt at his impatient gesture, materializing his own outfit at the same time. He had a feeling he didn't want to be naked for this conversation. "The thing is...you might not find it there."

Ivan froze in the act of buttoning up his slacks, his features smoothing out into an unreadable mask. "And why wouldn't I find it there?" he asked, his voice soft and deadly. "Where I left it?"

"I think your cousin Cooper might have accidentally picked it up."

Ivan narrowed his eyes. "It was in my desk drawer, Nix. My *closed* desk drawer."

"I might have accidentally banged it open with my hip."

"Twice you've used the word 'accidentally.'" Ivan stepped close, nose to nose with Nix. "Don't. Lie. To me."

"Fine." Nix rolled his eyes, resisting the urge to step back. He was a demon; he wasn't going to be intimidated by a human mobster, no matter how well he fucked. "I might have *purposefully* banged it open with my hip and then told Cooper he missed one and pointed to it and watched him pick it up."

The temperature of the air in the room seemed to drop a few degrees. "*Why?*" Ivan hissed.

"I have a friend in there. He deserves a chance to be summoned."

"Even if it fucks with all my plans?"

"We don't even know if he'll get summoned," Nix reasoned. "It's not like your shy little cousin knows how. He just...deserves the chance. If the Book's locked away, he'll never even get it. You can't summon another demon anyway."

"And you didn't think to tell me?"

Nix hadn't thought to, actually. For all his experience with desire, Nix didn't have much experience with partnership.

Maybe Ivan wasn't the only one bad at communication.

Ivan's fists clenched at his sides at Nix's silence. He looked like he wouldn't mind wringing Nix's neck, but for once he kept his hands to himself. "And is this friend of yours likely to be a threat?"

"Um...doubtful?" Nix hedged. "He might set a few fires here and there, but it's unlikely he'd be much interested in Mafia business."

"A few fires," Ivan repeated flatly.

"Only if he gets bored?"

"Of course." Ivan stepped back, turning away. "I'm going to finish getting dressed. Make yourself presentable. We'll be leaving in a half hour."

Nix's heart sank at the dismissive tone in Ivan's voice. He didn't even sound angry anymore. But what little warmth Nix had coaxed out of him—the little cracks in Ivan's armor he'd fought so hard for—was all gone.

It seemed like, after all that teasing, Nix had finally managed to truly piss Ivan off.

11

Nix

The car ride to Maine was about as icy as could be. Not the roads—it was still too early in the season for snow, Nix was sorry to note—but Ivan himself.

"Why couldn't you just break into Coop's place and have a little look-see for the Book?" Nix asked once again. He'd been ignored his last two attempts, but he was hoping the third time was, in fact, the charm.

They'd gone to Cooper's apartment building after he hadn't picked up Ivan's calls, but there'd been no answer at his door. Apparently Ivan's shy cousin hadn't been at home.

"His security is insane," Ivan finally answered, his hands clenching hard enough on the steering wheel to whiten his knuckles. They'd left sweet Oleg behind, in the hopes that his presence in the city would suggest to Sergei that Ivan had remained in New York, and Ivan was driving them. "I can't break through it without help, and we don't have time for that."

His eyes stayed straight ahead even as he spoke to Nix. As if he was too focused on the road to even glance Nix's way.

Except Nix knew better.

Nix, for his part, was slouched in his seat, his legs up on the dashboard despite Ivan's insistence they remain on the floor. If he was going to be given the cold shoulder, he was at least going to be annoying about it.

So, okay, maybe he should have realized this would be a big deal to Ivan, considering how adamant he'd been that Sascha not hold on to the Book. But Nix had thought it was more about Ivan's fixation with his brothers than actually wanting the damned thing close.

Nix narrowed his eyes at Ivan's hands on the steering well. He didn't like them there. At least, not both of them—one of them should have been on Nix's thigh, gripping tightly. That was their *thing*, even when Ivan was pretending to not be into it. He'd fake indifference, but his actions would say otherwise.

Now, though, Ivan's actions were sending the message that he didn't give a flying fig if Nix was there or not.

It made for a very long drive to Seacliff.

An eternity or so later (wherein Ivan wouldn't even allow Nix to listen to some decent music on the radio, too busy stewing in frigid silence), they arrived at a sweet-looking coastal town, eventually pulling up to a Victorian home not far from the downtown area.

It was Sascha who opened the door, his eyes wide in surprise even as Kai loomed over his shoulder, all big and blue and horned —meaning he'd heard them coming and knew not to bother with a human disguise.

Apparently he hadn't had time to inform Sascha, because the human was gaping. "Ivan... What—?"

Nix gave Ivan a sidelong glance. "You *did* tell your brother we were coming, didn't you?"

Ivan ignored him, looking to Sascha. "You said I was welcome."

Sascha crossed his arms, his brows dropping. "I said you were welcome if you were able to not act like a complete dick."

"You said I needed to act human. You didn't say anything about not being a dick."

Sascha's lips twitched, much in the same way Ivan's did when he was trying his best not to smile. He sighed, stepping back from the door and opening his arm in reluctant welcome. "Well, I didn't think you'd take me up on it, like, immediately, but come on in."

Some of Ivan's frostiness eased, just a touch. Nix could see it— if only for the briefest moment—how fond Ivan was of his brother, before Ivan swept past Sascha and Kai into the house like they didn't exist, leaving Nix on the porch with them.

Sascha seemed unfazed by the rudeness. "Hello," he said to Nix, adorably shy all of a sudden.

Nix grinned at him. "Hi, cutie."

Kai cleared his throat, the scowl on his face a marked contrast to Sascha's shy smile. "What are you two doing here?"

Speaking of rudeness.

Nix batted his lashes, knowing it would piss Kai off. "Maybe we wanted a cozy little getaway."

Kai scoffed. "Doesn't look very cozy to me."

No, it didn't, did it? Nix pressed his lips into a pout, looking to Sascha for commiseration. "He's angry with me."

Sascha waved a dismissive hand, leaning back against Kai, his shyness seeming to ease with a familiar topic of conversation. "He's always angry. What does he think you did wrong?"

"Something he's decided is some sort of betrayal."

Sascha's smile dropped. "Oof."

Oof? What the fuck did "oof" mean? Nix had been looking for reassurance, not confirmation that he was completely fucked. "Is it that bad?"

"Well, our brother, Alexei, supposedly betrayed him about

two years ago. He stayed away, but Ivan still held a massive grudge and may have fired a gun at him the next time they saw each other."

Ah, yes, the attempted fratricide. Well, that had clearly been Alexei's first mistake—staying away. A man like Ivan couldn't be left to stew in his own miseries. It gave him too much of an opportunity to shore up his defenses.

Nix wouldn't be making the same mistake.

They found Ivan in the living room, standing over what at first glance appeared to be a pile of blankets. Except, at second glance, there was definitely a hooded head poking out of it. A young man stared up at Ivan, big brown eyes blinking rapidly.

There was another resident in the house.

"I forgot about the stray," Ivan said, looking down at whoever he was.

And apparently Ivan already knew about him. Nix tried not to pout. He hated being left in the dark.

"Be nice to Matteo," Sascha scolded, shooting the young man a reassuring smile.

"Why?" Ivan asked, his eyes still on the "stray," as he'd called him.

"Because otherwise you have to go," Sascha told him, a bit of brattiness in his tone now. "It's his house now too."

Ivan turned to shoot him a look. "I *bought* this house."

"And what an investment," Sascha said dryly. "There's only one other guest room made up, but I can—"

"Nix and I will stay in the same room," Ivan interrupted.

Nix perked up at that even as Sascha blinked in surprise.

"Oh." Sascha cocked his head, studying Ivan. Or, most likely, studying the impressive array of hickeys Nix had left the night before. "Okay..."

"I want my demon close at hand." Ivan raised a brow, as if daring Sascha to question him. "Is that a problem?"

Kai growled. "Speak to Sascha nicely or I'll throw you out myself."

"I think—I think I'll go upstairs," the young man Sascha had called Matteo stammered, climbing out of his nest of blankets and bolting away.

Well, weren't they all off to a lovely start?

Some hours later, dinner was no less tense. Ivan clearly didn't want to get into the reason for them being there, so they all made awkward small talk, followed by slightly less awkward talk about the business he was setting Sascha up with.

"You still like it here?" Ivan eventually asked Sascha.

Sascha's lips quirked into a small smile. "You mean have I changed my mind since a few weeks ago?" He shook his head. "I still like it here."

Ivan sneered in the direction of the window, where dark clouds had gathered. "I hope you like it just as much when you're snowed in for months on end."

There was resentment there, pulsing out of him in little waves, and not directed at Nix for the moment. Did Ivan not like that his little brother had relocated? Maybe for all his posturing about his useless brothers, he'd enjoyed having Sascha close.

"Oh, Kai will keep me warm," Sascha crooned, finally showing a hint of sass. Nix approved. "Demons run hot, you know." Sascha's eyes flicked to Nix, then back to Ivan. "Not that you'd know anything about that, would you, Vanya?" he asked sweetly.

Matteo, who'd crept back down to dinner at the very last minute and was nibbling at his pizza crust like a little mouse, choked.

Ivan only cocked a brow coolly. "I must keep him fed, mustn't I? He's an incubus. His tastes are...specific."

"The contract should keep him fed well enough," Kai broke in, sounding disapproving.

Nix stuck his tongue out at him. He didn't need his meddling.

"I'm afraid I need him in top form," Ivan countered. Meanwhile, he still hadn't so much as looked at Nix this entire dinner.

"What does an incubus eat?" Matteo asked, his curiosity seemingly stronger than his timidity for the moment.

Ivan glanced at him. "He's a sex demon, little stray. What do you think?"

Matteo immediately flushed beet red, dropping his gaze back to his plate.

Nix shot him a wink anyway.

————

IT WAS hard to shock Nix, but he was still a little bit surprised when, after shutting themselves in their shared bedroom, Ivan began undoing his belt buckle, his eyes suddenly molten hot.

"Strip," he ordered, his voice somehow still as cold as it had been all day, in sharp contrast to the heat of his gaze.

Nix gaped at him. "Excuse me?"

"Strip."

So Nix hadn't misheard. *This fucking human.*

"No." Nix's tail flicked in agitation even as heat pooled in his belly at Ivan's commanding tone. That wasn't his fault though. His body was all hardwired to find Ivan's bossiness sexy. "You're too angry with me for that."

Ivan narrowed his eyes at him. "I'm tense and annoyed. I like to fuck when I'm tense and annoyed."

Nix hummed, stepping to the bed and taking a seat on the foot of it, crossing one leg over the other. "Sounds delightful," he said truthfully. "But not when you're annoyed with *me*." He pursed his lips into a mock pout. "I'm very sensitive, you know."

Ivan seemed to realize only then that Nix was serious in his denial. He paused by the door, his hands still on his belt. "I thought you liked that I'm vicious," he said coolly, managing to sound accusing. Like *Nix* was the problem here.

"Oh, I do, darling. But there's vicious, and there's...this." Nix waved a hand to encompass all Ivan's nonsense. "You don't get to ice me out and then fuck your anger out on me." He cocked his head, bouncing his foot. If they were talking things out all of a sudden... "Why *are* you so angry?" he asked.

"You know why."

Right, right. Betrayal and messing with his plans and blah, blah, blah. That explained the source of Ivan's annoyance but not the depth of it. Nix clucked his tongue. "Try again."

Ivan stared at him for a long moment, and then it was like a dam burst, his frozen exterior cracking and real frustration breaking through for the first time since the apartment. He jerked a shaky hand through his hair. "I don't *know*. I just...get like this."

Now they were getting somewhere, at least. Nix fought back a smile. He didn't want Ivan to think he was teasing him. "When someone does something you don't like?" he asked.

"When someone...undermines me."

"Is that what I did?"

"Yes."

"It wasn't my intention."

Ivan rubbed a hand over his eyes. "Intention doesn't matter. End results matter. Disobedience is the first step to losing control. And loss of control means death."

"Another lesson from Daddy Dearest?"

Ivan glared at him through his fingers. "Just because he was an asshole doesn't mean he was always wrong."

"As far as I'm concerned, it does."

Of all the ridiculous lessons to teach someone. Had Ivan's father wanted him to fail, or had he simply been *that* misguided? And would it be wrong to find out where Ivan's father was buried just to piss on the grave?

"I loosened the leash on Sascha for the first time, and look what happened—he's married to a demon."

"He seems happy enough with his choice to me." Nix could see it—and feel it—well enough at dinner, even with the tension between Ivan and everyone else. Sascha had a way of gravitating toward Kai, and Kai toward him in return. The big warrior demon was clearly Sascha's place of safety.

"Happy to be away from me, more like," Ivan said bitterly. "He hated being under my control." Pale-blue eyes met Nix's. "Will you grow to resent me in the same way?"

"I can stand up for myself."

When Ivan continued to stand there, frozen like a statue, Nix sighed, deciding to go the way of patience rather than petulance.

"You can never have perfect control over other people, Ivan," he found himself explaining, as if he were the human and Ivan a demon new to this realm. "Even if you lead by fear. Even if you're the scariest motherfucker in the entire universe and they know one misstep means their balls are getting chopped off. Do you know why?" he asked.

Ivan only stared.

"Because every individual has their own desires, and sometimes those will interfere with yours. You wanted the Book under your control. I wanted to give my friend a chance. Conflicting desires. Not betrayal. Not the end of the world."

Ivan slumped back against the door. "Are you a therapist as well as a sex worker now?"

Nix huffed a breath. "If only. You could use about a decade's worth."

"If I can never have perfect control, then what's the point of our little change of leadership tactics? Sounds like I'm fucked either way."

Nix leaned back on his hands. "Generally, followers who are given respect give respect in turn. It's more effective than fear. But if you're really so paranoid about the Mafia shit blowing up in your face, why not go legitimate? You can be rich and powerful without playing at gang wars."

Ivan pinched at the bridge of his nose, as if Nix's very sound reasoning was giving him a headache. "It doesn't work like that. You don't get to just...go legitimate."

"Who says?" At Ivan's face, Nix cackled meanly. "Of course. Your father." He put as much disdain into the title as he could manage.

Ivan released his hold on his nose, glaring. "I don't want to talk about this anymore."

"Fine."

Ivan stared at him, his eyes tracking Nix's crossed legs. He growled in frustration. "I want to fuck you."

"Too bad."

"Closing your legs indefinitely because I've pissed you off? Might as well be my wife."

Nix narrowed his eyes. "Misogyny aside, don't tempt me with a good time." He sighed again. He really should be billing hours for this conversation, shouldn't he? "Your want for me is too tied to your frustration right now. And while I've been used by humans for a variety of purposes, none of which had to do with me, it hasn't been like that with you, and I don't want to start a new pattern. Got it?" He patted the covers invitingly. "I'll still share your bed tonight. I'll even pet your hair the way you like because I'm a fucking saint like that. But your cock will have to fend for itself."

All at once, Ivan's ire deflated again. He dragged his hands down his face. "I don't know what the fuck's *wrong* with me."

"Too many things to count," Nix told him cheerfully. "But luckily I am, as we've already established, a fucking saint, so I have the infinite patience needed to deal with all of them."

Ivan took a step away from the door. "I'm still angry with you."

"I'm sure you are. Want to cuddle about it?"

Ivan whipped his belt out of his pants, tossing it on the floor. "I don't cuddle."

"Now who's the liar?" Nix let his clothes disappear off his body, leaving him in tight black briefs. He lay down over the covers.

"No lacy panties?" Ivan asked.

"You don't deserve them." Nix pointed a finger at him, repeating Ivan's earlier words, "Now *strip*."

Ivan scowled but did as Nix commanded, stripping down to his underwear and showcasing that delicious bulge Nix wanted to put his mouth on more than a little bit. But that would undermine all that hard-won communication they'd just sort of succeeded at, so instead he turned to his side.

"Spoon me," he ordered.

Ivan climbed onto the bed and lay behind him, wrapping an arm around Nix and tugging him close. So close it might have been hard to breathe, if Nix had needed to do so. A heavy leg draped over Nix's thigh, Ivan's erection snug against Nix's ass.

Nix settled into the hold, feeling at ease for the first time all day. "For someone who doesn't cuddle, you're very aggressive about it."

Ivan's fingers curled into Nix's chest. "It's because you're so infuriating. I have to get my frustration out somehow."

"And is it helping?" Nix asked, stroking the blond hairs on Ivan's arm.

There was a long silence, and then Ivan's forehead settled against the back of Nix's neck, his answer muffled but unmistakable. "Yes. It's helping."

12

***

Ivan

Ivan woke up on top of the incubus.

He'd fallen asleep spooning Nix, and he still had an arm and a leg thrown over him, but at some point in his sleep, Ivan had shifted so he was almost completely on top of the demon. Pressing him into the mattress, as if to keep him from leaving.

His erection was also pressed against Nix's firm ass, but of course, Ivan wasn't allowed to use it.

With no one to see it, Ivan's lips quirked into a small smile at the memory of Nix telling him off. Telling him no. It had been infuriating, but also...comforting, in an annoying way. Nix wouldn't let Ivan steamroll him, even if—even *when*—Ivan wanted to.

The last person Ivan had been able to say that about had been Alexei, but Alexei's defiance had come from a very different source. Hatred, maybe. Disgust, definitely.

Nix might misbehave, but he wasn't seething with ill-concealed disdain for Ivan like Alexei had always been. And he wouldn't be like Sascha, either, quietly resenting Ivan until the day he was finally able to escape his clutches.

The demon was different from both of them.

And Ivan hated to admit it, but the cuddling had helped calm him down. He felt less jagged than yesterday. Less out of control. His wrath had been overwhelming, when he'd found out Nix had slipped the Book away from him. As his anger always was.

Maybe everyone was right, and that was something to work on.

Or maybe Nix would hold Ivan at arm's length every time his temper got the best of him, and that would do the trick.

"Are you *smiling*?"

Ivan smoothed his expression, his gaze darting to Nix, only to find Nix's eyes were still closed, his face pressed into the pillow.

"How would you even know?" Ivan asked, his voice rough with sleep.

"I could feel it," Nix said with a small grin, eyes shut tight. "It was like your soul piece got all...fizzy."

Right. Because there was a piece of Ivan's soul residing in Nix's chest, keeping the demon in the human realm. And apparently letting him know when Ivan smiled. It was hard to remember sometimes—it wasn't like Ivan could tell a piece was missing. Was that because his soul was too tarnished to feel whole in the first place? Probably. Too late to fix that. And anyway, losing a piece of it was worth it to keep this demon at his side.

But for how long?

There had been another element to Ivan's ire, besides Nix's abject disregard for his orders. Sascha had said he and Kai needed the Book to bond. And Nix had said Kai and Sascha's bond was a way to keep Kai in the human realm even after his contract was finished.

So for Nix to stay...

It wasn't like Ivan wanted to *marry* the demon—wanting to

fuck him at every turn didn't mean Ivan was in the market for some supernatural husband—but he also didn't want Nix leaving before Ivan was ready either. And having the Book close at hand seemed to be the only way to prevent it.

And when will you be ready for him to leave?

Ivan scowled at his own question. He'd know when, of course. They couldn't continue on like this indefinitely, could they? Happy endings didn't exist in Ivan's world.

His mother had been proof enough of that.

"Oop. There goes the fizz." One of Nix's purple eyes popped open. "What's got you in a tizzy already?"

"Maybe I'm just pent up," Ivan told him, ridding himself of his useless thoughts and biting at Nix's neck. "Am I still forbidden from touching you?"

"That depends." Nix arched back, teasing his ass against Ivan's hard-on. "How were you planning on touching me?"

In answer, Ivan shifted all the way on top of Nix, pressing him into the mattress on his belly, rutting his erection between Nix's cloth-covered cheeks, wishing they were both nude already.

He gripped Nix's wrists with one hand, holding tightly. There was something intoxicating in the way he could hold the incubus as tight as he wanted, without causing him pain. Without Nix pulling away.

That had always been Ivan's problem—gripping things too tightly and losing them anyway when they chafed at his hold. But with Nix, he could grab on as hard as he could, and the demon wouldn't balk.

Nix chuckled, the sound slightly muffled by the pillow. "That's all well and good for *you*, but what about— *Oh*." He groaned as Ivan slid his other hand into Nix's briefs, rubbing Nix's cock in time with his thrusts. "Oh, that's lovely."

Ivan would have to agree. He'd grown fond of the feel of Nix's cock. The demon's skin was soft and warm, and his absurdly viscous precum always made for a smooth glide. It was fascinating to Ivan, how similar in mechanics it was to touching himself, and yet how different it was in so many ways.

Nix, shameless as ever, wasted no time, humping against Ivan's hand, his dick pressed tightly between his hip and Ivan's palm. His actions had the fortunate side effect of his ass pressing against Ivan's hard cock again and again, and Ivan took full advantage.

It was a ridiculous way to get off—like Ivan was a teenager again, fucking against his mattress and hoping no one roaming the hallway would know what he was up to.

And yet it was nothing like that at all, because Nix's body was firm against his, his skin smelled like spice and smoke, and his grunts and groans sent shivers up and down Ivan's spine.

Ivan had wanted him so badly last night, even in his anger. He'd wanted to bury himself in his heat, to feel Nix's warmth against him.

And now he had him, even if he was too impatient to claim him completely.

And Ivan would keep him, here at his side, until he was ready to let him go.

Ivan grabbed Nix's chin with his free hand, claiming Nix's mouth as he rutted furiously against him. His incubus tasted oddly sweet, as he always did. Ivan probably tasted vile, but Nix didn't seem to mind, sucking on Ivan's tongue deliriously as he worked toward his finish against Ivan's hand.

"That's right," Ivan murmured against his lips. "Come for me, demon."

Nix did come first, greedy for it as ever, and Ivan groaned at the feel of Nix's hot release spilling over his own fist. It didn't take Ivan long to follow, a stuttered moan leaving his lips as the wave of pleasure took him under.

He rolled off Nix afterward, facing him on his side, sticky in his briefs and momentarily sated. He brought a finger to his mouth, curious. The taste of Nix's cum was as smoky as Nix's scent.

Nix grinned wickedly, a glow to his purple eyes. "That's a mental snapshot I won't be forgetting anytime soon."

Ivan grunted, licking the last of the taste off his lips. He sat up, tugging Nix's arm until he followed Ivan out of bed.

They were lucky enough not to run into anyone in the hallway, and Ivan cleaned them both brusquely in the shower, not allowing for any of Nix's games, no matter how his hands wandered. Ivan could tell by the light that it was already later than he usually slept, and he didn't want to give Sascha a reason to come looking for them before they were presentable.

They found the house's strange trio of residents in the kitchen.

Sascha and Matteo were eating cereal at the kitchen table, while Kai was standing against the counters, gulping out of a horrifically large mug of coffee that still managed to look relatively tiny in his hands. He was a huge creature—there'd been a reason Ivan had wanted a warrior demon of his own.

But there was something oddly distasteful about it now. All that brute force, with no finesse to speak of. Ivan preferred the subtle strengths of his incubus.

He'd gotten the better deal in the end, hadn't he?

He sat at the table and poured himself a bowl of cereal, starved after barely touching his dinner the night before.

He looked up halfway through to find Nix seated across from him, staring at him raptly. Ivan paused, his spoon halfway to his mouth. "What?"

Nix raised his brows. "Nothing."

Sascha grinned around his own mouthful. "It's weird, isn't it? When he does mundane stuff."

Ivan gave his brother an unimpressed look. "It's cereal."

Although, it was true Nix hadn't seen much of Ivan at home

yet, not when Ivan had been running to and from the office at all hours when they'd been in New York.

"I don't know what I was thinking." Nix leaned back in his chair, making a show of his surprise now. "Maybe that you'd be eating bullet casings soaked in whiskey for breakfast."

"We're Russian," Ivan deadpanned. "They'd be soaked in vodka."

That pulled a giggle from Matteo, though he went silent, his face paling, when Ivan looked his way. He was a strange sort. Unreasonably timid, considering he'd been raised around Mafia men, same as Ivan and his brothers. Kai and Sascha had rescued him from the Carusos, where he'd been—according to Ivan's informants—treated none too kindly by his stepfather, Luca Caruso.

What he was so scared of now, after that family had been taken down, was anyone's guess.

Maybe he was just too traumatized to pull it together.

Either way, Ivan needed him out of the house, or at the very least the room. Ivan shot Nix a pointed look, reminding him of what they'd discussed in the shower, and his demon cleared his throat. "So I was thinking, Kai," Nix said brightly. "That you and Matteo could show me around town."

"Why?" Kai asked bluntly, either genuinely not understanding or stubbornly refusing to take the hint.

"Because I'd like to speak to Sascha alone," Ivan told him just as bluntly.

Kai set his coffee down, crossing his arms. "No."

"Kai," Sascha chided gently.

Kai looked at him beseechingly, like a dog who'd been reprimanded for guarding the home. "I don't trust him," he growled as if Ivan weren't right there.

Sascha shared a long look with him, the two of them seeming to come to some sort of unspoken agreement, and then turned to

Nix. "How about you and Matty start out, and Kai will follow after we know what Ivan has to say."

Ivan ground his teeth, a familiar hot rush of anger coursing through his veins. "I'm not allowed to speak with my own brother alone?" A hand landed on his shoulder, and Ivan shot Nix a frosty look. "*What?*"

Nix raised a brow at him. When Ivan didn't react, Nix mouthed the words *control issues* at him.

Ivan scowled. If Nix was referring to their conversation from the night before… "It's different," he argued.

This wasn't about him being a control freak. It was about the principle of the thing. He and Sascha were tied together by blood —Ivan should be allowed to speak to him without that big brute of a demon husband butting in.

But Nix only cocked his head. "Is it really?" he asked mildly.

Goddamn it.

Ivan relaxed his jaw with effort, setting down his spoon. "Fine," he said, pushing his bowl away from him. "We can have the chaperone."

Kai raised his mug smugly. "As if you had any choice."

————

AFTER NIX LEFT with Matteo (the little stowaway looking aghast at finding himself running off solo with an incubus), Ivan remained in the kitchen with Sascha and Kai.

Kai who had set aside his coffee once again, his arms crossed over his chest in a way that made his enormous biceps bulge, as if the kitchen needed a paranormal bouncer to protect its occupants from Ivan.

Sascha seemed to ignore Kai's ridiculous posturing easily enough. He had his own coffee steaming in front of him. As did Ivan, although he preferred tea.

"So what's up?" Sascha asked, worrying the sleeve of his brightly colored shirt. "You change your mind about me running one of your clubs?"

Just the suggestion of it had Kai growling at Ivan, like Ivan had said the words himself.

Ivan raised a brow at him, refusing to be cowed. "Charming," he sneered. He turned back to Sascha. "No, I haven't changed my mind. I—" He paused, realizing he had no idea how to say what he wanted to say.

I've been fucking my incubus, and it turns out he has some decent business ideas?

I've been fucking my incubus, and now the intolerance I've let slide for so long is no longer acceptable?

Or better yet...

I've been fucking my incubus, and I'm realizing our father was not only a deranged psychopath but a fallible one.

He cleared his throat, tapping at the table with one finger. He settled on the vague statement, "Nix has some ideas about restructuring."

"Okaaay...," Sascha said slowly, clearly needing more detail.

"We're looking to change up the men," Ivan told him. "Get rid of those that hold father's old...ideals."

"Get rid of how?" Sascha immediately asked, suspicion lacing his voice.

"They'll be given a chance to walk away," Ivan said easily.

He didn't add what would happen if the men refused that chance. Sascha was flighty but not stupid.

"What kind of ideals are you looking to weed out?"

"The hair-trigger violence. The changeable loyalties. The...bigotry."

Sascha's face gave nothing away, even though Ivan knew for a fact he had some strong opinions on the way their father's men had always looked at him. The way they'd judged him. The way

Ivan had...strongly suggested Sascha dress and act a certain way to prevent them from doing so.

"Why now?" was all Sascha asked.

"I never considered it an option before. But it would...ease things, to have a less hostile group. Less paranoia on my end, you might say."

Sascha had always accused Ivan of that: paranoia. He thought Ivan was too controlling. Too suspicious. Ivan had resented him for it. Resented that Sascha wasn't the same way. That he hadn't been forced to be by their father.

"Your mole," Sascha said suddenly. "You figured out who it is?"

Ivan's finger stopped its tapping, fists clenching instead. "Sergei."

"Sergei?" Sascha let out a disbelieving laugh. "He raised you. And Alexei. And me, if I hadn't been away at boarding school so much."

"Father raised us," Ivan corrected. "Sergei only...helped."

"But...why? Why would he do that?" If Sascha was hurt by one of his guardians being the reason he'd gotten stabbed, he didn't show it. Confusion seemed to be his main emotion.

Ivan shrugged a shoulder, the movement jerky. "I don't know why."

"Is he dead?"

"Not yet." Ivan grimaced. If fucking only. "Jace has eyes on him for the moment. Sergei put out a hit on me, but its failure seems to have left him scrambling."

Sascha nodded thoughtfully. He toyed at the handle of his mug. "Why are you telling me this, anyway? You've always liked keeping me in the dark."

"We could use a show of strength," Ivan said shortly, his eyes darting to Sascha's demon.

Sascha straightened. "You want Kai."

"Yes."

Sascha and Kai shared a look. "We said no more Mafia stuff," Sascha said with a heavy sigh, slumping slightly. "But let me think it over."

"It could be a step toward legitimacy," Ivan found himself saying, thinking of his conversation with Nix the night before. "A step away from the less savory aspects of the business."

Sascha met his gaze. "Don't say it if you don't mean it," he said, a surprising amount of steel in his tone.

"This whole plan was Nix's idea?" Kai asked in his low rumble, speaking for the first time since the conversation had begun.

"Yes. He's been...useful to me," Ivan admitted. "He reads people well. He can help figure out those who are truly loyal and those that will need to be removed."

"He does read people well," Kai agreed. Then, abruptly, "He likes the human realm."

"I know."

"He was desperate to return to it," Kai continued, his gaze locked onto Ivan's now. "Desperate enough to take an unfavorable contract."

Ivan's fists clenched again. He didn't like to think of the contract as unfavorable so much as...flexible. "So it seems," he said coolly.

"So desperate to stay in the human realm he'll even put up with the likes of you."

"Again," Ivan said through clenched teeth. "So it seems."

"I'd be careful if I were you. If he brings up talk of a bond...just know it's nothing personal." Kai's blue eyes started to take on a subtle glow. "Desperate desires lead to desperate acts."

Sascha turned in his seat, wide-eyed. "Kai!"

Kai scowled guiltily, reminding Ivan of a toddler caught misbehaving, the glow in his eyes subsiding. "I'm only saying."

What the fuck *was* he saying? Ivan let anger over the demon's unwelcome meddling push aside the unexpected pang Kai's comments had wrought. It was stupid of him, that he hadn't considered Nix was putting up with him just to stay. It was only... Nix seemed to delight so in tormenting him.

But maybe Nix delighted equally in tormenting all humans.

Maybe Ivan was nothing special to a demon like that.

"He's just being protective is all." Sascha laid a hand on Ivan's clenched fist, like Ivan needed comforting.

Ivan shook off his unease, leaning into the familiar anger instead. He drew his hand back. "Protective of his demon kin. Protective of you too." He narrowed his eyes. "Tell me, Sascha, why would your demon need to protect you from me?"

For all their brutal upbringing, Ivan had never once harmed Sascha. No matter Sascha's forgetfulness, or flightiness, or sass. Ivan had never laid a finger on him.

Old Sascha—the one from before the stabbing, before Maine, before Kai—would have taken the hint from Ivan's words and said something silly or inane. But this new Sascha met Ivan's gaze squarely. "Because you *have* hurt me in the past, intentional or not." He sipped his coffee, clearly not expecting a response to that, and they sat in silence for a moment.

Ivan could let it be. He always had before, when Sascha acted up about their dynamic. When he brought up Ivan's supposed failures as a brother.

Instead, he said quietly, "Not." At Sascha's raised brow, Ivan clarified, "You said intentional or not." He met Sascha's gaze evenly. "Not."

Sascha hummed, keeping the eye contact for a prolonged moment, then turned to Kai. "If you want to join Nix and Matty, I wouldn't mind some time alone with Ivan."

For all his posturing, Kai didn't hesitate once Sascha made his wishes known. He bent low for a kiss, shot one last glare at Ivan, and walked out of the kitchen.

Ivan waited to hear the front door shut before he spoke again.

He'd thought to tell Sascha more details of what he and Nix were planning, but instead found himself asking, "Do you remember the man you walked in on being tortured?"

It was a stupid question, and maybe a cruel one. Ivan already knew Sascha remembered. It was the reason Ivan's brother couldn't stand the sight of blood. He'd been too young to see such butchery—a full decade younger than Ivan at the time—and it had taken its toll.

Sascha paled but nodded. "I do."

"He was the son of a local mob boss." Ivan could see him now, as he'd looked before the torture. Relatively young and plain-looking, but strong. He'd seemed quite strong, actually, before Ivan's father and his men had gotten their hands on him. "Not any huge organization, but big enough to have our father's attention. The man's father had passed, and he tried to take over, as had been planned." Ivan tried and failed to relax his fists. "He failed. A brother or a cousin set him up and he ended up in our hands. You know what happened then." Sascha nodded, his face still ashen. "After you left, Father had me put a bullet in him to end it."

Sascha gripped the table, as if to steady himself. "*Ivan.* You were only, what, sixteen?"

"My first kill." Ivan's lips twitched into a bitter smile. "Father wanted me to know the consequences of failure."

"That's fucked up," Sascha hissed, some of the color returning to his face. He seemed to let it sink in for a moment, then repeated, waving a hand in agitation, "That's *so* fucked up. And it's fucked up that you've believed him for so long. Not every mistake ends in gruesome death, Ivan. Jesus."

Sascha didn't wait for Ivan to argue, just frowned down at his mug, speaking thoughtfully, "If Nix...if having him around is helping you rethink some of the ways we were raised, then..." He met Ivan's eyes. "I don't care if he's desperate or has ulterior motives. Keep him around. And we'll help, with the...restructuring. Me and Kai."

Was that why Ivan had told Sascha the story? To manipulate him into helping? Or had he been looking for some sort of catharsis? Ivan didn't know. He couldn't tell anymore. It was probably Nix's fault somehow. He was turning Ivan into something soft. Into the type of person that *shared* things.

But if it brought Ivan's brothers around...

"You think you can talk Alexei into doing the same?" he asked.

"Unlikely. Very unlikely."

Ivan nodded. He hadn't expected any different.

They passed a moment in silence before Sascha said, frowning down at his mug again, "We should put whiskey in this coffee."

"It's ten a.m."

"So? You just told me about your first murder. As a *teenager*."

Ivan shrugged. It wasn't as if the memory was new to him. But also...what else did he have to do in Maine?

He raised his mug. "All right, then. Let's get drunk."

13

Nix

Nix and Matteo walked the short distance downtown, neither of them speaking.

It wasn't in Nix's nature to stay so quiet, but Matteo was an odd one, and Nix wasn't quite sure how not to scare him off. He was once again swimming in a hooded sweatshirt about three sizes too large for him and radiating a massive amount of discomfort.

Nix might have thought he was shy, or maybe socially anxious like Ivan claimed Cooper was, but it wasn't anxiety leaching off Matteo.

It was fear.

So *much* fear, as soon as they'd left the safety of the house he shared with Sascha and Kai.

It made Nix's skin itch a touch. Fear wasn't his emotion of choice, or even among his top ten. It was too ashen for his taste.

Nightmare, on the other hand, would be well sated in Matteo's presence, with fear like that to feed off of. Except Nightmare was picky as hell about his contracts. He didn't seem to care if he was stuck in the Void for all eternity.

Maybe he would even prefer it.

But as Nix was the demon at hand, it wouldn't do to let Matteo stew in his misery. He slowed down his stride, pleased when Matteo changed his pace to match.

"So," Nix said conversationally. "I know I'm not as big and tough as Kai, but I promise nobody's going to be able to hurt you with me here. I'm stronger than I look. And meaner. And faster."

Matteo's head jerked from under his hoodie, his gaze darting to Nix and then away again. He had absurdly large eyes, their size only emphasized by his short buzz cut, but he didn't seem too fond of eye contact.

The fear emanating off him lessened, although not as much as Nix would have liked.

"Do you want to talk about what you're so afraid of?"

Matteo shook his head forcefully, pulling his hood back up.

"Is it me?" Nix asked, only half-teasing. "I promise I don't bite." He pretended to consider. "Well, I bite Ivan, but he likes it, I swear."

He caught sight of a blush on Matteo's cheeks, but the young human shook his head again. "Not you," he said quietly.

"You're not scared of Kai, are you?" It wouldn't quite make sense, with how much Matteo's fear had increased when he'd left the house, but it didn't hurt to double-check. Nix supposed it would be a shock to find oneself living with a seven-foot-tall horned demon all of a sudden.

"No," Matteo told him, surprisingly fierce. "Kai *saved* me. Him and Sascha."

"Oh. Well, good," Nix said, horribly awkward. He wasn't too proud of his efforts here, but there was just too much negative in Matteo for Nix to get a read on the positive. Although, Matteo's loyalty was clearly strong. Nix would just have to settle for not being the world's best conversationalist, no matter how much it hurt his pride. "Where should we go while we wait?"

Matteo answered quickly, "There's a bakery they like."

"Do *you* like it?"

"The guy's nice."

"Is he hot?" Nix asked, wondering if he could get another blush from him.

But Matteo only nodded solemnly, leading him to a small bakery called—most apt—the Bakeshop.

They walked in together, and a round-cheeked young man, his brown curls pulled back with a cloth headband, smiled widely at their entrance. "Matty!"

Matteo gave a shy wave.

"Who's your new friend?" the young man asked, eyeing Nix. Then, before Matteo could answer, "I'm Seth. I love your outfit. And your hair. And the tattoo."

Nix grinned. He was never one to turn down a compliment or two. "Well, I like everything about you," he purred. He was tempted to add, "And if you like me like this, you should see me in my demon form," but he supposed that wouldn't be very hush-hush of him.

"What can I get you?"

Nix had no interest in human food, so he turned to Matteo, but Matteo, for all that he'd suggested they go there, shrugged, looking uncomfortable. "Oh, um, I don't—"

"We have some lemon bars I made today," Seth told him kindly. "I was messing with a new recipe, and they're absurdly sweet. Like, take the enamel off your teeth."

Matteo gave a small nod. "Okay."

Seth smiled at him, bagging up two of them and handing them over. "On me."

Matteo didn't seem to know what to do with that, bobbing his head awkwardly and shuffling out the door. Nix gave a cheery, "Toodles, Seth!" and followed.

"You got a crush on him or something?" he asked Matteo as soon as they were out the door. He didn't scent any desire or anything delicious like that, but crushes took all kinds of forms.

"What? No." Matteo actually frowned at him, like Nix was being ridiculous. "He's just...kind."

Nix was distracted from any further teasing by the sight of Kai approaching in his human form. Matteo visibly relaxed more the closer he got, his shoulders no longer hanging out somewhere around his ears.

Like having a huge demon around was a source of comfort. Interesting.

Kai ignored Nix, gesturing to Matteo's bag. "What do you have there?"

"Lemon bars."

"Seth's?"

"Mm-hmm."

"They'll be tasty, then. Want to eat them by the ocean?"

Matteo nodded eagerly, giving Kai a genuine smile. "Yes, please."

Nix found himself absurdly touched by the exchange. He hadn't thought Kai liked any humans besides his own mate, but he was being awfully sweet with the traumatized young thing. Apparently he was capable of not growling and grunting at every little statement, as long as it wasn't Ivan or Nix talking.

Kai directed them to a path along the coast, and Matteo walked slightly ahead of them, looking back every now and then as if to make sure they were still there.

Nix nudged Kai with his shoulder, laughing when the touch made Kai scowl. "So you've decided Ivan's not going to do away with Sascha in your absence?"

"I've decided no such thing," Kai growled. "But Sascha wanted a moment alone with him."

"He's trying, Kai. Ivan."

Kai scoffed. "Is he?"

Nix fought against the surge of protectiveness that threatened to make him match Kai's grumpiness. He kept his tone light and airy. "Well, look who knows how to hold a grudge."

"Why wouldn't I? He's selfish and cold, and he's caused my mate immense distress. I don't know how you can stand his soul piece in your chest."

"Funny," Nix said, his tone not quite as light anymore. "Because he thinks of Sascha and Alexei as the selfish ones."

Kai kicked a rock off the path forcefully. "He's unreliable in his judgments."

"Or maybe Sascha is."

"Watch yourself." Kai stopped and turned to face Nix. Some yards ahead of them, Matteo stopped as well, waiting at a distance. "You've aligned yourself with a cruel man, incubus. Be done with your contract and find another. Sascha and I will do our best to make sure you're summoned again."

As if Nix would settle for another human. He cocked a hip. "And what if he wants me to stay?"

"You're blinded by your wish to remain in the human realm. I told him as much."

What. The. Fuck.

Nix stepped forward and gripped Kai's arm, relishing in his wince when Nix's talons came out against his will. He spoke slowly, despite the heat flushing through his body. "What exactly did you say, Kaisyir?"

"I told him you were desperate to stay. And to be wary of any mention of a bond."

"And why in the *fuck* would you do that?"

"I don't want you to regret tying yourself to a monster just because you want to keep out of the Void."

Nix wasn't sure if he'd ever felt rage like this before. If he had, it surely hadn't been toward one of his friends. It was hot and bitter and horrible, making his skin burn and his jaw clench.

He hadn't even been thinking of a bond, mostly because the terms of his contract should have been enough to keep him earth-side a very long time. But now that Kai had mentioned it...

Why *shouldn't* Nix bond with his human? There would be no wife for Ivan, after all. Nix would never allow it. There would be only Nix. Not a spouse, but a mate.

Oh, Nix liked that idea very much.

"Kai," he purred, sweet as sugar, his talons digging in hard enough to pierce even Kai's thick skin.

"Yes?" Kai asked, eyeing Nix warily, ignoring the blood beginning to run down his arm.

"Stay the fuck out of it."

Kai's heavy brow furrowed. "You care for him."

The surprise in Kai's voice was...irritating, for some reason. "And why is that so hard to believe?" Nix asked. "He had the same fucked-up upbringing as your mate. Just because he developed different coping mechanisms doesn't mean it was all his fault."

Kai shook off Nix's hold, his wounds healing immediately. "You watched too many human talk shows in the Void. You think you understand him."

Nix narrowed his eyes. "I *do* understand him, Kaisyir."

They remained in a standoff for another long moment, and then Kai raised his hands in surrender. "It's your mistake to make. I'll stay out of it from now on."

That would have to do.

Kai waved at Matteo to continue, then pulled out a small gadget from his pocket when a dinging sound rang out.

"You have a phone!" Nix gasped, grabbing for it and pouting when Kai lifted it out of his reach. "I want one."

"It's Sascha," Kai said after looking at the screen. "He wants more time with Ivan."

Well, if that didn't make Nix feel all sorts of smug. "Would you look at that. Not gonna check to make sure Ivan doesn't have him tied up somewhere, sending out messages pretending to be him?"

Kai's fist clenched, and his poor little phone's screen cracked.

Nix rolled his eyes. "I'm joking. Don't be daft. You'd be able to tell."

Kai's bond with Sascha would alert him to any mortal peril or extreme distress Sascha could be experiencing. Not that much could hurt Sascha with a bond in place, anyway.

Yet another reason for Nix and Ivan to have one.

They followed the path down to a pleasing little cove, the ocean a remarkably beautiful sight. Even Matteo seemed pleased to be there.

And despite Kai's bullshit, Nix was feeling remarkably good himself. It was nice to have goals, wasn't it?

Except for the fact, of course, that due to his own actions, the Book wasn't actually in their possession. They really would need to track down Cooper (and Chaos, if he'd been lucky enough to be summoned, however unlikely that outcome). Nix would add it to the list.

Item one: Fix Ivan's empire so dear Vanya could relax a smidge.

Item two: Make Ivan fall completely and irreversibly in love with Nix, so much so that he'd decide he needed Nix to stay at his side forever.

Item three: Find the Book and make it happen.

Three simple steps. Easy as pie.

———

Nix, Kai, and Matteo returned to the house to find that Ivan and Sascha had migrated from the kitchen to the couch in the living room, where Sascha's wild giggle and the loose set to Ivan's shoulders—not to mention the massive bottle of whiskey on the coffee table—suggested both brothers were quite tipsy.

Nix stopped in the doorway, Kai and Mateo behind him. Ivan welcomed him with a smirk, and Nix matched it. "And here I thought you said it would be vodka."

"Sascha only had this." Ivan lifted his mug, his smirk deepening. "He's shaming the family name."

"Hey!" Sascha protested before falling into giggles again. "It came with the house," he said when he caught his breath. "Plus, the family name totally deserves it."

He and Ivan clinked their coffee mugs together, but Ivan froze with his halfway to his lips. "You just...found this?" he asked, eyeing the whiskey bottle like it had personally offended him.

Sascha rolled his eyes so hard it looked almost painful. "It's not poisoned or anything."

"Mm." Ivan glared down at his cup but drank anyway.

Too cute, Nix's tipsy, paranoid human. He sashayed over, clucking his tongue. "I'm beginning to think you have a problem, Vanya."

Ivan snagged Nix's wrist and tugged him sideways into his lap, wrapping one arm tightly around his middle. "Two times does not a pattern make," he said before pursing his lips. "And it was Sascha's idea, anyway."

Nix made to tease Sascha for his corrupting ways, only to find him staring at them, wide-eyed, his mouth hanging slightly open.

Ivan noticed at the same time. "*What*?" he asked his brother pointedly.

"Um..." Sascha's eyes darted between them, then down to Ivan's arm around Nix's waist.

Ivan didn't move an inch. "You already knew I was fucking him."

"Right." Sascha nodded dazedly. "I just thought you'd be all furtive and repressed about it."

Nix cackled. "Oh, he's been plenty repressed, don't you worry."

Ivan's fingers dug into Nix's side. "Behave," he scolded.

"You're drunk and it's not even noon. I'm not the one who needs to behave."

Ivan eyed the whiskey bottle like he was considering pouring himself more. "We're holding a wake."

"Who for?" Nix had been under the impression the father had died years ago, but maybe they were belatedly mourning the bastard.

"Me," Ivan told him solemnly.

"Oh my." Nix patted at Ivan's cheek, laughing when Ivan tried to bite at his fingers. "I see we've reached the maudlin stage already." He shot Sascha a wink. "He's a very tragic drunk, you know."

Ivan buried his head in Nix's shoulder. "I am not," he mumbled.

"And very free with his kisses."

Sascha, who looked like he didn't know whether to be horrified or delighted by the proceedings, lifted his cup to his lips, only to freeze when a large blue hand halted his progress. Kai had settled on the arm of the couch next to him at some point, looking fairly ridiculous perched there, considering his size.

Sascha pouted up at him. "*Hey.*"

Kai's eyes were soft, but his voice was firm. "You'll be very put out if you're hungover this evening, zaychik. Remember last Saturday, after the dancing?"

Sascha sighed but ultimately set his mug on the coffee table. "You're right. It's time for a nap." He lifted both arms in the air. "Carry me."

Kai looked pleased as punch to be asked. He hoisted Sascha up bridal-style, and Sascha immediately tucked his head against Kai's broad shoulder. "Mm," he hummed. "Warm."

Now that Sascha was...relaxed, Nix could tell just how on guard he'd been around Ivan until now. His behavior at the moment seemed truer to his nature, from what Nix could read. A little spoiled and a lot sweet.

Ivan didn't seem to take much notice of Sascha's antics, too busy toying with the ends of Nix's ponytail, his forehead rubbing back and forth against Nix's shoulder.

And as for the fifth...

"Where's Matteo?" Nix asked.

Sascha lifted his head and frowned, looking around like Matteo might pop up from behind the couch. "I guess in his room. Outings kind of take it out of him."

"You don't know what he's so frightened of?"

"We're waiting for him to tell us. It didn't seem right to push him too hard after everything he's been through. But for now—" Sascha gestured toward the hallway that led to the stairs. "Nap time for everyone."

Kai carried him obediently, shooting a last, distrustful look toward Ivan and Nix. As if he couldn't help himself.

"Sascha used to have a higher tolerance," Ivan murmured, tugging gently at Nix's hair. "Domestic life has softened him even more."

Nix leaned back until Ivan was forced to lift his head, catching Ivan's eye. "And is that such a bad thing?"

"I don't know anymore," Ivan told him, his brow furrowing.

He looked so adorably disgruntled, although whether it was with his brother or himself or just life in general, it was hard to tell. No matter the answer, it was probably best for him to sleep it off. Nix escaped his grasp, jumping off the couch. "Come," he said, holding out a hand. "Nap time for you as well."

Ivan's frown deepened. "I don't a nap."

"I'll let you fondle me in your sleep."

Ivan cocked his head, seeming to consider it. But he didn't stand just yet. "Can *you* get drunk?" he asked.

"Not from liquor, no," Nix told him. "Sometimes when I feed on enough desire, it's a little like how humans describe being drunk. The world gets...fuzzy. Soft around the edges."

Ivan's gaze heated. "Does my desire do that to you?"

"Mm, of course it does," Nix purred. "You have so much of it, when it comes to me."

Ivan didn't refute the point, and Nix waggled his hand. "Come."

He was able to coax Ivan up into the room with a mix of teasing and subtle manhandling. Nix didn't strip him, though he was tempted. But Jace had brought Ivan spare clothes before their departure from Maine, and his selection was more casual than what Ivan was usually found in. It would do for a nap.

So Nix tucked Ivan under the covers as he was, sitting on the edge of the bed next to him. "Was it nice to have bonding time with your brother?"

"Mm," Ivan mumbled noncommittally, his eyes closing seemingly in spite of himself.

"See? He doesn't hate you. Maybe Alexei will have a change of heart too."

"One time, Alexei was off with another of my father's men," Ivan said, the words coming out quickly but without inflection, his eyes still shut. "My father had me call him, over and over. His man was reporting back to him, and every time Alexei didn't pick up, Sergei was instructed to sock me in the stomach."

A strange chill flushed through Nix—an uncharacteristic, icy rage. He had to swallow hard and gather himself before speaking, and even then his voice came out harsh. "What the fuck for?"

Ivan's brow furrowed slightly, but his voice stayed toneless.

"Something about the consequences of not being able to garner my brother's total loyalty. He knew Alexei didn't fear or respect me. He wanted me to know he knew it."

"And Alexei— Did you tell him about it afterward? "

"No."

Of course he hadn't. Nix resisted the urge to throw something. "Why not?"

"It wouldn't have changed the outcome, would it? And I thought it would be...better not to know." Ivan opened one eye, peering at Nix through pale lashes. "My own mother didn't want me. She was going to take my brothers, you know."

Nix didn't know much about a mother's love, but he knew enough to know the lack of it could fuck a human up. "Maybe she knew your father wouldn't give you up," he soothed. "You were his heir."

"He never even liked me." Ivan shook his head, shutting his eye again. "There's something...rotten inside me." He lifted a hand to his chest, where his heart was. "Something intolerable."

Unlovable, he meant. "I carry a piece of your soul in my chest," Nix told him firmly. "Your very essence. And there's nothing rotten in there. Bitter in places, perhaps. Broken. But not rotten."

Ivan let out a choked sound, his features tightening. "You can't say things like that."

"Why not?"

"It...hurts."

This human. Nix brushed his fingers against Ivan's cheek. "You're much too vulnerable when you're drunk, darling. You should consider becoming a teetotaler."

Ivan leaned his head into Nix's touch. "I think you like me vulnerable."

"I like you all ways. Does that hurt to hear too?"

"Yes."

Nix smoothed the blankets around Ivan once again, letting their conversation fall into silence.

He had thought Ivan was asleep already when the human spoke again. "It's better like this though. Love gets people killed. Or drives them to do the killing. It's a rotten business either way."

Good heavens. Nix shushed him, running a hand through his hair until Ivan's brow smoothed and he began sleeping for real.

Tucking his human into bed, comforting him after horrifying, gut-wrenching truths. It was all domestic as hell, wasn't it? Nix was going to be an amazing mate, now that he'd decided to be. And he'd never met anyone more in need of a mate than his Vanya.

Now he just had to convince Ivan of that fact.

14

Ivan

The familiar restaurant was dimly lit, the dark-red booths each with their own small candle. It had been Sergei's idea to hold the gathering here, but Ivan supposed it was appropriate. It had been their father's favorite place to do business, besides the warehouse. The owner was always willing to look the other way for regular patronage and a little extra cash.

Now it was the spot for his father's wake. A sea of men in black, with enough food to feed ten armies, some of it from the restaurant itself, the rest courtesy of the wives.

Ivan held his chilled glass of vodka, his thumb swiping back and forth across the condensation. For now, he was only holding it. Every man there was eager to refill it as soon as he took a sip, and he needed a clear head. Or as clear as he could make it. He barely remembered the service as it was.

His father wasn't supposed to die. Not so soon. Not like this.

An aneurysm. A fucking ruptured aneurysm—that was what the autopsy had said.

All Ivan knew was that one moment, his father had been talking about business, and then he'd winced, said, "My head's fucking killing me," and slumped in his seat. Sergei had called 911—probably the first time in his life he could say he'd done so—and Ivan had tried to resuscitate his father.

He'd failed at that, clearly.

"You're not drinking enough," Alexei chastised, sliding into the booth next to him. His dirty-blond hair was swept back into its usual bun, his broad form stuffed into a black suit. He looked...tired, his hazel eyes red-rimmed and heavy-lidded.

"Someone has to be sober," Ivan told him, another round of raucous laughter from the men punctuating his point.

"And it should be our new revered leader, hm?"

"And is there a problem with that?" It may not have been meant to happen for another decade, but Ivan had been raised to lead, Alexei meant to stay one step to the side.

One step behind.

And fuck, did Alexei seem to hate that. Ivan had never been able to figure out why, exactly—it wasn't like Alexei wanted to lead himself. He could hardly care less about the entire business.

"Our father is dead," Alexei said bluntly instead of answering Ivan's question.

Ivan contained his eye roll, if only barely. "Yes. I'm incredibly aware."

Alexei lowered his voice and lifted his drink, his lips now hidden behind his glass. "If there was ever a time to leave all this behind, it would be now."

It was a fucking dangerous thing to be said out loud, even as quietly as that.

Ivan gestured to the gruff men surrounding them, the scars and tattoos, guns hiding within suit jackets. No loose women, not with the wives around, but that would happen later, as the night went on and the wives went home. More than half the rabble were watching Ivan and

Alexei from the corners of their eyes, even those laughing among themselves. "Does this look like something that gets left behind?"

Alexei leaned closer. "If we did it now—"

"We'd be as dead as our dear father. You know this. You know this," Ivan repeated, his frustration hard to contain. "Why do you make me say it?"

Alexei's jaw tightened, the only sign of how pissed off he might be at Ivan's refusal. "We might be dead either way."

"What the fuck does that mean?"

"You think you can keep all these people on the same tight leash our father did?"

Ivan narrowed his eyes. "You doubt it?"

"He was a mean son of a bitch."

"And I'm not?"

They stared each other down for a long moment. Too long, considering how many people were watching them. Then Alexei sighed, rubbing a hand across his forehead. "No, you're right, Vanya. You're fucking perfect for the job."

It should have been a victory, however minute, but somehow it didn't feel like Ivan had won. "Where's Sascha?" he asked, instead of investigating why that might be.

"Getting completely shit-faced."

Of course. Their baby brother was maybe one of the few people truly sorry their father was gone. He had a right to mourn. But still, there were dangers in Sascha losing control on a night like this.

"Watch him," Ivan ordered.

Alexei raised his glass in a mock salute. "I always do."

He rose from the booth and shuffled away, brushing off the men who tried to drag him into their booths for a toast.

Alexei wasn't completely off course with his misgivings. Their father had fought his way up the ranks through cruelty and violence, and now the men who had served him so faithfully would be waiting to see if Ivan could measure up. Looking for any sign of weakness.

Ivan eyed the room over his glass. These men had been part of his family for almost as long as he could remember. But now they were competition, of sorts.

Succession of a business like this was never a sure thing, was it?

A shadow fell over the table. Sergei, swaying slightly as he loomed over Ivan. It wasn't surprising he was letting loose—Sergei had been with Ivan's father from the beginning, and he wasn't afraid of a little vodka making him lose esteem among the men.

"Where are your brothers?" Sergei asked, his words surprisingly clear considering how much alcohol he must have had in his system.

"Alexei went to corral Sascha."

"Good," Sergei said shortly. He'd never approved of Sascha's coddling; Ivan knew that much. He'd heard Sergei argue against it with his father more than once. One of the very few things the two hadn't agreed on.

Sergei shoved his way into the booth with significantly less grace than Alexei had. "When something—or someone becomes a liability—" he said, not at all subtle. "You cut it loose. Even family."

Ivan nodded, not ready to get into the age-old argument over Sascha. "I'll keep that in mind."

Sergei sat there, sipping his vodka for a few minutes, then spoke again, "Your father. He loved your mother. It almost cost him his sons." He sneered, his eyes unfocused over his glass. "He was right to do what he did."

Images ran through Ivan's mind, swift and horrible. A pale corpse. Bloodstains on a faded yellow sheet. "Of course he was," he said evenly.

He couldn't feel his face for some reason, but he was skilled enough now at controlling it that he was almost certain it was giving nothing away.

Sergei stared at him, steely-eyed, for a long moment, then it was as if a flip switched, and he was all smiles. He clapped Ivan on the shoulder, grinning broadly. "You'll be a good leader, hm? With Sergei here to help."

"I want to modernize," Ivan told him, almost before he could think.

There wasn't much he could reform—not without making himself a target—but he could do away with the dank warehouse his father had used as his meeting room, forgo the scent of mold and old blood.

"Of course, of course," Sergei told him, magnanimous. "You're in charge now." He swayed toward Ivan across the table. "Just not too many changes, hm? Makes the men restless."

Ivan looked out at those men again. It was suddenly harder to focus on individual faces—they were just one cohesive mass, all staring, their eye sockets bottomless pits. Alexei and Sascha were nowhere to be found, or maybe they'd become part of that staring mass.

Maybe Ivan had downed too much vodka after all.

He wasn't used to drinking during the day like this, and it was sure to go on all night. There wouldn't be a moment alone, not until well after dawn. It wasn't as if Ivan could leave either. Not when it was his father they were celebrating.

He was trapped.

Sergei stood, raising his voice to be heard over the din. "Dimitri's last words were to our Ivan here!" he bellowed, and the men silenced immediately. "His Vanya. How proud he was of him. He'd been preparing for Ivan to take over for a long time now, hm? It happened a little sooner than expected, but—" He shrugged a shoulder. "—such is life." He raised his glass. "To Dimitri Kozlov and his son Ivan."

"Dimitri," everyone repeated. "And Ivan."

Sergei shot Ivan a wink, and Ivan nodded in return, complicit in the lie.

His father's last words had been nothing of the sort, of course. He hadn't had a chance to say anything profound—he'd died too quickly. And never once had he said he was proud of Ivan. He'd probably rather have bitten off his own tongue than let such praise leave his lips.

Still, Sergei had given him an endorsement, no matter how false.

Ivan tried to think of his last conversation with his father that hadn't been about business logistics.

It had been a week or so before his death, he was pretty sure. His father had just executed someone he'd suspected of sharing information with another family. He'd been cleaning his gun, Ivan standing at the ready next to him, waiting for the cleanup crew.

"Vanya," his father had said. "You know how I knew it was him?"

Ivan could have hazarded a guess, but it was always better with his father to admit ignorance than pretend knowledge. "No, I don't."

"His wife. She was sick. Very sick. Medical bills, you know?" his father had explained, tucking his weapon away. "He's always been loyal to her. He needed the money, and it made him stupid." He had stepped closer, catching Ivan's eye. "What's to be learned from him?"

Ivan had glanced at the body at his feet, then back to his father. "You never betray the real family. Our family."

"No, Vanya." His father's hand had whipped out, gripping Ivan's chin hard enough to hurt. "It's that love makes you stupid. Makes you weak. And then someone smarter and stronger puts a bullet in your brain."

Ivan had nodded as best he could within the tight grip. His father had grinned suddenly and dropped his painful hold. "But he doesn't have to worry about his wife anymore, hm?"

"Because he's dead," Ivan had said dully.

"Because Sergei is on his way to their house." His father's grin had sharpened. "No more medical bills."

A beautiful lesson from father to son.

Now Ivan took a swig of his vodka after all. He supposed he could have made that sage advice into a toast, but it didn't seem like it would have had the same effect as Sergei's lies, did it?

And what did it matter anyway? His father was dead.

His words could die with him.

———

IVAN HUNG UP THE PHONE, cursing.

Jace had lost Sergei. Or at least, the useless fool thought he had. It was possible Sergei was holed up in his apartment, but if that was the case, he'd been in there since before the assassination attempt on Ivan.

It was unlikely, to say the least.

Jace hadn't heard any word on whether Sergei was attempting to make deals with any other family, and Ivan couldn't get a hold of Cooper to find out if he'd been able to track anything pertinent electronically.

The silence from Cooper was...concerning.

"Problem?" Nix asked from his spot on the porch's Adirondack chair, his legs slung carelessly over the side.

Sascha had informed them he had a "no Mafia business in the house" rule, one that was obviously made up solely to piss Ivan off, but Kai had seemed only too willing to enforce it, so Ivan and Nix had removed themselves to the front porch for Ivan's call.

Nix was wearing what he must have considered some sort of vacation wear. His propensity for sheer or silken shirts had been replaced by some knit thing. It was too thin for the weather, but then Sascha had been right—demons ran hot. It also had a loose enough collar that it kept slipping over Nix's shoulders, leaving the skin bare.

It was no doubt meant to entice.

It was working.

"The usual incompetence," Ivan muttered, jerking his gaze away from Nix's silken skin. He was feeling irritable again, although he had no one to blame but himself. He'd slept off the drunkenness from that morning with an extended nap, one full of half-remembered dreams and distorted memories, and it had been dark when he'd woken up. A fact that made him pissy in and of itself—there was an entire day wasted. That compounded with the persistent headache he had from his overindulgence, and he was just about ready to snap.

Maybe Nix was right and Ivan needed to cut off drinking

entirely, at least until this mess was sorted and he was feeling less...jagged. There was something too tempting about liquor these days, about the way it made him just a touch looser. The way it made it easier to let go.

He'd said foolish things that morning, admitted to hurts he was always better off ignoring, but he couldn't even regret it fully.

Nix would keep his secrets close. Even Ivan—mistrustful as he was by nature—knew that much.

The way he felt when drinking was similar to the way he felt around Nix in any state, tempted by the notion that it was okay to lower his defenses just a smidge. That Ivan could be soft for a moment and not regret it later.

But was that feeling truth or a trick? There was Kai's warning to consider.

Desperate desires lead to desperate acts.

But between the two of them, Ivan and Nix...which of them was the desperate one? It was impossible to answer. Maybe it was both of them.

"Is the incompetence the only thing that has you scowling?" Nix asked, his chin propped on one hand.

"I'm not scowling," Ivan told him. He wasn't either. His looseness from the morning was nowhere to be found, and he had a firm rein back on his facial expressions. So Nix was just being a little shit.

"You're scowling on the inside." Now Ivan did glare, which Nix met with a grin. "And now your outside matches your insides. Isn't that lovely?"

Ivan stalked over to him across the porch. "I'm more than a little irritable and annoyed at the moment, incubus. And you're not nearly as charming as you think."

"Is that so?" Nix swung his legs off from the side of the chair and widened them invitingly. "Because a little birdie told me you like to fuck when you're annoyed."

"Mm." Ivan leaned over the ridiculous chair, resting his hands on its arms, inhaling Nix's smoky scent. "Give me your mouth, then."

"With pleasure," Nix murmured, closing the distance between them.

His mouth was hot, and his tongue was eager, and Ivan groaned, pressing a knee onto the chair's seat for stability and fisting a hand in Nix's hair.

He could give up liquor easily, if *this* was always available to him.

His demon drug.

Nix pulled away to mouth at Ivan's jaw. "Wanna see how far we can get before the neighbors call the cops?"

Ivan tugged him back, cocking a brow. "I generally try to steer clear of law enforcement."

Nix smirked. "What a pity."

Ivan hesitated, his hand in Nix's hair, studying his incubus. There was no point in saying anything, was there? Whatever came out of Nix's mouth could be a lie anyway, so why bring it up? Still, he found himself asking, "Are you like this with all your contracts?"

"Like what?" Nix quipped. "Horny?"

When Ivan didn't respond, Nix's smile dropped slowly. He sighed. "Did Kai happen to say something to you?"

Ivan stiffened, his stomach dropping. That was as good as an admission, wasn't it? That Kai had something to say. He dropped his hand out of Nix's hair. "And what would Kai have said to me?"

"Listen, Ivan—"

Nix stopped midsentence, his gaze darting out over Ivan's shoulder. There was a black car pulling up, a quietly expensive model. Not one Ivan recognized. He reached for his gun as the car pulled in to the drive, only to remember Sascha had made him leave it in his room.

Why the fuck had Ivan listened?

Nix was in front of him before he knew it, somehow out of the chair and blocking Ivan in the blink of an eye. "Inside," he barked, like Ivan was supposed to follow his orders.

"Not until we know who it is."

But Ivan didn't recognize the man who exited the driver's side of the vehicle. He had light-brown hair and sharp cheekbones and was dressed in a patterned suit like some sort of eccentric professor.

Ignoring Ivan and Nix on the porch, the stranger opened the door to the passenger seat, drawing out a conventionally attractive blond man around Ivan's age who was dressed much more casually, like he'd just come from a backwoods hike.

The two strangers faced them, the professor type standing in front of the blond, much in the same way Nix stood in front of Ivan.

But it was the blond who spoke. "Sascha?" he asked hesitantly. "Or..." He cocked his head. "Ivan?"

"Not that we don't love surprise visitors," Nix drawled. "But who the fuck's asking?"

"I'm Eric," the blond said, not looking too put out by the rudeness. He pointed to his companion. "This is Wolfe. Alexei sent us?" He made it sound like a question rather than a statement.

The one identified as Wolfe made a vaguely disgruntled noise. "We were not *sent*," he corrected. "We were already in the area. And we found something of yours." He steered his partner to the back of the car, popping open the trunk.

It would be stupid to walk over, yet Ivan found himself too curious to resist. But before he could step off the porch, Nix froze in front of him, halting his progress.

"What is it?"

Nix sniffed the air like some sort of bloodhound. "Vampires," he accused, loud enough for Eric and Wolfe to hear.

"Yes," Wolfe said coolly, arching a brow. "Was that not clear? We've already stated we're...friends of Alexei's. What else would we be?"

There was a time—merely a few weeks ago, in fact—when Ivan would have assumed the worst from that statement. Would have thought Alexei had sent these two to do his dirty work—to hit Ivan when he was already down. He would have rushed back into the house with Nix at his heels. Or, more likely, fled the state entirely, convinced Sascha had done his part to set him up.

But now, for whatever reason, he found himself urging Nix forward, approaching close enough to peer into the trunk.

For a moment, he was at a loss for words, even as Nix cackled at his side.

Eric cleared his throat. "Did we do it right? I've never really abducted someone before."

There was a first time for everything, apparently.

Because there in the trunk, bound and gagged and clearly unconscious, was Sergei.

15

Ivan

"I don't like this," Sascha moaned, wringing his hands like some despairing maiden. "I do *not* like this."

When Kai glared at Ivan with glowing blue eyes, Ivan shrugged. "It wasn't my doing. You have Alexei to blame."

Their group—including the two newcomers—was gathered in the living room, which was feeling quite crowded with the three couples, even with Matteo hiding upstairs.

There'd been quite a bit of hubbub initially when Kai had realized a duo of vampires had arrived. It had involved Kai transitioning into his demon form and letting his wings out, a sight Ivan had already had burned into his brain from his last visit to Maine. Nix had transformed as well, seemingly out of a desire to disrupt more than some instinct to protect, since he'd already decided the two were friends rather than foe. Wolfe had told them all matter-of-factly that he and Eric meant no harm but that if either of the demons disturbed even a hair on Eric's head, he'd rip off the wings and the tail and stuff them down their throats.

It had calmed down a bit after that.

Although, Ivan noticed Nix still had a wary eye on the vampire Wolfe, even now. And he'd been unusually quiet during the whole exchange, considering his usual mouthy demeanor.

In some fit of mass paranoia, everyone was standing—Kai and Sascha in the back corner, with Kai's arm wrapped around the front of Sascha's shoulders; Ivan and Nix behind the couch, Nix cocking a hip up against the upholstery; and Eric and Wolfe closest to the door, Wolfe's hand on Eric's shoulder.

Ivan hadn't missed the way Wolfe had assessed the room and quickly placed Eric and himself where they could escape easiest.

Eric, for his part, seemed to be doing his best not to gawk at Kai in his demon form, but his best was...horrendous. His eyes kept darting over to the massive blue demon and lingering on his shoulders, as if he was expecting the wings to make another appearance.

Sascha stuck his tongue out at Ivan, presumably for shifting the blame to their brother, then faced Wolfe and Eric with a considerably more polite expression. "Did Alexei really send you?"

It was a question worth asking, as overall it seemed unlikely. Besides the fact that Alexei would be hesitant to spit on Ivan if he was on fire, as the saying went, it was also that Eric and Wolfe were a strange duo. Eric seemed like nothing more than a regular man, one raised in the suburbs rather than dingy basements and docks, and Wolfe seemed...oddly blank. Like he was uninterested in these proceedings, even if he'd been the one to initiate them.

Eric drew his gaze off Kai with a noticeable effort, making an awkward face at Sascha. "Well, it was more like he and Jay were complaining about Ivan asking for help after...everything." His cheeks flushed pink, and he gave Ivan an apologetic shrug before continuing. "And we were already in the area..."

"My pet wanted to play at mobsters," Wolfe drawled, running a possessive hand over Eric's shoulder.

"Hey!" Eric's flush deepened, even as he leaned back into Wolfe, not seeming to notice Wolfe wrapping an arm around Eric's middle, or the pleased smirk Wolfe made when he did so. "I just thought it'd be interesting. And we've helped, right?"

"How did you find him anyway?" Sascha asked.

"He was at the gas station here," Eric said, almost sheepish. "Jay had snapped a photo of him last time he came to town, so we knew to run him off if we ever saw him. We just...took the opportunity presented to us."

"And yet Alexei should be under the impression that Sergei still works for me," Ivan pointed out.

"I told him about the betrayal," Sascha said, a defiant tilt to his chin. He frowned. "But now I have a mobster tied up in my basement, and I was really trying to avoid that kind of thing here."

"He won't be here for long," Ivan muttered darkly.

Sascha scowled at him. "You are *not* killing a man in my basement!"

If only that were the plan. Ivan would like nothing more than to put an end to this here. But he still needed Sergei to be useful one last time, so the execution would have to wait.

He was supposed to be learning to act without anger getting the better of him, after all.

And then he wouldn't have Sascha sulking at him for the next three months.

"I'm not killing anyone in your basement," he conceded, pleased when Sascha's mouth clamped shut abruptly, as if he hadn't been expecting Ivan to agree. "We'll be taking him back to New York with us."

"Is that wise?" Kai asked. "He's a known enemy. Wouldn't it be better to end it now?"

Ivan sneered at him. "Worried for our safety, are you?"

"I don't wish for Sascha to be inconvenienced more than he already has."

Before Sascha could add his two cents—whether to confirm his inconvenienced state or deny it—Wolfe interrupted. "Are we done here, then?" he asked in a flat tone, as if the conversation was boring him beyond belief.

Ivan would have been more than happy to let the two go, but it would be stupid of him to turn down the opportunity of two vampires when they were already here.

"I could use you—use your *help*," Ivan amended, when Wolfe's eyes flashed dangerously, "one more time, if you will. A meeting in New York. Since Alexei won't come himself."

Wolfe tutted. "We're on a fishing trip." He drew his blond mate closer. "For Eric. And I don't believe there's any fishing for him in New York."

Eric tilted his head back to murmur, "I've never been to the city though."

Wolfe eyed him thoughtfully, then pursed his lips into a small smile. "We'll stay at the most expensive hotel I can find," he said as if in warning.

Eric grinned at him. "You think I'm going to argue?"

Feeling oddly like a voyeur, Ivan cleared his throat, gaining their attention again. "The meeting won't be for another two days," he told them. "That gives you more time to...fish."

"Very well." Wolfe unwrapped from around Eric, taking his hand instead. "We'll be going now. This has already taken up too much of our time."

He led Eric to the front door without further ado, leaving it to the blond to turn and give them all an apologetic wave.

"I'd be careful there," Nix murmured after they'd left.

Ivan glanced at him in surprise. Nix had been quiet, yes, but Ivan wouldn't have thought two vampires would be enough to give the two demons in the room any trouble. "Why?"

Nix's brow furrowed. "The bloodsucker Wolfe. There's not much there, emotions-wise. Other than some pretty obsessive adoration for his mate. It's the one overpowering scent he gives off." He wrinkled his nose. "Psychopath, I think."

Ivan shrugged. "I don't really care one way or another, if they can do what we need them to do."

"Great," Sascha groaned. "Mobsters *and* psychopath vampires."

"Again," Ivan hissed. "He is *Alexei's* friend."

Sascha pouted, seeming put out that he couldn't throw the blame on Ivan, then pulled his phone from his pocket. "I'm calling him." He rushed out of the room, already holding the phone to his ear.

Ivan had to bite back the immense surge of bitterness—Alexei would answer Sascha, no doubt. They would probably have a long, lovely conversation. Perhaps make Christmas plans together.

Nix's hand fell, hot against the back of Ivan's neck. "Are you spiraling?"

"No," Ivan sighed. Not spiraling, exactly. But he did need to focus.

He had a meeting to attend, after all.

He glanced at Kai, who was already watching Ivan intently. "Would you care to be a tool for intimidation?"

"This Sergei is the reason Sascha was stabbed."

Ivan wasn't sure if it was a question or a statement, but he answered either way. "Yes."

Kai grinned at him with a mouth full of sharp teeth. "Then I would. With pleasure."

———

THE BASEMENT WAS DIMLY LIT, the overhead light ancient and dusted over. There were boxes shoved in different corners—some had brighter, fresher cardboard, possibly odd bits from Sascha's move, and some clearly had been there for quite a while, remnants from the old owner.

It smelled musty and damp, in the way the warehouse Ivan's father had operated in had always smelled.

Maybe Ivan was destined to always be finding himself in dark, dank places.

He entered with Kai at his back. The demon had chosen his human form for the moment, for whatever reason. He was still intimidating enough, six and a half feet of pure muscle, with a belt full of daggers he'd brought out for the occasion.

Sergei was as they'd left him—tied to a small wooden chair they'd found, the white paint on it cracked and peeling—although he'd woken up at some point while they'd been inside discussing, and his eyes were open. The vampires hadn't been too rough with him—more was the pity—but he had a split lip and some impressive bruising. To his credit, whatever he might have been feeling at finding himself tied up at Ivan's mercy, there was no telling just by looking at him. His roughhewn features were blank.

But Kai sniffed the air as he leaned against the wall by the basement door, directly in Sergei's line of sight. "He reeks of fear," he rumbled.

"Is that right, Sergei?" Ivan murmured, approaching the man who'd helped raise him. "And what would you have to fear from me? Your *family*?"

Sergei didn't answer. Of course, he couldn't, not with that duct tape slapped across his mouth. Ivan walked over and ripped it off, wincing in a show of sympathy as he did so. "My apologies. Our new compatriots seem to be a fan of doing things the old-fashioned way."

Sergei looked at Ivan as if he were an unruly child. "Untie me, Vanya."

"No."

Ivan could imagine the calculations going on in that thick

head, even if he couldn't see them in Sergei's expression. To continue to pretend or to beg for mercy? To plead complete ignorance or to plead for his life?

After a long moment, Sergei let out a sigh, clucking his tongue. "You already know, hm? I thought as much."

"Yes," Ivan confirmed. "I know."

He thought it would be more climactic, the moment where the lies were over, but Sergei only let out a harsh breath. "Then time to kill me." His gaze darted to Kai. "Is that what the brute is for?" Sergei bared his teeth in a false smile. "New hire?"

"You're not already familiar?" Ivan asked, shaking his head. "You should get better intel. That's Sascha's new...partner."

Sergei sneered. "Partner," he muttered, and spat on the basement floor.

That earned a low, rumbling growl from Kai, although he still didn't shift into his demon form.

"Watch it, Sergei," Ivan said lightly. "He's testy."

He stood there for a moment, considering Sergei. The best thing to do—for himself if not his plans—would have been to end it right away. To remove any temptation to give in to wondering. To questioning. But still he found himself asking, "Why did you do it? Why change loyalties?"

Sergei gave him a scathing look. "What does it matter?"

"It matters," Ivan told him through clenched teeth.

A gleam entered Sergei's eyes, and he let out a bitter laugh. "Always so angry, Vanya," he taunted. "That's your problem, you know. Too emotional. After Alexei left?" He clucked his tongue again. "A disaster. You think Sascha is the liability in the family, but it's you. *You* let Alexei leave. *You* let Sascha run wild. No control of yourself, no control of them."

Never mind that Sergei had been the one to return from Colorado without Alexei, scared off by him and his vampire. But Ivan supposed enough time had passed that Sergei had conveniently forgotten that fact. Maybe he'd convinced himself monsters didn't exist after all.

And maybe Sergei was right about some things, because Ivan *was* angry. So angry it burned, itching under his skin and pulsing in his chest. "You didn't think to tell me any of that before stepping straight to betrayal?" he asked, fighting to keep his voice from cracking with rage. "You were supposed to *guide* me."

"There was no need. You're unfit, Vanya. You always have been." Sergei narrowed his eyes, and there was finally a flash of real hatred there, some hint of his true feelings. "Given long enough, your father would have passed the family onto me. The Carusos were happy to right his mistake."

"You really think that?" Ivan laughed, disbelief momentarily taking over his rage. "Now who's the one letting his emotions get the best of him?" He leaned in, the scent of copper from Sergei's split lip filling his nostrils. "My father may have hated me, but I was still his blood. And that narcissistic bastard cared more about that than anything as ephemeral as your fucking loyalty. If he was here, he'd shoot you himself."

Ivan's gaze roamed over Sergei's too-familiar face. "How many times did you beat me, do you think, under my father's orders?" Ivan paused, but the old mobster didn't take the bait. "I always considered it water under the bridge," he continued. "You were only following orders, hm? But whose orders are you following now? Because they sure as *fuck* aren't mine."

Sergei stayed silent.

Ivan shook his head. "I should be grateful you beat the sentimental side right out of me. Otherwise, I might even regret killing you. But I'm not shooting you tonight, anyway." He stepped back from the chair. "We're making changes, Sergei. Big changes." He flashed his teeth. "The kind that make the men *restless*. So bear this a little longer, hm?" He headed toward the door leading into the house, ready to be out of this room and away from...all of it.

"Water," Sergei said quickly, a bit of panic in his tone.

Ivan waved his hand without looking back at him. "In the morning, if I'm feeling generous. In the meantime, Kai here has some *emotions* about the knife that got stuck in Sascha's arm, thanks to your betrayal. So I'm thinking I'll let him repay the favor." He tossed a glance to the demon. "Does that sound like something you're interested in, or are those daggers ceremonial?"

Kai's grin was the broadest Ivan had ever seen on him. "I'm very interested."

Ivan paused at the door, turning back to Sergei. "That's the thing about the Carusos. You thought they were the bigger power in town, but they were only little fish in a very big pond. My brothers and I have some new allies. You remember how Alexei changed, the last time you saw him?" There was a flash of fear in Sergei's eyes, there and gone. He did remember, no matter what denial he'd put in place since then. "The eyes, you kept saying." Ivan cocked his head. "I wonder which part of Kai will stick with you the most. Other than his knife, that is."

Ivan didn't have to look at Kai to know he'd changed forms. The high keen of fear from Sergei was sign enough.

"Try to avoid any major arteries," Ivan said as he walked through the door. "I don't want him bleeding out just yet. And put the tape back on his mouth, will you? Sascha wouldn't want to hear the screaming."

16

Nix

Nix lay on his back on the guest room bed, his feet propped up against the wall toward the ceiling, his tail slapping against the mattress.

It was possible he was pouting. But he was a little put out, if he was being honest, that Ivan had wanted Kai for backup and not Nix. Sure, Kai was massive, and a warrior demon, and his battle prowess was the whole reason they'd come to Maine in the first place. But still...

Nix frowned, staring up at the cracked plaster. He'd lost his own point somewhere along the way.

Ah yes. The point was that he didn't want Ivan pushing him aside when it came to business once they were bonded. Nix would essentially be Ivan's mob wife, and weren't mob wives supposed to be at their mobsters' sides?

Actually, come to think of it, no. From what little Nix knew, the wives were left behind, weren't they? With the house and the brats.

Well, that was fine. Nix had misspoken—he wouldn't be some

mob wife anyway. He'd be a mob *mate*, and that was a whole different kettle of fish. He'd be at Ivan's side through all of it.

And Kai would stay in Maine, where his big blue butt belonged.

The bedroom door opened, and Nix's tail paused midsmack. He sat up immediately, scooting to the end of the bed and wrinkling his nose. Those were not good vibes his future mate was putting off. Not at all.

Ivan looked terrible. There was a harsher set to his jaw even than usual, and it looked like he'd been running his fingers through his hair. And the emotions wafting off him? Bitter resentment and rage, tangled up nicely with despair, shame, and guilt.

Nix tsked at him. "Really, Vanya. I should be the only one making you this undone."

Ivan scoffed. "After we kill Sergei, I'm sure you will be." His tone was cold enough when discussing the prospect of killing his right-hand man, but the veritable tornado of emotions roiling within him said otherwise.

"And when will that be?" Nix asked pointedly, eager to be brought back into the fold. In all the hubbub with the newcomers and their unexpected gift, Ivan had forgotten to tell his darling Nix the details.

Ivan leaned heavily against the bedroom door. "After the meeting with the men. I figured it'll be easier for you to suss out who may have been working with him if we can shock them a little with the sight of him."

It was smart enough. And Nix was pleased the plan included his own skills. But really, who cared about the fucking business when Ivan looked so wrecked?

Nix patted the bed. "Come here."

Ivan didn't. He walked over to the bedroom window instead, looking out, his back ramrod straight. After a moment, he spoke. "He says I'm too emotional. Sergei. That it makes me a poor leader." He tapped a finger against the window. "It's a bit funny. My brothers have always complained I'm ice-cold."

It showed how much Ivan's brothers knew. Perhaps they'd been fooled because of their father, who by all accounts had been icy inside and out. But Ivan was more like a dormant volcano in winter. There might have been snow at the top, but the fire simmering under the surface could take out a city.

"Well, you put on a good facade," Nix said. "But yes, Vanya, you're quite emotional. Most big, scary men are, as much as they hate to admit it. But it won't be a liability to your leadership," he reassured.

"And why not?" Ivan asked without looking over.

"Because I'll be here to keep you in line."

Ivan tapped the glass again. "Until you leave."

Nix sucked in a breath. "Ivan—"

Ivan whirled around, his expression blank. Icy on the surface indeed. "I don't want to talk about that now," he said dismissively.

As much as Nix wanted to disagree, it was probably best not to. Not when Ivan was such a powder keg at the moment.

Talking wasn't the best strategy with this one anyway.

"Come here," Nix repeated.

Ivan did as he asked this time, approaching the bed until he was standing between Nix's legs. Nix cocked his head, his tail flicking out to slide against Ivan's hip. "Would you like me to make you feel better?"

"What are you, my nursemaid?"

Nix tutted, his tail slapping lightly against the fabric of Ivan's pants. "Try again, Vanya."

A muscle twitched in Ivan's jaw, but he answered, "Yes." And then, without Nix even asking for it, "Please."

Oh, what a good boy. Nix let his clothes disappear off his body, leaving him in another pair of lacy panties. He widened his legs, enjoying the way Ivan's gaze immediately trailed over him, hot and hungry. "Tell me—have you ever sucked a cock before, Vanya?"

Ivan's perusal stopped in its tracks, and he frowned at Nix. "You know I haven't."

"Would you like to suck mine?"

Ivan let out a heavy breath, and Nix thought for a moment he might not answer at all. But then— "Yes."

Nix wanted to purr or preen. He did so love to get the exact answer he wanted. But he kept his voice firm as he ordered, "On your knees, darling."

Yet Ivan stayed standing—acting as his own worst enemy, as usual. Getting in his own way. As evidenced by the skepticism in his next words. "You think getting on my knees for you will make me feel better?"

"I do." Nix wrapped a leg around Ivan and grabbed his shirt-front, pulling him in close. He pressed his cheek against Ivan's, whispering in his ear, "You don't have to be in charge here, Vanya. Did you know that? You boss me around only when you *want* to. The rest of the time, you can let your devoted demon take care of you. How does that sound?"

"And why would you want to?" Ivan asked, after a strangled breath. "Take care of me?"

"Because it pleases me to," Nix told him. "And I'm all about pleasure." He pressed the lobe of Ivan's ear between his teeth, lightly enough that his fangs didn't puncture, then released it. He leaned back to catch Ivan's eye. "You want to get rough and fuck me into the mattress like there's no tomorrow, we can do that. I'll follow your every order like the devoted demon I am. But if you want a little rest from all that? Then you'll let me do what I think best." He tugged Ivan's shirt again. Hard. "Won't you, Vanya?"

Ivan held himself unbearably still for a long moment, then slumped in Nix's hold, forehead landing against his. "Yes."

Nix kissed him for his honesty, then pressed lightly on his shoulders. Ivan followed the cue, sliding down to his knees.

"Shirt off," Nix told him.

Ivan raised a brow at Nix's tone but tugged off his shirt. Nix was shameless in his ogling. He'd acquired a beautiful human. He liked that Ivan was a bit older too. It was as if he was...slightly worn in, one could say, in a way that tickled Nix's fancy. And he had wonderfully well-formed shoulders, with that lovely light dusting of hair on his chest.

Ivan snapped the waistband of Nix's panties against his skin irritably. "These are in my way."

Nix disappeared those too, letting his cock fall free. He was already half-hard, both from the sight of Ivan on his knees and the anticipation of what was to come. It was sure to be clumsy. Inept.

But it would be Ivan, and that was enough to have Nix salivating.

Ivan eyed Nix's cock warily before letting his gaze roam over the rest of Nix, surprising him with his next words. "You're stunning. You know that, don't you?"

Nix stroked a finger down Ivan's cheek. "I do, yes. But I don't mind hearing you say it."

Ivan's lips twitched, and then he went back to staring at Nix's cock.

"It won't bite," Nix teased.

He received a glare for that. "I'm aware," Ivan said archly, wrapping a strong hand around it. "I like the way you feel," he murmured. "How hot you are in my hand." He rubbed his thumb gently across the tip, and Nix hissed at the contact. "How silky your skin is here."

"And what about my taste?" Nix asked pointedly.

Ivan continued circling his thumb. "I've already tasted your cum."

"Mm." Nix grinned. "I remember."

"It was smoky. And sweet. I don't usually like sweet."

Usually, Nix noted. "Why don't you taste it from the source?"

He received another glare for some reason, as if Ivan hadn't just been reciting an ode to the joys of Nix's cock. Then Ivan licked a stripe up him, from base to tip.

More blood rushed into Nix's cock, and he went immediately from half-mast to full. "Mm." He sighed. "Lovely. Now—"

Whatever instruction he'd been going to give—and who the fuck could remember?—was cut off as Ivan wrapped his lips around Nix's tip, sucking aggressively.

Nix arched his back, one hand flying to Ivan's shoulder. "Oh *fuck*. S-Sensitive there."

Ivan popped off, licking at his lips. "I know." He smirked. "Too much for you, demon?"

In answer, Nix cupped the back of Ivan's head, pulling him back down.

What followed was an aggressive exploration. Ivan sucked Nix down, testing how far he could get, and promptly gagged and popped back up, glaring at Nix's cock like it had offended him. He tried again and again, ruthlessly persistent until he was deep-throating him, swallowing convulsively around the head of Nix's cock, spit gathering and dripping from his lips.

He didn't leave the exploration to Nix's cock alone. He would pop off every now and then, sticking his face into the crease of Nix's groin, inhaling deeply while jacking him off with strong, sure strokes. He squeezed and tugged at Nix's balls, murmuring about the lack of hair.

In all, Nix found himself fighting for his fucking life, toes curling and tail twisting.

He should have expected it, he supposed: the ferocity. Ivan wasn't one to go about something half-assed. But Nix hadn't quite expected the rising desire in the air, the way it built and built just the same as when Ivan fucked him. Like he couldn't get enough of Nix, even like this.

What a waste that Ivan hadn't sucked cock until now, with the appetite he had for it.

It was even worse when Ivan found his rhythm, just as aggressive as what had come before, a hand at the base of Nix's cock while he hollowed his cheeks and sucked like a fucking vortex. Nix could barely move, his hand digging into Ivan's shoulder and his back in a constant arch, not sure whether to fuck into Ivan's mouth or away.

He couldn't even find it in himself to tease. All he could do was gasp and warn, *"Coming."*

Ivan let out something remarkably close to a growl in response, but he didn't let up. Nix practically swallowed his own tongue as he emptied into Ivan's mouth, head flung back and eyes shutting against his will as the world swirled around him.

"Holy hell," he muttered when he was able. Ivan let out something that sounded suspiciously like a laugh.

When Nix got his strength back, he ran a foot along the impressive erection Ivan was sporting. "Did that turn you on, Vanya?" he asked, aiming for sultry but probably coming out wrecked. "Would you like to come on me, perhaps? You can. Anywhere you like."

Ivan leaned back and spit a glob of Nix's cum into his hand, thick and viscous. He hadn't swallowed all of it, then. "I already know where I want to come," he said in a voice like gravel before standing and tugging his slacks down with one hand, slicking himself up with Nix's cum. "Inside you."

And then he was flipping Nix over and hauling his hips up. Nix barely had a chance to gasp before his cheeks were parted and Ivan was spitting on his hole, one finger sliding in.

The desire in the air was delicious beyond belief, heavy as

coastal fog. Nix had just orgasmed, but he still found himself ravenous for it. "Hurry," he urged. "You don't have to—"

Ivan caught his drift, because his finger withdrew, and then he was notching his cock against Nix and slamming in.

Nix keened.

It wasn't painful, not with his natural lubricant, but there was an intensity to it, to being filled so suddenly. Ivan wasted no time fucking him like he meant it. Fucking him into the mattress, just as Nix had teased. Nix couldn't even touch himself, too busy drinking in the desperation in Ivan's thrusts, the way he seemed to be trying to meld their bodies together, one punch of his hips at a time.

"My demon," he growled, his arms like a cage around Nix's head, his body heavy over him. "Fucking *mine*."

Nix wanted to agree, but the words were lost somewhere in the high-pitched moans he couldn't seem to contain.

It wasn't long after that Ivan's rhythm faltered, and he slammed in one final time, his whole body shuddering as he emptied into Nix.

"Oh my," Nix said when he finally could, Ivan's weight solid against his back. "Did you like sucking me off that much?"

Ivan pulled out with a groan, falling bonelessly onto the bed next to him. "It wasn't the worst thing I've done."

Nix tutted at him, rolling over so his head was on Ivan's chest, his hand trailing over the lovely cool skin there. "You'll hurt my feelings," he warned.

Ivan tucked a hand behind his head, smirking up at the ceiling. "I liked it. Obviously."

Nix preened. "I told you I'd make you feel better."

"Mm."

"You're quite ferocious at it, you know. If only your enemies knew what a terror you could be with a cock in your mouth."

In the answering silence, Nix wondered for a moment if he'd gone too far. Ivan was so testy about business. But there was a steady shaking underneath him and a low rumbling coming from Ivan's chest.

A laugh.

"You're such a—" Ivan began, then stopped.

"Such a what?" Nix prompted.

"Such a demon."

"Mm." Nix pinched Ivan's nipple lightly, laughing when he swatted his hand away. "That I am."

They lay there together. Nix could bring it up now—his desire to stay, his hope for a bond between them. It could be the right time, while they were warm and lax and soft with each other. But odds were that it would tense Ivan right back up, and all the glorious work Nix had just done in smoothing his rough edges would be wasted.

So he propped his chin on his hands, giving Ivan a lecherous grin. "Vanya?"

"Mm?"

"Can I suck yours now too?"

He grinned when Ivan's softened cock stirred against his hip.

"Jesus." Ivan rubbed a hand over his eyes. "Give me ten minutes."

Instead, Nix slid down, inhaling Ivan's musky scent as he went, and darted his tongue out to dip into Ivan's navel. "Oh, I think we can do better than that."

17

Nix

It was a lovely day for returning to New York. The birds were singing, the weather was clear and cool, Nix had wrung three orgasms out of Ivan the night before, and they had Ivan's scumbag of a traitor in their trunk.

Or they would, as soon as Kai and Ivan finished transferring him.

Nix had already said goodbye to Matteo, who'd been back in his blanket bundle on the couch, probably thanking the heavens that the intruders were leaving already. And now Nix was getting a lovely hug from Sascha on the porch.

"Thank you for your hospitality, sweetums," Nix said.

"Oh." Sascha's cheeks turned a lovely pink as he blinked up at Nix. "Of course. And we'll be there tomorrow."

He sounded like he wasn't sure Nix would believe him, so Nix patted him on the shoulder. "I know you will. You're a very good brother."

"Right." Sascha craned his neck past Nix. Looking to see if the others were still occupied, perhaps. "Listen." He tugged on Nix's shirt lightly. "My brother pisses me off."

Well, then—Nix bit back a smile—it seemed like they were getting right into the meat of it.

"He forgets to be human more often than not," Sascha continued with a frown. "And he uses his control over others as a crutch, instead of just dealing with his emotions or going to some goddamn therapy. But he's been better with you here." He took a deep breath, then met Nix's eyes. "You should stay," he said firmly, then blanched at his own words. "I mean, obviously, it's your choice. But he might not be able to tell you that he wants you to stay even if he does. And he does."

What a lovely little speech. Nix had to press his lips together hard now to contain his grin. He leaned down. "Don't you worry," he whispered. "I won't let Ivan scare me off."

Sascha nodded, then bit at his lower lip. "But *you'll* be happy too, right? If you stay?"

After all that, was he worried he'd just coerced Nix or something? Nix chuckled, patting Sascha's reddened cheek. "You're very sweet, did you know that?"

Sascha sighed, his lips pursing into a pout. "That's what Kai says."

Nix hummed. "Even a broken clock is right twice a day."

Sascha's pout turned into a grin. "You really irritate him, did you know that?"

"I'm very aware. It's good for him. As are you."

Nix wasn't even flattering the little human. The warrior demon had been miserable in the Void. Actually, he'd been miserable even in the beginning, when all the demons had been summoned to the human realm regularly. Kai had gotten his kicks battling and all that—to each his own—but there'd always been a certain air of discontent about him. Honestly, it had been part of what made him so fun to tease.

But that air of misery was gone now. With Sascha at his side, Kai was at peace in a way Nix hadn't known he was capable of.

Any other future brother-in-law bonding was put on hold as Ivan and Kai appeared, their task complete.

Ivan stood in front of his brother for a long moment, then nodded stiffly. "Until tomorrow."

Sascha rolled his eyes, wrapping his arms around Ivan in a hug. Ivan patted his back as stiffly as he'd nodded, and Nix had to contain his own eye roll. Ivan seemed to sense it anyway, scowling at him as he tugged him off the porch.

Nix waved at Sascha and blew a few kisses at Kai. "Toodles, Chez Sascha!"

"Chez Kozlov," Ivan corrected as they got seated in the car. Either Sergei was bound tightly or they'd knocked him out, because Nix didn't hear any pounding from the trunk. "I'm the one who bought the house."

"Well you can buy another one if you're so determined to be lord and master of it," Nix told him, slouching down in his seat as Ivan pulled away from the curb, tickled pink when Ivan's hand landed heavily on Nix's thigh.

"Why would I?"

"So we have a place to stay near your brother when we visit. Unless you'd rather stay *with* him when we vacation in Seacliff, but that does limit our bedroom activities to the actual bedroom, which is a bit of a shame." Nix had a feeling Ivan could get very creative with locations for hanky-panky given the chance, and it would be such a waste to tie his hands that way.

"And when would we be taking these vacations?" Ivan asked in a tone Nix couldn't quite read. He wasn't angry, exactly. Pensive, perhaps?

Nix shrugged. "Annually? Biannually? I don't know, but either way, you should adopt a European work schedule. Take a month off every summer, at the very least." Nix may have been looking to bind himself to a mob boss, but that didn't mean he had to be tied to a workaholic. There was too much of the human world to explore to spend every hour in the office.

"And you're planning to stick around that long, are you?"

Nix gave Ivan a sharp look. "Are you planning otherwise?"

He was met with silence.

It might not be the perfect time, but Nix was starting to realize there might not ever *be* a perfect time with Ivan. Not with those few walls he still stubbornly kept up standing in Nix's way.

Nix cleared his throat. "If we bonded..."

Ivan cut him off immediately. "You wouldn't want a bond with me."

See? Walls.

"Says who?" Nix asked lightly. He was met with silence again. He went another route. "Would *you* want a bond with *me*?"

Ivan's hand clenched on Nix's thigh. "I would like for you to stay." A lightness filled Nix's chest, until his stomach sank as Ivan finished his sentence. "Until *I'm* ready for you to go."

Of all the bullshit repressed-emotion statements.

Nix had to fight not to grit his teeth. "And if you're *never* ready for me to go?"

"You wish to stay in the human realm," Ivan said, neatly avoiding Nix's question.

"Yes."

"You've always wished to."

"Yes." Nix eyed Ivan's clenched jaw. Oh, his human didn't like that. "Two things can be true at once, you know. Wanting to stay in the human realm and wanting to stay with you."

A muscle in Ivan's jaw ticked, and then he relaxed with visible effort. "It's a moot point anyway," he said. "Until we get back the Book you lost."

"I didn't lose it," Nix told him archly. "I gave it away."

Nix wasn't anywhere near done with this conversation, but

Ivan's phone rang through the car's Bluetooth before he could respond to that, Cooper's name flashing.

"Speak of the devil!" Nix crowed.

Ivan side-eyed him as he accepted the call. "Cooper."

"H-Hey, Ivan. Hey." Cooper sounded out of breath. And possibly a bit terrified? It was hard for Nix to tell over the phone. Stupid technology got in the way.

"I've been trying to reach you." Ivan made the sentence sound like a threat.

"I know. My phone was—I couldn't get to my phone. But, um, so—"

Ivan cut through the rambling. "You have something of mine, Cooper."

"Right. Sure. But I just need to ask—one of the books you gave me, does it—" Cooper laughed, and the sound was tinged with hysteria. "Have you ever summoned a demon with it?"

Nix's heart soared. Chaos was there, wasn't he? No wonder Cooper sounded so flustered.

But he tried not to look too delighted, not when Ivan was immediately looking so irritated.

Ivan sighed heavily, his hand tightening again on Nix's thigh, as if he could sense Nix's joy anyway. "Where are you?"

Cooper's laugh cut off. "Me?"

"*Cooper.*"

"My apartment. But—"

"Stay the fuck there," Ivan ordered and hung up the phone.

———

Now that he wasn't completely in the doghouse like the last time, Nix had a chance to properly appreciate Cooper's apartment building and how close it was to Ivan's own. "You must pay him well," he pointed out after the doorman let them in.

"I pay for the apartment on top of his salary," Ivan told him. "It's part of the deal."

"I'm surprised he wanted to go into the family business at all." From what Nix had seen, Cooper didn't seem like the type.

"He didn't. His father came to my father," Ivan explained as they got onto the elevator. "My mother's brother," he clarified, which made sense to Nix, considering how little Cooper looked like Ivan's father's side of the family. "He was struggling after moving here from Russia, wanted to secure a life for his son. Decent man, but a fucking mess." Ivan shook his head. "My father wasted Cooper on gopher duties. He was...mistrustful of tech. After he died, I changed Cooper's workload. He was shit at gopher duty, anyway. Too thin-skinned around the men."

Maybe it had been wrong of Nix to push the Book into Cooper's hands after all. He sounded like the kind of person Chaos would eat alive, even if it was more out of carelessness than malice.

"I may have miscalculated," he murmured.

Ivan only gave him a look as he rapped his knuckles sharply on the apartment door.

There was the sound of what seemed like twenty different locks unlocking, and then Cooper's auburn head poked out, something between a smile and a grimace on his lips. "Ivan."

"Cooper," Ivan greeted shortly. "Where's the demon?"

"No demons here!" called out a very familiar voice from somewhere in the apartment, bright and chipper.

Cooper rubbed a hand over his eye with a nervous laugh and opened the door wider, letting them in.

No matter how much he might have fucked up, Nix couldn't contain his grin. Because there, sitting cross-legged on top of a dinged and dented coffee table, was Chaos.

A sight for fucking sore eyes, even if Chaos *was* in his human form.

"*This*?" Ivan asked Nix under his breath, eyeing Chaos across the room while Cooper looked on nervously, chewing on his thumbnail.

Nix supposed it *did* look unlikely. It had been a while since he'd seen Chaos out of his demon form, and while his face was familiar, he was still remarkably...unassuming. Or at least in this current version.

He was slightly shorter than Cooper—who already wasn't a very tall human—and slender, all big eyes and elfin features. His hair at the moment was a rather dull brown, with an eye color to match. He seemed to have borrowed some of Cooper's clothes, for whatever reason. That sweatshirt he was wearing was definitely the same one Nix had seen on Cooper before, at least.

Chaos cocked his head at Cooper, and the human went to stand next to him, still nibbling on his fingers nervously.

They looked kind of cute side by side like that. Definite twink-for-twink vibes.

Ivan was still looking at Nix expectantly, so Nix gestured from Ivan to Chaos and back again with a flourish. "Ivan, meet our chaos demon."

Chaos shook his head, pouting at Nix. "No demons here," he said again pointedly, like Nix was ruining his game. "I'm just a very mortal, human friend of Cooper's here."

Ivan pinched the bridge of his nose. "How—"

"I was uploading the ledgers you gave me," Cooper said hurriedly. "I wasn't quite sure why you wanted that old weird book with them, but I didn't want to miss it if you needed it, so I did it anyway, and then it just kind of—" He raised his hands, fingers spread wide. "—happened."

"You summoning a demon just kind of happened," Ivan said blankly.

Cooper paled a bit but nodded. "Yes?"

"And where is the Book now?"

"I still have it."

Ivan narrowed his eyes. "I should fucking hope so."

Quicker than even Nix could follow, Chaos was off the coffee table and in front of Ivan, every part of him held in eerie stillness, as if he hadn't moved at all. Except his eyes, which cycled through a range of colors—aquamarine, violet, hot pink—before settling on bright, fiery red.

Not a great sign, that. Nix began to shuffle closer to Ivan but stopped when Chaos's gaze darted his way.

When Nix was sufficiently stilled, Chaos returned his focus to Ivan. "Hi," he said brightly, his tone incongruous with his blank face. "You're scaring Cooper."

Nix slowly—very slowly—laid a careful hand on Chaos's shoulder. "Chaos," he warned.

Luckily, Ivan seemed to sense the threat. For once, he didn't scowl or scoff. And he didn't make any sudden movements, thank the Book. "I didn't intend to scare him," he said slowly. "I'm simply...irritated."

"Irritated...," Chaos mused. He cocked his head. "If I set that suit of yours on fire with you inside it, do you think you'd be more or less irritated?" He asked the question like he was genuinely interested.

He probably was.

"Chaos," Nix said again. Then, "*Bracchus*."

At the sound of his given name, Chaos finally turned his head to look at Nix fully, his eyes still glowing red.

"I'm rather fond of this one," Nix told him quietly. "I'd like to keep him in top condition."

"Oh." Chaos blinked, and his eyes shifted into the form Nix was most familiar with—golden, with vertical slit pupils, like the eyes of a fox. His hair, for whatever reason, shifted into a bright purple color. "Why didn't you say so?" He grinned, revealing a dimple in his left cheek. "Hello, Nix. You could tell it was me?" He asked it as if Nix hadn't been calling him out from the first moment.

And then he was crashing into Nix's arms for a hug. Nix steadied himself against the force of it, patting his back gently. "Hello, sweets."

He was pleased to see his friend—pleased that Chaos was getting a chance to experience life outside the Void again—but he was also realizing how badly he'd miscalculated the timing.

It had been so long since Chaos had been summoned—and much longer than that since Chaos and Nix had been summoned at the same time—that Nix had forgotten how his friend was in the human realm. Namely, like a human child let loose in a candy shop.

And in this case, more like a starving human child deprived of sugar for centuries let loose in a candy shop.

Oopsies.

Cooper cleared his throat. "Let me just grab that Book for you."

He ducked into another room briefly, then returned with it in his hands, passing it over to Ivan, who was still holding himself stiffly, watching Chaos out of the corner of his eyes.

"There's a meeting the day after tomorrow," Ivan said after a moment, his words a bit stilted. "If you and your demon would like to attend."

Nix bit back a smile as he released Chaos from the hug. He'd definitely messed things up a bit, but it was still remarkably charming watching Ivan do his best to be polite. It definitely didn't come naturally to the poor thing.

"Um..." Cooper didn't seem to know what to do with Ivan's hesitance. "What about?"

"We're making some changes. Getting rid of the rest of Sergei's men, for one."

"Does that mean you found him?" Cooper asked. He sounded relieved.

"He's in the trunk of our car."

"Will it be fun?" Chaos asked, tugging on Nix's arm. "The meeting."

"You might get to kill someone," Nix told him with a smile.

"Fuck," Cooper swore, then blanched as they all looked his way.

Chaos flounced back to the coffee table at Cooper's side, perching on top of it like a gargoyle.

"Cooper doesn't involve himself in the violence, usually," Ivan explained, narrowing his eyes at Nix.

"He won't have to, though, if I'm there." Chaos patted Cooper's hip reassuringly. He'd pulled the human in close, and Nix didn't miss the way he was still tracking Ivan's every move like a hawk.

Or like a minuscule dragon guarding his treasure.

Yep, Nix had definitely miscalculated.

"Cooper will let you know," Chaos told them. "Or he won't. But you two can go now. You're still scaring him."

A vein in Ivan's temple throbbed, and he seemed to lose his battle with politeness. "Are you sure *you're* not scaring Cooper?" he asked icily.

Chaos's eyes flashed red with flames, then back to gold. "It's different when it's me. I'm afraid your tiny human brain wouldn't understand."

"Um, you can send me the details," Cooper told Ivan, his gaze bouncing between the two, seemingly torn between his employer and the overprotective demon at his side.

"You're sure you two will be all right?" Nix asked. He wasn't usually too fussed about the welfare of humans he didn't know, but this whole situation *was* just a teensy bit his fault.

"Go away, Nix," Chaos said breezily.

Cooper shrugged helplessly.

So Nix and Ivan left, the twenty different locks engaging again behind them.

Ivan turned to Nix immediately. "*This* is why I didn't want any other demons summoned."

"This exact scenario?" Nix asked skeptically.

"You know what I mean. Can you honestly say we have any control over that situation?"

"I'm sorry," Nix told him. "I don't know what else to say. He's my friend."

It showed how far they'd come that Ivan only scowled, grabbing his hand and tugging him down the hallway. "Come. Before our car gets impounded with our very illegal cargo inside it. I don't have time to be angry with you."

Nix smiled as he was pulled away.

They might have a few fires—literal or otherwise—to put out down the road, but on the plus side, Ivan was obviously totally sweet on him.

Nix would take his wins where he could get them.

18

Ivan

Ivan resisted the urge to press his fingers against his forehead yet again in an effort to counteract the tension headache that had been steadily forming the last half of the day.

Whether the brutal ache was caused by the residual stress from the encounter with Cooper's wayward summoning or the tangle of logistics Ivan was dealing with, it was hard to tell.

At least they had Sergei stowed away safely, and Nix had—perhaps wisely—denied Ivan any further conversation with him. ("He'll have nothing useful to tell you, and it'll only make you crabby," he'd insisted.)

Nix hadn't exactly been wrong that any conversation with Sergei would have left Ivan on edge. Or more on edge than he was already. But they also both knew by now that Nix would have been able to soothe away the sting afterward.

They both knew Ivan was putty in Nix's hands.

Was it folly to rely on one person so much? Undoubtedly. This...dependence was a situation Ivan had worked his entire adult life to avoid. Whether that person be family, minion, or lover, he'd never opened up, never thawed, never lowered his walls even once.

Because then what did one do when that person inevitably disappointed? When they disappeared? What would *Ivan* do when Nix returned to the Void he'd sprung from?

But of course, Nix claimed he didn't have to go anywhere. That he and Ivan could tie themselves together permanently by way of a demon bond. He'd offered Ivan a path to ensuring he stayed forever. Tied to Ivan forever.

It was a thousand times worse than a marriage, wasn't it? A demonic matrimony that had, as far as Ivan knew, no divorce clause. The thought should have been fucking horrific.

It wasn't.

Even if the demon in question was currently sprawled on his back on Ivan's office rug in some sort of dramatic demonstration of his boredom.

Nix had at least been silent for the past hour or so, but he registered Ivan's attention immediately, lolling his head back and forth and whining, "What exactly is there even for you to *do* at this point?"

Ivan pressed his fingers to his forehead after all, hard enough to hurt. "I may lose half my men tomorrow, either to defection or... otherwise, and I need to make sure things can run smoothly in the meantime. Until they can all be adequately replaced."

Still, he shut his laptop, conceding that he may have reached the limit on what he could prepare ahead of time.

Nix rolled onto his stomach and propped himself up onto his elbows, his legs swinging in the air behind him as he watched Ivan. "How many men will be there tomorrow?"

"Thirty, give or take a few. I have five main lieutenants below Sergei in my operations. Jace you've already met, plus four others, and they're each bringing their most trusted soldiers." Ivan stretched his neck from side to side, wincing at the ache. "There are more men in the organization, but they're grunts, easy to replace at the drop of a hat. They don't need to be there."

Nix nodded absently, fingers tracing the abstract design on Ivan's rug. "Can I ask you something without you biting my head off?"

"Probably not."

Nix grinned at him cheekily, clearly not taking the threat seriously. And he was obviously correct not to, what with Ivan's weakness toward him.

If any other bastard had pulled off the major fuckup of that chaos demon being summoned, they'd be dead to Ivan, most likely literally. And yet the only chastisement Ivan had been able to summon for Nix at this point had been a scowl and about five minutes of a surly mood.

Even now, it took everything in Ivan not to shudder at the memory of that creature standing in front of him in Cooper's apartment. The brutal violence he'd been able to feel roiling under the surface, only waiting for an excuse to come out.

He was deadly, that one. And Ivan's only hope to harness any of that power was for Cooper to talk him into aiding him at the meeting tomorrow.

Assuming the chaos demon didn't decide to set Ivan on fire instead.

"In the shows and movies, mob bosses are always surrounded by men," Nix said, bringing Ivan's attention back to him. "At the very least a few key players. And yet you're always alone, except for when Oleg drives you."

"Ah." Ivan leaned his head against the back of his chair, staring up at the ceiling. "It used to be more like that here. The way it was with my father. But then Alexei left, and I...lost my temper, you could say." Ivan ignored Nix's wry chuckle at his phrasing. "And then with Sergei's betrayal...." Ivan shrugged. "I've kept the men at a distance. The whole business is probably fucked at this point."

It was his first time admitting that out loud. That maybe he'd damaged things beyond repair. That maybe Sergei had been right to doubt his leadership.

"Well, we'll fix that," Nix said easily. "I'm great with people."

"Because you're staying." Ivan refused to phrase it as a question.

"Yes, I'm staying," Nix answered anyway. He rose from the floor, gliding over and hopping onto Ivan's desk, bracketing Ivan with his legs. "So tell me why the thought of that makes you grumpy. You should be delighted to have me. I'm delightful."

Ivan was too tired to hedge his words. "Kai told me you'd want to stay no matter what." He arched a brow. "He told me you're using me."

Nix scoffed. "And *I* told you both things can be true—wanting to be here and wanting you."

Ivan scowled at him, something bitter churning in his gut. "And that pisses me off."

"You don't like when my desires conflict with yours, and now you don't like that they align?" Nix asked, making it clear how idiotic he found the concept. "I want to stay in the human realm, yes. I also want to stay with you."

"You should want me more," Ivan told him, aware that the demand made him sound like a child. "You should want me *most*."

It might not have been logical or healthy or sane, but there it was. Ivan didn't like to hear that Nix had other reasons besides himself to stay. It was that horrible, controlling, possessive part of him that needed Nix to covet him exactly as much as Ivan had grown to covet the demon.

Nix let out a frustrated breath, kicking gently at Ivan's chair. "Do you want me to tell you if it was a choice of here without you or the Void *with* you, I'd choose you? Fine. I would." He narrowed his eyes. "But then we'd both be miserable because the Void is boring as fuck and there'd be no one for you to boss around but me."

Ivan snaked a hand around Nix's ankle, tugging him to the edge of the desk. "And that's all I would need."

A flash of something crossed Nix's face—some bit of true surprise, maybe. Despite his irritation, Ivan was almost pleased to have managed it. The demon was hard to shock.

Until Nix spoke.

"Vanya," he asked, his voice a silken purr. "Do you *love* me?"

It was Ivan's turn to scoff. He didn't know anything about love, except as a poison that weakened a person beyond repair. The very word made him want to tear something to shreds. "I need you," he corrected. "Here. With me."

That much he could admit.

Nix grabbed his tie, tugging until he'd drawn Ivan up from his chair and he was standing between Nix's legs. His eyes searched Ivan's face, but Ivan kept his expression blank.

"Demons don't talk about love, you know," Nix said after a moment. "It's all about mating, or soul bonds. But as much as a demon can love, I love you." He cocked his head. "How does that make you feel?"

"Ill," Ivan admitted.

Nix grinned, all sharp teeth. "Of course it does." He pulled Ivan in for a chaste kiss, then swiped his tongue along Ivan's lips. "I'm sorry I make you sick."

He didn't sound sorry at all.

Ivan dropped his head onto Nix's shoulder with a groan, his hands grabbing at Nix's hips. "You're like a disease. You've infected me, and now there's no getting you out."

Nix scratched his fingers into Ivan's hair. "Why, that's the most romantic thing you've ever said to me."

"Enough," Ivan growled, half demand, half plea.

It was enough talking. Enough emotions. Enough laying bare his weaknesses for all to see. He certainly couldn't handle any more teasing. He dug his fingers into Nix's hips. "Take the clothes off," he ordered.

Nix huffed a laugh, but he complied, his clothes disappearing in an instant.

But of course he complied. He always knew exactly what to do. Exactly what Ivan needed from him.

And what Ivan needed was this—all that lush lavender skin laid on a platter before him.

Except what was covered by the lace fucking panties Nix refused to get rid of.

Red again.

And—because while Nix always knew what to do, he still loved to torment Ivan anyway—this pair had an opening in them. A very convenient one.

Nix caught him eyeing it and spread his legs wider.

Ivan ran his hands up those spread thighs, fingers dipping toward the swell of Nix's ass. "All I can think about, at any given time, is touching you," he murmured, unable to stop himself from confessing his own lunacy. "Touching you. Tasting you. Fucking you. My entire empire could fall apart tomorrow, and all I can think about is you."

"It won't fall apart," Nix told him, the words ending in a gasp as Ivan's thumb dipped into his hole. "It'll—it'll grow stronger."

Ivan hummed his skepticism, but his focus was already centered on what his thumb was doing. The convenient wetness it found. He dipped it in and out, pressing and circling, listening to Nix's breathy sighs until he couldn't take it anymore.

He unbuttoned his pants and lowered them enough to pull his hardened cock out, hitching his hands under Nix's thighs and sliding him until his ass was half off the desk. He wrapped an arm around Nix's waist and lined his cock up.

"Yes, Ivan," Nix purred, arching into his touch, his tail wrapping around Ivan's forearm. "Yes, yes, yes."

Ivan pushed in, groaning in relief as he was encased in that infernal heat.

This was what he needed.

What he always needed.

He fucked Nix on his desk in hard, steady strokes. His free hand wandered, grasping Nix's chin, his cheek, his hair. He felt fevered and strange, torn constantly between claiming Nix's mouth and lowering his head to watch the obscene sight of his glistening cock leaving Nix's body, the way Nix's leaking cock peeked out of his panties.

It was harsh and brutal and rushed, and Nix keened his encouragement, wrapping his legs around Ivan's waist and pressing into every thrust.

Ivan's orgasm was quick and vicious, an earthquake from deep within him, and he didn't pull out when he was done. He was too busy biting at Nix's neck, mouthing at the silken skin while Nix stroked himself to completion, his talons digging into Ivan's scalp and his legs still wrapped around Ivan's hips.

He fed his cum to Ivan afterward, and Ivan took it without question, licking at his fingers and savoring the sweet, smoky taste.

"We'll bond after the meeting," Nix told him after swiping his tongue one last time over Ivan's lips, catching the drops of his release Ivan hadn't swallowed. "It's not safe to do it before, not when there's no telling how the bonding ceremony will take it out of you."

"Are you commanding?" Ivan asked idly, stroking his hand along Nix's side, his back, down to the velvety-smooth furred skin of tail. He was all too aware Nix didn't have to command him to do anything. He'd meant what he'd said about needing the demon.

He'd been weak for him from the very first moment, but Nix's fate had been sealed the night before, when Ivan had left that basement raw and open. Nix could have done anything with him, and Ivan wouldn't have had the defenses to do much about it. Nix could have taken advantage and demanded a bond right that moment, if he were really so eager to use Ivan. He could read Ivan well enough that he must have sensed the opening.

But instead Nix had...cared for him. He'd soothed and coddled in a manner that was all Nix—with his body, with his touch, with his surrender to whatever Ivan needed of him.

Ivan had never had that. He'd never had any of what Nix gave him. The care. The snark. The constant provocation.

Ivan wanted to keep it all. Every bit of it.

"I *am* commanding, I'm afraid," Nix told him, tucking sweaty strands of Ivan's hair back into place. "Because while I can't say I've ever been likened to a disease, you're right about one thing, Vanya darling. There's no getting rid of me."

IVAN DROVE them to the meeting spot the next day, forgoing a driver altogether.

He'd already assigned Oleg to drive Jace and Tag—they were carting Sergei with them, and had been instructed to bring him in when the time was right.

Nix was slumped in the passenger seat of Ivan's car, chin in hand, frowning out the window.

Ivan squeezed his knee. "Why are you pouting?"

"I'm not pouting," Nix told him with a little pout. "But I thought Oleg would be driving us."

"You'd prefer that?" Ivan didn't quite manage to hide his surprise. He hadn't realized his incubus was so fond of his driver. He wasn't sure if he liked that at all.

Maybe he needed to fire Oleg.

Nix heaved a sigh. "I was just really hoping you'd finger me in the back of the town car one of these days."

Provoking. Always provoking.

And in spite of himself, something hot ran through Ivan's lower belly, an image of exactly that flashing through his mind. Nix, writhing in his lap, three of Ivan's fingers working him into a puddle while Oleg drove them steadily on.

Jesus.

He pinched Nix's thigh. "Don't distract me, demon."

"Would that I could." Nix clucked his tongue. "I've never seen you this tense, and I've seen you plenty rigid, Vanya, darling."

Well, who the fuck could blame him? The only backup Ivan was 100 percent certain would be arriving for this little tête-à-tête with his men was Kai and Sascha. Which would mean a total of two demons to intimidate thirty violent men. He was hoping Wolfe and Eric would show as well, for the novelty if nothing else, but Ivan had no idea about Cooper and his chaos demon.

Alexei he could count right the fuck out, bitter as the thought made him.

Ivan had learned long ago not to depend on his middle brother.

So they'd make do with what they had. Kai in his demon form was enough to make most men piss themselves, and Nix was definitely...inhuman. Just because Ivan had come to associate his demon form with sex and seduction didn't mean his men would.

And speaking of seduction...

Ivan had the Book tucked into his jacket pocket, ready to be used to bond the moment business was done with. No matter what else, the demon was staying at his side.

"Where are we?" Nix asked as they pulled into the back parking lot, peering out at the brick building.

"A restaurant my father favored for business," Ivan told him.

"It's under our protection still." He paused, then added, "We held his wake here."

"And now we'll bury him for good," Nix said with satisfaction.

Ivan hummed his agreement, even if a final "fuck you" to his father wasn't really the point of the whole thing. He'd come to enjoy how much his demon hated him, even though the man was long dead and gone.

They entered through the back. Sascha and Kai were already holed up in one of the booths, as expected. Ivan had asked them to come early so Kai could ensure no trap had been laid for him. Something unclenched within Ivan when he saw Wolfe and Eric with them.

The vampires had shown.

Sascha gave a poor semblance of a smile as Ivan and Nix approached. "I haven't been here since..."

Ivan cleared his throat. "I'm aware."

The restaurant hadn't changed a bit since their father had passed. Not since their childhood, really. It was still owned by the same family, kept as a time capsule of a different era.

Sascha swallowed hard before getting a hold of himself. "So where's the staff?" he asked much more brightly.

"Paid off for the night."

The side door Ivan and Nix had entered through opened again, and Ivan had his gun drawn and pointed in an instant.

But it was only Cooper poking his head through, nodding when he saw them all, unfazed by Ivan's gun pointed in his direction. He led his chaos demon by the hand. The creature was still in his human form, his hair and eyes back to brown. He hissed at Ivan's weapon, and Ivan lowered it immediately.

Kai growled, turning on Nix immediately. "What did you do, incubus?"

Nix's eyes widened in faux innocence. "Me?"

The chaos demon grinned, an innocuous-looking dimple flashing in his left cheek. "Hello, Kaisyir."

Kai swore softly, tugging Sascha closer in the booth.

Ivan could barely contain his smile. That was three demons and two vampires on their side. Much better odds than he'd hoped for.

Introductions were made to those who hadn't met before, and the chaos creature remained surprisingly docile after Ivan had stowed his gun. He seemed unconcerned by Kai's wariness, or his bitter mumblings.

Maybe he was shoring up his bloodthirsty ways for what was to come.

Ivan could only hope.

He took the remaining time to discuss what would come next, once the men arrived. By the time he was finished, Jace, Tag, and Oleg were coming through the door to the kitchens, signaling to Ivan that things were ready on their end.

Something hot ran through Ivan's veins, anticipation setting his skin buzzing. It was time. No going back. Changes would be made today, bloody and permanent.

The front door opened, the first of the men arriving earlier than anticipated.

But it wasn't one of Ivan's men who came through the door. Or at least not one still loyal to him.

It was Alexei, tall and broad and stern-faced as ever, with a small dark-haired man at his side. His vampire.

Two years after his betrayal, Ivan's wayward brother had come home.

19

Nix

Nix had never been so blue-balled by a family reunion in his life. It was frustrating to the point of maddening, considering how much pain and resentment he knew Ivan harbored over his middle brother.

If Nix hadn't recognized the vampire with him, he might not have known the man was Ivan's brother at all. Alexei looked nothing like Ivan or Sascha, his features more rugged, his hair a dirty blond rather than the icy color of the other two, his broad frame packed with muscle.

A swell of emotions had filled Ivan at the sight of Alexei at the door, strong enough that Nix could feel all of it—the shock, the tentative hope, the familiar bitterness, the ever-present suspicion —but not a bit of it had shown on Ivan's face. He'd been placid as ever, and the brothers had only given each other the barest of nods, Ivan murmuring, "Alexei," as if the man's arrival hadn't been a complete surprise.

And that had been it. The tall, man-bunned figure Nix had

heard so much about had simply joined the fold with his partner, who'd waved shyly at all of them, miles away from the exuberance the little vampire had shown over their FaceTime call.

It wasn't like there had been time for much else, not with the men arriving, but still.

What the fuck?

When this damn meeting was done with, Nix would be making sure there was more between Alexei and Ivan. He'd tackle the burly middle brother himself if he had to.

But for now, they were all gathered at the front of the restaurant, an open area that must have been used as a stage for live music some nights. Ivan was facing the men, Nix at his side (as he damn well should be). Sascha and Kai were off to their left, with Cooper and Chaos beyond them, and Alexei and his vampire, Jay, were to Ivan and Nix's right, with Eric and Wolfe close by.

Jace and Tag were with the men but off to the side toward the kitchens, ready to bring in their cargo when the moment was right.

There was a heady sense of anticipation all around, and Nix drank it in. It was clear the men recognized Alexei and that his presence was a surprise to them.

The men were giving off a lovely perfume of nerves and fear and confusion as well. Not enough for Nix to gather what was innocent anxiety and what was more nefarious in nature, not all tangled together like that, but that would come as Ivan spoke.

Which he seemed ready to do now. Ivan didn't say anything, didn't ask for quiet—he just looked on in much the same way he had been. But the men sensed it anyway, their nervous murmurs quieting until there was nothing.

Nix had meant what he said about true loyalty trumping fear, but he supposed fear did have its perks.

"It's come to my attention that we as a business—as a family— are at a crossroads," Ivan said, his voice quiet but firm, looking out at the small sea of faces. "I admit the recent years have been... messier than I would have liked, and I take responsibility as your leader for any unease you might have been feeling." Not one of the men was stupid enough to confirm or deny, and Ivan continued, "But doubt does not allow for betrayal. Not in a business such as ours."

One of Ivan's main lieutenants, one of three Nix hadn't met before, emitted a thick tendril of fear at those words. Nix kept track of his face, aware the others in their group would be looking to him for guidance. Although, that fear had been strong enough he was sure even the other demons and vampires had sensed it.

"What do we do with men who betray us?" Ivan asked, his voice deceptively mild.

Not a single man answered.

Nix's human was magnificent like this. Immaculate in his appearance, poised and ice-cold, not a chip in his armor to be seen. Whatever Ivan thought about his shortcomings, he had the makings of a leader in him. His father had twisted and turned around his better instincts, but they were there.

Nix would make sure they were straightened out.

Ivan nodded to Jace and Tag, and they went back to the kitchens, returning with Sergei, gagged and bound once again to a steel chair. The man had certainly seen better days—he was bruised and battered, a makeshift tourniquet around his arm where Kai had presumably sliced into him. Nix loved to see it. He'd have loved to seen him torn apart by wild dogs, to be honest, although he didn't think that sort of punishment was quite the rage anymore.

Nix had no sympathy for the one who'd hurt Ivan so, both as a child and as a man.

Sergei's appearance finally lifted the silence, the men murmuring among themselves. There were several more sharp spikes of fear, some tinged heavily with guilt. Nix clocked them all.

"Sergei here didn't like the direction I was leading us in," Ivan announce coolly. "But we're making changes, heading toward the future. We no longer have the time or patience for small-minded bigotry holding us back." Ivan's hand came to rest on Nix's lower back, and Nix slid an arm around his waist, settling in close, grinning sharply at the crowd as he nuzzled into Ivan.

He scented the shock coming from the crowd at the little display of intimacy. No surprise there. There was some disgust too, and Nix kept close track of where that came from.

"I'm giving those who haven't acted in secrecy a chance to walk away if we're no longer a fit," Ivan announced, his hand stroking Nix's back. "For those that remain, my new priority will be making sure we're all well provided for. Secure and safe. But for those who went behind my back, who thought to betray my family..." He narrowed his eyes, the first sign of his anger. "You may have thought we were weak and fractured, that it was a good time to strike. But as you can see, my brothers stand beside me still, and we've gathered new allies, ones I doubt any of you have the gall to cross."

That was the signal. All those among their group who could change forms did, Nix included. There was a cacophony from the crowd of men, curses and shouts. Nix supposed it was to be expected. Kai was a giant blue monster, after all, and even the vampires were intimidating, with their black eyes and fangs. And while Nix personally thought Chaos was adorable in his demon form, with his black feathered wings and monkey-like tail, he supposed others might find it...intimidating.

"What the fuck is this, Ivan?" one of the men Nix had clocked as a traitor yelled, his gun drawn.

"Why, Gregor," Ivan purred, still stroking Nix's back, Nix's tail curling around his calf. "What the fuck does it look like?"

"It looks like fucking—fucking Halloween tricks," Gregor protested, all indignation and false bravado, even as Nix breathed in the ripe stench of fear off of him. "A smoke screen. You think this is enough to scare us off?"

"For fuck's sake," Wolfe murmured. In a flash, he was off into the crowd, grabbing the dissenter and tearing his throat out with his teeth, leaving the man to bleed all over the floor. Before human eyes could register it, he was in front of Sergei's chair, serving him the same.

Well.

Apparently Chaos hadn't been the loose cannon to worry about.

There was a sliding sound and a thump, and there was Sascha unconscious. Kai had him over his shoulder in an instant, growling curses at Wolfe. Meanwhile, the crowd was registering the dead men in their midst, and the blood all over Wolfe's fanged face.

There was a surprisingly high-pitched scream. "What the fuck *was* that?"

Wolfe ignored the crowd, turning back to his companions, blood all over his bespoke suit. When he found Ivan and Alexei glaring at him, he arched a brow. "Wasn't that the point of identifying the traitors? So we could do away with them? Eric and I have places to be."

His words served as a cue for another one of the traitors to attempt to flee, and then it was Chaos leaping into action, knocking him on the floor and slicing through his chest with his talons.

Cooper yelped at the sight, shutting his eyes behind his glasses, but he didn't pass out, so Nix had to give him points for that.

And then all was pandemonium.

Guns were fired. Men were screaming. Chaos was cackling like a fiend.

Nix kept Cooper and Ivan—their two vulnerable humans—

behind him once the guns started going off, and the rest of their supernatural companions worked to corral the men. Those Nix had already identified as traitors were disarmed and held by Wolfe and Eric, with Alexei sternly informing Wolfe to "keep your fangs to yourself for five fucking minutes."

Nix had a hard time containing his smile.

Who knew Mafia meetings could be such fun?

———

THE REST TOOK TIME.

An annoying amount of it, in Nix's opinion, as Ivan worked to convince the rest of the men that they truly could leave if they wished it.

"Only those who've already acted against us—those who already conspired to take my brother's life," he said, in a pointed reminder, "have been punished. The rest of you may leave, or you may stay. I simply ask that if you go, you remember what might happen should you try to turn against us."

With three demons and four vampires standing in front of them, it seemed unlikely anyone in the building would forget.

In a surprise to absolutely no one, not a single man was willing to say he wished to go. It was Nix who had to work through them one by one, to suss out who was afraid because they'd seen a vampire rip out someone's throat, and who was afraid because they wished to leave and worried their throat was next.

In the end, the numbers came down to this: they had four rats besides the two already gone, and ten more men who wished to leave, or who Nix had decided would be more trouble than they were worth if they stayed.

Those who left were allowed to keep their memories intact. The rest of the men in Ivan's organization who were staying were subjected to vampire compulsion, courtesy of Wolfe, Eric, and

Alexei. They would remember the violence, that those men who'd betrayed the family had been dealt with, but they wouldn't remember the monsters.

That had been Ivan's suggestion, and their supernaturals had agreed. In Ivan's words, "I'd rather the rumors swirling around us come from the outside. Those within won't be able to confirm or deny. It will keep things vague and threatening, and no one's identity will be at risk."

It was surprisingly thoughtful of him. Nix was proud.

When they'd separated the wheat from the chaff, and adjusted those memories in need of adjusting, Ivan had more work to do. He held a more...generic meeting, one in which he explained in further detail what he expected from his men, the changes that would be taking place within the business.

As delightful as his first speech had been, it hadn't exactly been a plan of action.

It seemed a little strange to Nix to be holding a real business meeting with two corpses and quite a few bloodstains on the carpet right next to them, but he supposed Mafia members were used to such things. Kai, meanwhile, had taken Sascha to the kitchens so he wouldn't be subjected to any more blood sightings when he woke up.

When the meeting was finally over, and the loyal men had gone back to wherever they'd come from, Ivan glared at the stains in irritation. "We'll have to buy the restaurant off them now. We've ruined the carpets. It goes against our agreement."

"You wanted bloodthirsty creatures to instill fear in the hearts of men, did you not?" Wolfe asked, clearly unapologetic. "Just remember you owe myself and my mate a favor, to be determined at my discretion." Then he grabbed Eric's hand and took him away.

Apparently they had a dinner reservation.

That left the traitors to be dealt with.

Nix watched, unmoved, as Jace and Tag took them out back to be executed. Chaos bounded after them, having agreed to incinerate the bodies with his powers afterward. Less work for the cleanup crew.

Alexei and Jay made their way to the kitchens, Alexei murmuring that he wanted to be present when Sascha woke.

Nix wrapped his arms around Ivan's neck, pleased to be alone, if only for a moment. "Did it all go as you hoped, darling?"

Ivan lowered his forehead to Nix's shoulder, letting out a sigh. "It was a fucking mess," he mumbled. "But I guess that's about what I expected."

"Mm." Nix tugged his head up gently by his hair, meeting his icy blue eyes. "And now I get what you promised me," he reminded. He wasn't going to let a few deaths and bloodstains distract his human from what was important.

"A bond," Ivan agreed. But his gaze flicked to the door to the kitchens.

Nix sighed. "I suppose you want to speak to your brother first."

Ivan arched a brow. "You say that as if you're not dying for me to do so."

Nix was, in a way, although not in the same way he was dying for a bond. He was aware Ivan had a certain fear that Alexei would disappear before they had a chance to really speak. That Ivan wanted to speak to him at all showed how much he'd grown.

Still, Nix couldn't help teasing him. "Will there be hugging? Or manly claps on the back?"

"We'll be fortunate if there aren't any more gunshots."

In a case of perfect timing, there were four subtle pops of a silenced gun, and Nix felt the four traitorous souls being snuffed out in the back.

That was all the betrayal dealt with. Sergei was gone, as were the men he'd managed to turn. The grunts, as Ivan had called them, would have to be parsed through at some point, but Ivan's core group was loyal now, and those who hadn't been would be replaced with better models.

It gave Nix a funny feeling, a strange tugging in his gut. Which was odd, considering he didn't care much about human lives.

It took the shock emanating from Ivan, now stiff in Nix's arms, for Nix to realize the strange feeling wasn't about the deaths at all.

His arms around Ivan's neck had gone transparent. Ah. That explained the tugging, didn't it?

Nix was being pulled back to the Void.

"Oh," he could only say dumbly. "I guess we met the conditions of the contract after all."

The last thing he saw of the human realm were Ivan's pale eyes widening in horror, and then Nix was taken away.

20

Ivan

Ivan's demon was gone.

Disappeared, in a puff of sweet smoke. In Ivan's arms one moment and dragged into the ether the next.

Ivan hadn't been ready.

I was never going to be fucking ready.

He barely registered the murmuring of voices until Jace was in front of him, his brow furrowed at whatever he saw on Ivan's face. "Boss?" he asked warily. "Things have been...dealt with. You need anything else here before we head out?"

Ivan should be telling him "well done," shouldn't he? Nix had been harping on him about verbalizing appreciation for his men more.

Nix would want him to be appreciative.

Ivan drew his gun and pointed it as his new main lieutenant. He distantly registered the shock and fear in Jace's eyes, but that wasn't important.

Only one thing in Ivan's life held any fucking importance.

"I do need one more thing from you, Jace," he said, in a voice that was nothing like his own. "And I'm afraid refusal is not an option."

He held the gun steady as he withdrew the Book from his jacket pocket.

"I need you to summon a demon."

21

Nix

Nix landed hard on the dusty cave floor.

He was usually more graceful returning to the Void, but he was too stunned to catch himself, and he ended up sprawled out on his back.

He'd completed the contract.

Obviously, since here he was, back in the Void. But worse—so much worse—was that when he reached for Ivan's beautiful, broken soul piece in his chest, it wasn't there. It was somewhere deep inside Nix, dormant with all the others.

Except, unlike with all the others that had come before, Nix felt like a piece of himself was now missing.

He supposed it was funny—his idea for a meeting had proven more effective than he could have imagined. Apparently the boost to Ivan's reputation it was going to give, coupled with the culling of his disloyal men, was enough to cement his foothold in New York and keep him and his brothers safe.

But of course, his brothers were already safe, bonded as they were to their respective vampire and demon.

Nix really should have taken that into account.

He wanted to scream. *I wasn't ready! I was never going to be ready.*

He'd been an idiot. He should have bonded with Ivan the moment the thought had entered his mind. He should have tricked him into it, if necessary. Should have sucked Ivan's brains out of his dick and pressed his advantage when the human was still gasping for air.

Now Nix did scream, the sound echoing off the cave walls, "I wasn't! *Fucking!* Ready!"

He jumped as a raspy voice sounded out from inside the cave, Nightmare's glowing white eyes like a beacon in the dark. "You're back."

"As you can fucking see," Nix snarled, cracking the dirt floor with his talons.

He knew better than to talk to Nightmare that way, but he didn't have it in himself to care. He didn't even have the energy to lift himself off the dirt to face him properly.

But there was no retaliation. No creeping, crawling shadows or horrific visions.

"You're crying," Nightmare told him instead.

"I'm not. I'm a demon. I don't cry." But Nix lifted a hand to his cheek anyway, surprised when it came back wet. Maybe he was bleeding from his eyes. It certainly felt like he had some sort of mortal wound.

"You're crying," Nightmare repeated, his tone unreadable.

Nix sniffed. "Maybe you should give me some privacy, then."

"You won't be here long enough."

It took a moment for the words to register, but then it was like a spark of lightning ran through Nix. He scrambled onto his knees, peering up at those glowing eyes. "Do you know something? Nightmare? Do you—do you know something I don't?"

There shouldn't be any reason he would. Nix knew for a fact that Nightmare never watched the portal to the human realm. But Nix wondered, not for the first time, if he had another connection none of them knew about. Another way of watching.

Or maybe that was only Nix's wishful thinking.

"You found a mate," Nightmare mused instead of answering his question.

"I did. But I fucked it up." Nix sniffed again, blinking back his not-tears. "And he can't summon me twice."

Would he even if he could have? Ivan had said he needed Nix, but that was when he'd had Nix up in his business twenty-four hours a day. Maybe given a moment alone—given some breathing room—Ivan would remember his life had been better without him. Smoother. Calmer. Under his control.

And it didn't fucking matter anyway, because what were the chances Ivan would let someone else summon Nix? Allow another demon into his world that he had no control over? The way he'd reacted to Cooper summoning Chaos...

If only Nix had been given more time. If he'd had more of a chance to burrow under Ivan's skin the way Ivan had gotten under his. More time to convince him what a good partner Nix could be. What a good mate.

But maybe...maybe Chaos would return the favor Nix had given him. Maybe he'd pull his attention from Cooper long enough to find a way for Nix to come back.

And then Nix would hunt Ivan down, and he would *demand* a bond in return for not burning down the whole fucking city.

But if Ivan wasn't the one who summoned him...

"Can we bond with a human who hasn't summoned us?" he asked Nightmare.

Nightmare hummed—a creepy, tuneless sound. "Goodbye, Nix."

His glowing eyes blinked out, and the cave was dark again.

And then for the second time that day, Nix was tugged away.

Nix

Nix was back in the restaurant.

No more dusty cave. No more traveling through the ether. He was back in the human realm, where he belonged.

And there was Ivan—*his* Ivan—looking more manic than Nix had ever seen him, his eyes red-rimmed and bloodshot and his chest heaving with heavy breaths. He had a gun pointed at Jace, who was holding a bleeding hand over Nix's symbol, which had been scrawled onto one of the restaurant's red tablecloths.

"Vanya." Nix rushed toward his human, only to be stopped by the invisible walls of the summoning circle.

It took Ivan a moment to speak, his red eyes roaming over every inch of Nix, drinking him in like he couldn't believe the sight.

"You're crying," he eventually said, an echo of Nightmare's words, his voice hoarse and brittle.

Nix didn't deny it this time. "I lost you," he said in explanation.

He couldn't feel Ivan through the soul connection anymore, but something horribly pained crossed the human's face, hurt wafting out of him, thick and potent. Ivan turned to Jace, his gun still level. "Finish it," he ordered.

Jace stared at him, wide-eyed. "I don't know how, boss."

Ivan snarled at him. "Make. A. Contract."

When Jace looked no less confused, Ivan turned to the back, where Sascha, Kai, Alexei, and Jay were watching in tense silence. Nix had no idea where Cooper and Chaos had gone, but it wasn't like Chaos to stick around once a party was over, so Nix wasn't exactly surprised by their absence.

"Kai!" Ivan barked. "Does he need a fucking contract? Or can we bond with him still in the summoning circle?"

"I—I know not. I'm not sure if you can bond at all. Not like this."

Ivan let out an inhuman sound, and Nix reached toward him, snarling when the summoning circle stopped him again. "We'll try," he told Ivan. He didn't know if it would work, either, but he did know if they didn't make some kind of move soon, Ivan was going to lose it. "Let's try, Vanya."

Ivan didn't lower his gun, but his eyes softened as he looked at Nix. "Tell me what to do, demon."

Nix gestured to the Book. "The last page."

Ivan's fingers shook as he turned to the last page of the Book, no matter that the hand holding the gun was still steady. He held the Book up so that Nix could see from his circle.

"Repeat after me," Nix told him. His own control felt frayed and tattered, his eyes still wet from the shock of his abrupt loss. But Ivan needed him to be steady right now.

So steady he would be.

Nix said the words in their demon tongue, the vow of bonding, body, heart, and soul. Ivan repeated each word exactly as Nix said it. He didn't ask for meaning or double-check with Kai as to their purpose. He seemed to be trusting implicitly that Nix was doing as he'd asked.

Nix hadn't known Ivan was capable of such trust.

Red smoke rolled over the restaurant floor, covering it completely. Nix let out a sigh of relief. It meant *something* was happening. "Put your hand in the summoning circle, Vanya."

Ivan walked toward him, close enough that Nix should have been able to catch his scent, if not for the damned circle. He stuck his hand inside and didn't so much as flinch when Nix bit his wrist, sucking in a mouthful of his blood. Ivan only kept his eyes on Nix's face, intent and unblinking, as if Nix was going to disappear again if he looked away for so much as a second.

Nix could understand the sentiment.

Nix bit through his own finger, smearing the blood on Ivan's hand. He didn't have to instruct Ivan—his human withdrew his hand and immediately sucked on the spot Nix had anointed, smearing blood on his lips.

He looked more unhinged than ever.

Nix loved him so fucking much.

He fell forward as the summoning circle evaporated in an instant, and Ivan caught him, crushing Nix tightly against him, so tight Nix could barely move.

"Everyone *out*," Ivan barked. "Now."

Nix was frozen in his arms, fearful and giddy all at once. He could *feel* Ivan again. Could feel his angry, broken, bitter pieces, his obsession and devotion. It was like a balm against Nix's own recent hopelessness, his fear and desperation.

He might have lost this.

He *had* lost this.

He could hear the shuffle of people leaving, the murmur of voices, but he couldn't see. Ivan was blocking his view, and he wasn't letting up his hold.

Nix tried to smile. "You missed me, huh?"

"I told you I need you." Ivan's voice was harsh and repri-
manding.

Now Nix did smile, his lips curling against Ivan's throat. "Well,
there's need, and then there's *need*."

"This is the latter." Ivan withdrew just enough to meet Nix's
eyes. "I've been taught my whole life that love gets you killed. I
never wanted it. I wouldn't have known how to reach for it if I did.
But with you—" Ivan swallowed hard, his hands like claws against
Nix's body. "It doesn't matter if it kills me. Because I refuse to live
without you."

"Oh, but, Vanya," Nix sighed, something warm and fluid
running through his chest. He lifted his hand to Ivan's cheek.
"Baby. I keep telling you—I'm an incubus. Loving me isn't going to
get you killed. Loving me is going to make you invincible."

Invincible might have been a bit of a stretch. But Ivan's lifespan
would be linked to Nix's, and that was quite a long, long time for
them both to live.

"I don't fucking care." Ivan dropped his forehead against Nix's.
"Just don't leave again."

"Never," Nix soothed, running his fingers through Ivan's hair.
"Never ever."

They spent a long moment like that, breathing each other's air,
and then the magic of the bond began to take its toll on them both
and Ivan let out a pained groan, pushing Nix down onto the
carpet, tugging at his clothes. "Off," he growled. "Get these fucking
things off."

Nix could have disappeared them, but Ivan seemed to be
getting some of his frustration out in the act of tearing them off
him, so he let it be.

It wasn't long before he was naked, spread out on the carpet.
Ivan's eyes roamed over him greedily, as if Nix had been gone for
centuries and not mere minutes. Nix should have been preening
under his gaze—he did so love to be appreciated—but his entire

body was trembling, the newly formed bond between them setting him alight.

Tremors racked Ivan's body as well, but his words were firm. "You're mine, demon."

"I've been yours since the moment you summoned me," Nix told him. "Big mistake, there. You were never getting rid of me."

His joke didn't even garner a smile, but that was hardly a surprise, as Ivan had begun to busy himself with a new way of getting his frustration out—biting at every inch of Nix's skin he could reach.

It was like he was testing the limits of Nix's demon strength, trying to mark him up against all odds. He rolled Nix over, biting at his shoulders, his spine, his lower back. He spread Nix's cheeks and licked at his hole, softening him until he could spear him with his tongue. He ate him out thoroughly, muttering steadily over Nix's moans. Oaths about keeping Nix forever. About how Nix was his. About how he was going to fuck him every day for the rest of eternity.

Nix was pretty sure he'd broken Ivan. But if this was him broken, Nix wasn't sure he was ever going to put him back together again. The manic possessiveness was exactly what Nix himself needed to soothe the horrible pain of their brief separation.

He'd never felt so wanted. So needed. So perfectly desired.

The carpet was rough against him, and he could smell the blood from the earlier meeting saturating the air. But Nix wouldn't leave this room for all the world. This could be his new Void. He could be stuck here in this godforsaken mobster restaurant forever, and as long as Ivan was with him, he wouldn't care. They could lose their minds together, slowly meld into each other, until their souls weren't only connected, but one entity.

Maybe this wasn't the healthiest relationship in the history of the world.

Ivan rolled him back over, biting at Nix's inner thigh. "Stop. Thinking."

"I'm thinking about you," Nix told him, sighing his pleasure when Ivan continued to bite at him viciously. "You're always fucking me in your suit. Get naked."

Ivan could easily have argued about how the doors were unlocked. That any of his men could come in at any time. That he didn't have Nix's handy power of making his clothes reappear at will.

But he started stripping, his brow furrowed. "I feel— This is—"

"It's the bond," Nix soothed. "You'll feel better after we consummate it."

Ivan laughed in disbelief as he shucked his underwear off, his hard cock bobbing in the air. "Will I? Will it ever be enough?"

"I don't know," Nix told him truthfully, holding back his thighs, presenting himself for Ivan to take. He needed Ivan inside him like he'd never needed anything. "But we have a very long time to figure it out."

23

Ivan

Ivan pushing into Nix's pliant body felt like coming home. The inhuman warmth of him, the tight grip as he took every inch of Ivan inside.

Ivan couldn't take his eyes off it—the spot where their bodies connected. Nix's tender skin was a deep, bruised purple, stretched tight around Ivan's glistening length.

Ivan had almost lost this forever.

He drank in Nix's moan, feeling crazed and giddy and ill all at once. He wasn't used to these kinds of emotions, and they were fucking with his head. Not to mention the new feeling he had blossoming in his chest—Nix's soul, if he wasn't mistaken. It was a twisty and serpentine thing, seductive and strange. It filled some gap in Ivan he'd never been able to place, a jagged hole the perfect size for it.

The feel of it inside him was soothing and maddening all at once.

Ivan couldn't focus. He couldn't find a rhythm. His hips kept faltering as he returned to Nix's mouth again and again, sucking on his tongue and biting at his lips. Trailing down to suck bruises into his skin, tiny purple shadows on Nix's neck and collarbone that disappeared as quickly as Ivan made them. He was mumbling nonsense all the while, frantic and foolish words he couldn't seem to swallow down. "Need you. Want you. Keep you forever."

Eventually Nix's heels dug into his ass. "Move, darling," Nix pleaded.

Ivan gathered his wits enough to start thrusting, angling Nix's lower half so he could get as deep as humanly possible. Nix had said they needed to consummate.

And it did get better, the agitation under Ivan's skin dissolving away as he sank deeper and deeper into his incubus, Ivan's sweaty, sticky skin pressing against every bit of him, their chests sliding together, the barbells in Nix's nipples cool against Ivan's fevered skin.

He was vaguely aware that any of his men could come back at any time, to find him completely nude and balls deep in his demon. But so the fuck what? Wasn't that the whole point of his reorganizing? Getting rid of the worst threats, keeping only those with the potential to change, so Ivan and his brothers could live their lives however the fuck they wanted?

Maybe it hadn't been for this *exact* purpose—fucking Nix into the carpet of the restaurant where a half dozen men had just died. But so Ivan could keep Nix at his side. Touch him where and when he wanted.

The incredibly selfish roots of Ivan's change of heart. If only his brothers knew.

Maybe they did.

Nix arched up against him, and Ivan reared back, taking Nix's legs into the crook of his elbows as he found a new, better angle.

He had rug burns on his knees, but he couldn't find it in himself to care. His demon looked too beautiful like this, spread out on his back, bared for Ivan's pleasure. The sight of him almost hurt, at the same time as it healed.

"Stroke yourself," Ivan ordered, his voice hoarser than it had ever been.

Nix grabbed his purple cock, stroking himself languidly as Ivan fucked him desperately, never taking his eyes off Ivan's. His were glowing, searing themselves into Ivan. Burning him, the way Nix's insides burned against Ivan's skin.

His release caught him completely off guard, a tidal wave that was brutal and fierce and all-consuming. Ivan dropped Nix's legs and fell onto him, batting Nix's hand away and taking over as his own body shook and shuddered, until Nix was trembling beneath him, spilling hot into Ivan's hand.

Ivan couldn't catch his breath, but maybe that was because he couldn't stop kissing Nix. His shoulders. His chest. His neck. His face. As Nix stroked his hands along Ivan's sides, murmuring sweet nonsense that Ivan couldn't listen to, at risk of losing it all over again.

He pressed his forehead against Nix's. "This is fucking terrible."

"What is?" Nix asked, stroking Ivan's hair, moving to press warm kisses to the side of Ivan's face.

"Loving you like this."

He felt Nix's lips curve against his skin. "I know, baby. I know."

Ivan rolled them over until he was on his back, Nix propped over him. Whatever crazy things the bond that had formed between them was doing to his body—to his soul—he was hard again already.

He slapped a hand against Nix's thigh. "Ride me, incubus."

Nix didn't need telling twice. He sank onto Ivan's length with a happy sigh and started rocking furiously. Gone were the languid movements he'd used to stroke himself. He seemed to have inherited Ivan's frantic energy. He stretched out over Ivan, and it was his turn now to bite at Ivan's chest. With his sharper teeth, Ivan could feel the harsh sting of him breaking skin.

Maybe Ivan would heal quicker, now that he was bonded to a demon. Maybe he wouldn't. Ivan didn't give a fuck either way. Nix's marks could stay forever, for all he cared.

Ivan busied himself with pulling and twisting at Nix's barbells, and Nix rode him until they were both quivering messes, cum streaking their bodies. And then Ivan, hard once again, took him bent over one of the booths, tugging hard at the base of his tail with every stroke, mindless with the way it made Nix keen.

They'd already covered the room in blood and smoke. Why not smear their cum and sweat and spit over every available surface?

When they'd both finally collapsed, half on and half off the bench of the booth, tangled and sweaty and exhausted on what seemed to be a spiritual level, Ivan finally felt halfway sane. Like he was more man than beast for the first time in hours.

He slid down, tugging Nix with him until they were fully on the floor again. "This entire place is a biohazard."

"Mm," Nix hummed, pressing a kiss to one of Ivan's many bite marks. "Ask me if I care."

Ivan wound Nix's ponytail around his hand, tugging his head back to meet his eyes. "Tell me again. That you're not leaving."

Nix's eyes softened. "I can't leave you, Vanya," he told Ivan, his voice gentle in its reassurance. "Even if I got tugged away to the Void somehow, or back to the demon dimension, you would be taken with me. Our souls are bound, baby."

"Good." The last of the horrid tension of the last hours left Ivan's body. "Good."

Nix grinned at him, bright as the sun. "It's good that you'd be sucked away into another dimension?"

"My life has always been a form of hell. What do I care if we make it literal? I'll leave my empire of crime behind. Become your human concubine."

The words left his lips easily, light and airy and ridiculous. It was possible he was delirious.

But Nix didn't seem to mind. He laid his head back down, laughing softly against Ivan's chest. "It's a deal. But just to be clear —I don't come from *hell*. It's just...another world."

"You'll tell me about it sometime," Ivan murmured, his eyes closing against his will. "You'll tell me everything about you."

"Yes, Vanya."

He could have fallen asleep like that, possibly for days, but the sound of the side door banging against the wall had his eyes opening again.

The bright, clear voice of his brother's vampire rang out. "I've been sent to tell you that you're not allowed to fuck for days while the rest of us stand around with our dicks in our hands," Jay announced. "Those are Alexei's words, not mine. He's not usually so crude, but we *have* been listening to you have sex for quite some time." The sound of his steps grew louder as he approached. "Oh, you're naked! And there's your tail!"

Ivan craned his neck to glare at the little vampire. "Stop ogling my demon."

"I'm ogling his tail," Jay said absently, not paying him any mind. "It looks soft."

A light weight settled over Nix and Ivan. It seemed as if Nix had summoned some sort of robe. He smiled at Ivan, the expression bittersweet. "I think it's time to get up now."

Right.

It was time for Ivan to deal with his family.

———

SOME TIME later Ivan and Nix were both dressed. The little vampire, Jay, had averted his eyes after Ivan had growled at him, but now he was back to ogling Nix's tail as Nix swished it back and forth for him.

At least Nix wasn't naked for it.

After one of the longest hugs of Ivan's life, Sascha and Kai had run off to who knew where, leaving Ivan and Alexei to survey the damage in the restaurant while Jay and Nix entertained themselves.

At least, that was what Ivan and Alexei were ostensibly doing. In reality, Ivan had people for that. It was only that he and Alexei were incapable of sitting across from each other civilly, and they both knew it. It was easier to talk when they didn't have to make eye contact.

And judging from the way Alexei was hovering—and how he'd sent his vampire in to corral them—he *did* want to talk.

Strangely enough, so did Ivan.

Now if only he could figure out what to say.

"I'm surprised you came," is what he settled on as he crouched down to catalog the different blood spatters on the carpet.

It was a neutral enough observation, his surprise. And not nearly as much as a minefield as asking Alexei *why* he'd come.

"So am I."

It seemed for a moment like Alexei would leave it at that incredibly uninformative response, but then he murmured, "Sascha was certain you're turning over a new leaf."

Ivan scoffed. "I'm not sure I'd put it that way."

It wasn't as if he was suddenly a better person than before. He was still just as selfish and controlling as his brothers had always believed him to be, at least by their standards.

He simply had a different...focus now.

Alexei leaned back against one of the booths, crossing his massive arms. Ivan had no idea where his brother's larger build had come from. Somewhere way back in the family line, perhaps. "I've never seen you look that way. The way you did when your demon disappeared."

Of course he would go right to the heart of it. Ivan contained his wince as a stab of pain ran through his chest at the reminder, right over the spot where Nix's soul connection now lay.

"And how did I look?" he managed to ask.

"Devastated," Alexei said simply. "Like a piece of you had been ripped out." He glanced away, toward Nix and Jay. "You didn't even look like that when Mom died."

Of course Ivan hadn't. He would have been punished severely for it by their father—for showing any signs of mourning for the one who'd attempted to betray him. The one who'd wanted to take his sons away.

And Ivan's mother hadn't wanted him, anyway.

But Ivan didn't feel up to hashing out any of the old arguments. He was past caring that Alexei believed him to be made of ice. It wasn't like it was his brothers who'd managed to thaw him in the end.

That had been all Nix.

Ivan rose from his crouch, making a mental note that the entire restaurant would need to be recarpeted. "And when do you flee back to Colorado?"

Alexei sighed, like Ivan was being difficult. "We're willing to stay for a bit. To help...rearrange things." He narrowed his eyes, a familiar look of suspicion taking over his rugged features. "Are you really going legitimate?"

"I'm considering. But it'll be a slow process." Ivan gave Alexei a pointed look. "It's not as easy as pressing a button."

"Of course not."

And that could be it. Ivan could leave it at that, and it would be the most civil conversation they'd had in years.

But the words were out of his mouth before he knew it. "But it was easy for you, wasn't it? Easy to leave." He turned his back as soon as he'd asked the question, hating how weak it made him sound. He was aware that for all their hushed conversation, Jay and Nix were surely listening in on the reunion. Still, he couldn't help adding, "*Why* was it so easy for you, Alyosha?"

Ivan had never understood it. They had both had the same upbringing, the same punishments for any misstep. There had been small differences in expectation—for Ivan to lead and Alexei to follow. But they'd taken, more or less, the same immense damage from their bastard of a father.

And yet Alexei had walked away.

Ivan could feel the weight of Alexei's stare, and it was a long moment before he answered, but when he did, the words were firm. "Because it was killing me, Vanya."

Ivan scoffed. "Mafia life so tough?"

Alexei let out a frustrated growl. "Maybe it was killing me to watch you become him," he snarled. "But also, yes. It *was* fucking tough. I hated it. We're allowed to hate it."

Of course they were allowed to fucking hate it. But Ivan had been so sure they weren't allowed to leave. That it would be sentencing them all to death to do so.

And Alexei hadn't fucking cared.

So why was *Ivan* the selfish one?

He forced himself to breathe. To focus on what they were saying and not the endless spirals of bitterness he was always sinking into around his brother. "You thought I was becoming him?"

"Weren't you?"

Ivan didn't know. In his mind, he'd been worlds away from the brutal psychopathy of their father. But maybe their father had also thought he was being reasonable, when he'd acted the way he had. That he was more measured than the mobsters who'd come before him.

"When our father died, " Ivan mused, toeing at a clean patch of carpet before he caught himself fidgeting and went still, "I thought his lessons—his poison fucking words—would die with him. I thought I'd feel...free of him. But I could hear him in my head, long after he was gone. Lessons like that...they stick, Alexei. They fucking stick."

Alexei's voice was soft behind him. "I know that."

Ivan whirled to glare at him. "Then why am I the only one you hate for it?"

"Because you remind me of him." Alexei's eyes tracked Ivan's face, catching his wince. "I'm sorry to say it, but it's true." His gaze darted to Nix, then back again. "But less so now. How you looked when your demon disappeared... Our father never looked like that. Not once."

Ivan ran a hand through his hair, wishing he could hit something. Or someone. "So what...we can be friends now? You can tolerate me because I have a—a boyfriend?"

Alexei's eyes widened, looking startled at Ivan's choice of words. Almost as startled as Ivan felt saying it. It was a stupid fucking word for what Nix meant to him, but it wasn't exactly incorrect either.

Alexei's smile when he recovered was bitter, but it was there. "We're not friends, Vanya. We're brothers. We always have been."

"Even when you ran?" Ivan snarked.

"Even when you shot me," Alexei countered.

Ivan let out a breath, refusing to laugh. "You healed quickly enough."

"You're an asshole."

"I'm aware."

Alexei swore softly, then turned on his heel, muttering over his shoulder. "Come meet Jay properly. Your mate has clearly already won him over. It's your turn to try."

It was an olive branch, even if it was a grudging one. And Ivan had to give Alexei credit for his choice of words.

Mate was a much better word than *boyfriend*.

24

Nix

Nix noticed something was different about Ivan after his talk with his brother.

It was interesting, since not much had been said—Nix and Jay had been eavesdropping shamelessly, even as Nix had been demonstrating the prehensile abilities of his tail—but nonetheless, the bitterness surrounding Ivan when it came to Alexei had tempered slightly.

With time, perhaps it would fade away entirely.

Which was all well and good, but now that the all-consuming lust from the bond forging had faded a bit, Nix could see how worn out his poor human was. The dark circles under his eyes were back, and there was a faint tremor in his hands.

Ivan would soon have a demon's strength to fall back on, thanks to their bond, but in the fragile aftermath of their souls colliding, what he needed at the moment was rest.

And Nix was all about giving Ivan what he needed.

Nix clucked his tongue as Ivan slipped an arm around his waist, returning to his side. "I'm taking you home."

"Are you?" Ivan asked mildly even as he tightened his hold, either in protest or agreement.

Alexei, in a mirror of Ivan's actions, wrapped an arm around his vampire. "Listen to your mate. You look like shit."

Ivan cocked a brow at his brother. "Time to go home, then. I wouldn't want to lose any beauty pageants." He made as if to turn Nix toward the door, then paused, a rare awkwardness to his hesitation. "But...you're staying?"

Just him asking the question was almost shocking in its vulnerability. Nix supposed that was his fault. He'd hacked down Ivan's walls, and apparently this was the result. Although, Nix wasn't sure how he felt about Ivan being vulnerable with others, even if it *was* his flesh and blood. All those unguarded, gooey bits were supposed to be for Nix alone.

He supposed he'd need to learn to share.

"For a time," Alexei told Ivan after a beat. He looked around at the room's destruction. "I'll tell Jace to get a cleanup crew in here."

Ivan nodded. "And make an offer on the restaurant before they put up a fuss."

Alexei hummed his agreement. "Tag can handle that easily enough."

It hit Nix that for all their sordid history, the brothers *had* worked with each other for a long time, prior to Alexei's disappearance. However terribly it had ended, they were falling back into it easily enough.

But Nix wanted the work to be done now. He needed to tend to his mate.

Luckily, a sight for sore eyes entered the building just then. "Oleg!" Nix cried happily. "Darling! Take us home."

"Don't call him darling," Ivan growled even as he let Nix lead him to the exit.

Nix ignored him, waving goodbye to the other couple and getting them the fuck out of there.

He sighed in pleasure as he slid across the leather seat of the town car. It was delicious to be once again in familiar surroundings, with Ivan close and grabbable.

Alas, there was no fingering, but Nix's dear husband was truly pooped, so Nix couldn't blame him.

Nix leaned across the partition. "Oleg, my love," he said, just to hear Ivan snarl in protest. "Did you know we got married today?"

"Not legally," Ivan murmured under Oleg's congratulations, his hand gripping Nix's thigh. "We'll need to rectify that."

Nix winked at Oleg before turning to Ivan. "Do I get a ring?"

He was only joking, but Ivan nodded, his eyes closing as he rested his head against the seat. "Mm. Amethysts. To match your eyes."

Nix wasn't able to hide his surprise. "You've thought about it?"

Ivan's lips twitched up at the corners. "I'm thinking about it now."

Well. Be still Nix's freaking heart.

The journey home was uneventful, and as soon as they were back in the apartment, Nix stripped them both, turning on the shower and watching it steam. He had to give a hats off to modern plumbing; that was for sure.

He pushed a disconcertingly docile Ivan into the shower and followed him in. Ivan was clearly flagging, but he also had smoke and blood and cum on various parts of his body, so a thorough soaping was necessary before bed.

Nix got to work, digging into Ivan's muscles as he soaped him up, just to hear his relieved groan. When he got down to the interesting bits, Ivan cracked an eye open. "I can't fuck you again," he protested, even as his cock twitched in interest at Nix's touch. "I'll die."

"You won't," Nix teased. "I wouldn't let you. But don't worry, this is strictly clinical."

It was. Mostly. It was possible Nix paid slightly more attention to some parts than others, but who could blame him?

As he hastily cleaned himself under the spray, Ivan spoke from behind him. "I've always craved loyalty," he said, his voice a low, husky murmur. "Or maybe even devotion. I thought Alexei would give me some version of it, as my brother and my right hand. I pushed him too hard, hoping for it. I thought I could force it out of him."

Nix turned to face him, and Ivan's pale eyes bore into him.

"But you give it to me so easily, Nix. My demon."

Nix pushed back his wet hair, frowning at Ivan. "Because it *is* easy to be devoted to you. Fuck everything and everyone in your past that made you think otherwise. You just needed the right person." He cocked a hip when Ivan didn't look convinced. "*I'm* the right person, in case you didn't get that."

"I'm lucky," Ivan said softly, his tone in stark contrast to the intensity of his gaze. "The way you...care for me. Losing it, even for a moment, was the most painful thing that's ever happened to me."

It was maybe the most straightforward declaration Ivan had ever made, outside of the heat of bonding sex, but Nix was at heart a little shit, so he couldn't help pressing, "Because you love me?"

Ivan didn't even flinch. "Because I love you."

Well, damn. He must really have been exhausted.

Nix kissed him, soft and slow and sweet in a way Ivan was usually too hungry and desperate to allow. "Good," he murmured as he pulled away, nipping at Ivan's lower lip. "You fucking better."

He led Ivan out of the shower, drying them both off quickly and tucking Ivan naked into bed before following right behind him. He drew Ivan to him after settling in, and Ivan placed his head on Nix's chest, sighing as Nix stroked his hair.

Nix loved Ivan's strength. His fire and his ice. But there was a certain sweetness to moments like these, when Ivan was soft and pliant, allowing such a tender touch.

"I'll keep caring for you, Vanya," Nix told him, barely above a whisper. "For longer than you can even fathom."

He'd thought Ivan might have already been asleep, but he was mistaken. "Because you love me?"

Nix grinned. "Because I love you."

A ghost of a smile graced Ivan's lips, and then in a surprising burst of energy, he rolled them over, pulling Nix on top of him, delicious bare skin against delicious bare skin. He pressed Nix's head down to his shoulder. "Come, demon. Sleep."

And the draining force of the bond forming must really have gone both ways, because Nix did.

———

THE NEXT WEEK was a flurry of activity as aspects of the business were rearranged, different responsibilities handed over to new, loyal men.

Alexei and Jay had stayed for longer than either Nix or Ivan had expected, but they'd eventually flown back to Colorado five days after the bloody meeting.

At their goodbye, Alexei had looked Ivan in the eye, both brothers tense and expectant. "We spend Christmas with our den," he'd said.

Ivan's lips had twisted into a bitter shape. "Noted."

"But there's always New Year's. Sascha would be pleased."

Ivan hadn't exactly smiled, but it had turned out Nix *did* get to see some manly clapping on the back. It had seemed like more a competition of strength than a sign of brotherly love, but he supposed it was all about baby steps.

What Nix hadn't gotten to see much of was Chaos or Cooper

around, but he hadn't really expected Chaos to participate beyond the initial bloodshed. According to Ivan, Cooper was still completing any work requested of him, so they knew the two of them were both alive and hopefully well.

Nix would give Chaos a few more weeks before he hunted him down. If it went much longer than that without word from his friend, he'd put up a fuss.

But for now it was Friday, and Ivan had been holed up in his office for far too fucking long. Nix flounced down the hallway, stopping to gab for a minute with Tara (he'd convinced Ivan it was a truly insane move to have his secretary on an entirely different floor) before barging his way into Ivan's office.

Jace and Tag were there, sitting across from Ivan's desk, but they didn't so much as twitch when Nix plopped himself sideways into Ivan's lap.

They'd gotten used to the sight in the past week.

Ivan for his part just wrapped an arm around Nix's waist and shifted him slightly to the side so he could still see his laptop. "And who do we have managing the last three nightclubs?"

"Well, Sascha has the one you gave him...," Jace said.

"Give him the other two, if he wants them. He can handle them remotely well enough. Just tell him to run it by you if he needs more help than we've given him."

"Sure, boss."

"Anything else?" Ivan asked his lieutenants.

Nix shut Ivan's laptop firmly before they could answer. "I'm afraid that's it, boss," he drawled.

Ivan arched a brow at him. "Tiring already of your interior decorating?"

Nix had been rearranging and redecorating Ivan's apartment so it wasn't so starkly depressing. It would do until Nix decided exactly what kind of human dwelling he wished to spend the majority of his time in. And Ivan had given him free rein because he was, underneath his stubborn bossiness, a very smart man.

"I've just had a ten-foot-tall nude portrait of myself commissioned," Nix told him, batting his lashes. "You don't mind, do you?"

Ivan smirked at him. "You can hang it in here," he said, calling Nix's bluff. "Give me something to look at while you're off spending my money."

"Or you can come home now and have the real thing," Nix countered.

Ivan ducked his head, running his nose along Nix's jaw as his hand trailed over his hip. "Why wait until we're home?" he murmured.

Nix shivered, ready to disappear his clothes right there and then. He hoped Ivan tugged at his tail again when he fucked him —the underside of the base was deliciously sensitive, and Ivan's rough handling in the restaurant had been a delightful revelation.

A throat cleared.

Ivan's face was an icy mask in an instant as he looked around Nix to his lieutenants. "Is there a fucking problem?" he asked, low and dangerous.

"No problem," Jace answered quickly. He and Tag were frozen in place in their seats. "We just thought maybe you'd want...privacy?"

"Be nice," Nix told Ivan under his breath when it looked like Ivan might bite Jace's head off at the mere implication that his lieutenants were reluctant to watch him fuck his husband right in front of them.

But really, they should be so lucky.

"Out," Ivan barked instead. "*Now*. I'm done with you."

The two scurried off but not before giving deferential nods to Ivan and Nix. So polite, these boys.

Nix swung his leg around so he was straddling Ivan, toying

with the buttons on his shirt. "I thought we weren't relying on fear anymore."

"A little fear never hurt anyone." Ivan slid his hands under Nix's blouse to caress his lower back. "I need to keep them in line. The way they look at you sometimes..."

"How do they look at me?"

"Like they wouldn't mind a ten-foot nude portrait of you hanging in my office."

Nix laughed. "Darling, you married an incubus. I'm a desirable commodity. Get used to it." He ground down in Ivan's lap, practically purring when Ivan began hardening against him. "Or maybe stop manhandling me in front of them, and they won't get naughty ideas."

Ivan raised his hips to meet him. "You're the one who jumped in my lap."

"And what are you going to do about it?"

Ivan captured his mouth in answer, kissing him hungrily. His hands were suddenly everywhere at once, stroking Nix's back, his hips, twisting the barbells in his nipples. "I want to fuck you over my desk," Ivan rasped, licking and biting his way down Nix's throat.

"Oleg's waiting for us," Nix told him even as he tilted his head back to give him better access.

"Let him wait," Ivan murmured against his skin.

It was a tempting fucking thought. Still...

"No, no, no." Nix gathered his strength of will and escaped Ivan's grasp, rising from his lap. "Because once your balls are drained, you're going to look longingly at your laptop and start working again." He held out his hand. "We're going home."

Ivan took his hand and stood, making no attempt to hide the bulge in his slacks. "I have an office at home. There's a desk there too."

Nix shook his head, grabbing Ivan's laptop and shoving it in his bag. "We're not setting foot in there tonight. I've always wanted to take a bubble bath—your presence is required for the experience."

Ivan cocked his head as he watched Nix furiously gather his belongings. "I've been working too much, haven't I?"

Nix fought the urge to roll his eyes. "Yes. You have."

"Aha. There will probably be another week or so of this, and it'll ease up as the others take on more responsibility." Ivan rubbed a hand over his face, as if dreading the next seven days. "I'm learning to rely on other people. Are you proud?"

His question had been sarcastic, but Nix answered sincerely anyway, "Immensely."

Ivan sighed heavily, slipping into his coat. "We need to tell Tara she can go."

"I already did," Nix told him with a grin. At the door to the office, he stopped Ivan with a hand on his chest. "Vanya." He grabbed Ivan's face, staring into his eyes and speaking firmly. "I am very, very proud of you."

Ivan blinked at him. "The things you say."

And Nix would keep saying them. The wounds Ivan had been given growing up ran deep and would take time and care to heal. Their soul bond had filled many of the fissures, and their physical connection was unlike anything else in this world, but sometimes Ivan needed the words, even if he didn't realize it.

And sometimes Nix needed to give them to him.

From the very first moment the summoning smoke had cleared, Ivan had seen Nix for who he was. Wanted him for who he was. No illusions, no tricks. And while Nix had never thought he could be satisfied belonging to one human for all eternity... well, that was before, wasn't it? Before Ivan. Nix may have dealt in desire, but he'd had no experience with connection. He hadn't realized what he'd been missing, but now he knew.

No one else would need and want him the way Ivan needed

and wanted him. No one else would feed Nix's urge to care and cajole and tease and torment the way Ivan did.

Nix didn't know what the fuck had brought him and Ivan together. He didn't know if it was blind luck or fate or the whim of unknown gods.

But whatever it was, they belonged to each other now, body and soul and heart.

"Come, darling." He grabbed Ivan's hand again. "I want to hear the things *you* say when you're fucking me over the rim of the tub."

EPILOGUE

Ivan

"Vanya. Vanya. *Vanya*."

Ivan pressed his nose harder into Nix's hair, inhaling his smoky scent. "Yes, my incubus?"

"You're going to ruin my panties."

Ivan chuckled darkly, crooking his fingers in a way that made Nix keen. "We both know you can conjure another pair. So hush. Take what I'm giving you."

"Mm," Nix moaned, writhing against the push of Ivan's fingers. "So bossy."

Ivan pressed in a third, smirking at Nix's gasp. His demon was already sopping wet, and he was making a mess of the town car's leather seat, never mind his fucking panties. Ivan would have liked to have him on his lap, to make good use of that eager writhing, but he had a meeting to get to, and he couldn't have Nix's slick all over his pants for it. The bond gave him certain advantages, but Ivan conjuring his own clothes wasn't one of them.

"Touch yourself," he ordered instead.

Nix immediately grabbed at his erection, cupping it over his panties and thumbing the leaking tip desperately.

He looked gorgeous like this, his head thrown back against the leather interior, his long, elegant neck on display, and his eyes shut tight, almost as if he was in pain.

Ivan crooked his fingers again, and Nix's eyes flew open. "I'm close," he whined. He turned his head, purple eyes beseeching. "Kiss me?"

Ivan captured his mouth, licking into it desperately and biting at his plush lips. His own erection was straining against his zipper, a delicious, painful ache.

He felt it when Nix came, his inner muscles clamping down on Ivan's fingers, his moan spilled directly into Ivan's mouth as his body trembled in his seat.

Fucking gorgeous.

"Now you," Nix panted.

"We don't have time," Ivan told him regretfully, withdrawing his fingers.

It wasn't nearly as long of a drive as Ivan would have liked, and he knew they were nearing their destination.

But Nix was already reaching for his zipper. "Oh, darling," he purred. "You underestimate me."

He freed Ivan's erection easily, leaning over his lap and laughing softly when Ivan wound his ponytail around his fist, his protestations already forgotten.

"Don't make a mess," Ivan ordered.

"Wouldn't dream of it," Nix murmured, lapping at Ivan's precum.

Ivan hissed at the tease, and Nix laughed again, swallowing him down in the next instant. His mouth was burning hot as always, and Ivan cursed, tugging sharply at his hair.

Nix popped off, licking at his lips and peering at Ivan through his lashes. "Just like that, Vanya. Be vicious with me, hm?"

Fuck. He always knew what buttons to push.

Ivan fucked up into his mouth, using his grip on Nix's hair to guide him just like he wanted. He was as brutal as Nix had requested, thrusting hard into Nix's throat with no thought to his need to breathe.

Mainly because Nix didn't need to.

Normally Nix was messy with his blow jobs—spit and precum bathing Ivan's lap by the end of it—but he was being obediently neat this time, suctioning his lips as tightly against Ivan's cock as he was able to with the violent rocking of Ivan's hips.

"Perfect," Ivan muttered, eyes rolling into the back of his head. "Fucking perfect."

He found his release just as they pulled into their destination, and Nix swallowed every drop greedily. Ivan panted in the aftermath, trying to collect his wayward brain cells. Luckily Oleg knew better than to open the door or lower the partition before they'd signaled they were ready.

Ivan's driver had learned that lesson the hard way.

Ivan released his tight grip on Nix's hair, stroking the strands as Nix busied himself licking Ivan's softening cock clean. He tucked Ivan back in almost daintily before zipping him back up with a fond pat.

He looked Ivan over skeptically afterward. "It'll do," he said after a moment. "Your lips are bruised from kissing, but nothing to be done about that."

Ivan scoffed. As if Nix could talk. He looked wrecked—his red hair in disarray, his lips puffy, and his eyes red.

And his panties were soaked, just as he'd worried they would be.

It was a good thing he wasn't the one with a meeting.

"You demanded a kiss," Ivan reminded him.

Nix sniffed haughtily. "I asked politely. Besides—" He gave a sly grin. "You're the one who attacked me in the first place."

Yeah fucking right. Nix had been a pest from the moment they'd gotten into the car. Dancing his fingers up Ivan's thigh, pressing his lithe body against him as he nuzzled into his neck. Ivan stuffing his fingers inside him had been the only way to get him to sit still.

Unashamed by his lie, Nix began pushing strands of his hair back into place, tightening his ponytail. "No sense playing the blame game," he said with a smirk that said he knew exactly where the blame lay. "You look mostly respectable, I promise. Are you still nervous?"

Ivan narrowed his eyes. "I was never nervous."

But perhaps he'd been...unsettled. He wouldn't put it past Nix plotting the whole seduction as a means of distraction. He was perceptive that way.

"You shouldn't be. There's nothing he can do to you." Nix snapped his fingers, and his soaked underwear was replaced with a clean pair. "And if all goes well, you can fuck me on the way home in celebration."

"And if it doesn't?"

"Then you can fuck me on the way home in consolation."

Ivan laughed as he smoothed down his shirt. Of course. It wouldn't be the first time Nix had ridden him in the cramped back seat. He could be remarkably creative in tight spaces.

Ivan's laughter had a soft smile tugging at Nix's lips. "You sure you don't want me to come with you?"

"I'm sure," Ivan told him, knocking on the partition. Five seconds later and Oleg was at the door, opening it for him.

Ivan pressed a final, filthy kiss to Nix's mouth before exiting the car. "Don't flirt too hard with Oleg while I'm away. I'd hate to have to kill my loyal driver."

"No promises!" Nix called after him.

THE OFFICE the assistant led Ivan into was smaller than Ivan's but tastefully decorated, with a certain warmth his had always lacked.

Anton Petrov didn't rise to greet Ivan, but he didn't look overly hostile at his arrival either.

He nodded at Ivan as he entered, pushing aside the papers he'd been glancing over at his desk. He was a relatively attractive older man, somewhere in his late fifties, with plenty of gray running through his dark-blond hair. "Ivan Kozlov. I admit I was surprised when you requested a meeting."

As he would be. Anton was the head of a rival Mafia family Ivan's crew brushed up against every now and then. They were relatively small potatoes, neither a threat nor a formidable ally, and Ivan had always ignored them as such.

Until now.

"Is that why you agreed to meet me?" Ivan asked as he took a seat. "Curiosity?"

Anton's lips curled into a small, secret smile. "Curiosity is one word for it. I've heard a lot of interesting rumors about your organization lately."

Ivan was sure he had. In the last year, his group had been surrounded by nothing but rumors. The frantic cries about monsters under his yolk had calmed somewhat in these last months, but whispers surrounding his family still abounded.

As they were meant to.

"I came here for something more concrete than rumors."

Anton hummed thoughtfully. "Your property at the docks."

"Just so."

Ivan had begun, ever so slowly, to rid himself of those aspects of his business that were less than legal, or at least the ones that were overtly so. The biggest hurdle by far was the control his family held over the docks. Quite a few other families relied on someone to look the other way for their less legitimate shipments, and they wouldn't take kindly to a change of ownership that wasn't...amenable to such things.

Someone had to be willing to take over. Someone already enmeshed in their world. And somehow, Ivan had found himself promising Sascha it would be someone who'd put a foot down when it came to shipments of people.

Enter Anton Petrov.

"It would be quite an extensive investment for us," Anton mused, as if it was his first time considering it and not something he'd surely gone over already with his accountant. "Not all of us have your ready funds."

"I'm well aware."

"But the returns..." Anton rubbed at the short beard on his chin, raising his brows at Ivan. "Why are you giving it up?"

There were a hundred ways Ivan could answer. A number of ways he *should* answer. Every one of them left him with a certain tightness in his chest, vestiges of panic left over from his father's many years of instruction.

In the end, he went with the simplest. "I'm getting out."

Anton's eyes widened in surprise even as he nodded. "Good for you."

And that was it. Ivan kept his shock to himself, but it was a battle. He'd been expecting some degree of pushback. Anton was closer to Ivan's father in age, the younger end of an older generation.

Shouldn't he be telling Ivan the only way out was death? Warn him that he was being cowardly and foolish and he'd end up with a bullet in his back?

Anton seemed to read *something* on Ivan's face. He leaned back in his chair, folding his hands over his stomach. "I've got a son," he said easily. "He's going to Stanford next year." He cocked a brow. "It's always a good thing when we can make a better life for our kids, isn't it? Give them choices we never had. That's supposed to be the point of all this bullshit."

Ivan took a moment to process the subtext. The idea that no one was actually required to pass on a blood-soaked inheritance to their unwilling sons. The fact that not all mobsters were like Ivan's father.

It had never been a Mafia thing. It had always been an asshole thing.

The confirmation didn't hurt as much as it could have. As much as it might have even a year ago.

They discussed business after that, agreeing to a meeting in the near future to sign all the necessary paperwork. It could be managed digitally, of course, but some things were still best left old school.

It was less than an hour before Ivan was back at his town car, opening the back door in a bit of a daze. Nix was leaned halfway over the partition, saying something that made Oleg laugh—a feat Ivan hadn't been aware was possible until Nix had entered his life.

Ivan slid in beside him, tugging Nix onto his lap and burying his head in his neck.

Nix was pliant, amenable to his manhandling. "That bad?"

"No," Ivan answered, his voice muffled against Nix's skin. "It went very well."

Nix hummed, the sound reverberating under Ivan's ear against his throat. "Back to the office, then?"

"No." Ivan raised his head. "Oleg, take us home."

Oleg grunted his agreement, raising the partition without being asked and pulling onto the street.

Nix began stroking Ivan's hair, his touch soft and perfect. "You don't have to give up the docks if you don't want to, darling. I don't mind."

"I'm aware."

It was a truth that had been burned into Ivan's very soul—that

Nix accepted all parts of him, even those jagged, bitter bits anyone else would throw out. Nix wouldn't mind if Ivan kept his bloody empire. He didn't care if Ivan went legitimate, either, as long as he didn't cut into their time together by working sixty hours a week.

Nix had been truthful in his claims—he *was* good for Ivan's organization. He knew all the men's names, remembered their families, their likes and dislikes, what made them rage or made them laugh. He made them all feel seen by him and, by extension, Ivan.

Thanks to him, Ivan could keep things dirty and still feel in control, if he wanted to.

But going legitimate wasn't for Nix. It wasn't even for Ivan's brothers, as much as it pleased Sascha that he was doing so. It was for Ivan. A final way to say "fuck you" to every single one of his father's teachings. A way to set himself free from shackles he hadn't even realized had been binding him.

Shackles Nix had seen for exactly what they were, from the very first moment they'd met.

Ivan leaned over Nix to knock on the partition. "Oleg. The package."

Oleg lowered the barrier and handed him the slim box. Ivan passed it onto Nix without a word.

"What's this?" Nix asked even as he opened it with eager fingers, gasping in delight at the jeweled necklace inside. It was a short chain embedded with diamonds and amethysts, a match to the ring on his finger.

"Happy anniversary, demon."

Ivan grinned at the expression on Nix's face. It wasn't often he caught him by surprise. "I summoned you a year ago," he explained.

Nix's brow furrowed. "I didn't—"

Of course he hadn't. Nix had spent centuries in the Void. His concept of time was different from any human's. Ivan had never expected him to keep track of some random date, even if it held a certain holy significance to Ivan himself.

"Don't worry." He leered at his demon exaggeratedly, gratified when it knocked the rueful look off Nix's face. "I'll be taking my gift from you in the way I like best."

"Oh?" Nix cocked a brow, shifting on Ivan's lap, practically purring at the bulge he rubbed against. He held up the necklace with a sly smile. "Put it on for me?"

Ivan took the necklace and clasped it around Nix's neck. It was short enough that it resembled a collar, and Ivan's cock hardened further at the sight, the same jolt of possessive satisfaction going through him as when he saw the ring on Nix's finger.

Mine, he thought. *My demon. My incubus.*

Nix stroked the pretty bit of jewelry. "This is very sentimental of you, Vanya."

"I'm afraid you've ruined me that way."

It was clear from the look in Nix's eyes that he knew exactly what Ivan meant as he kissed Ivan with rare, hesitant sweetness.

Because Nix hadn't ruined Ivan, as they both knew. He'd saved him. His life, most likely, and his soul, most definitely, all in one fell swoop. He'd dragged Ivan back from a precipice he hadn't even known he was standing on, and Ivan owed him everything for it.

It was highly possible Ivan didn't deserve good things in life. However shitty his father may have been, Ivan's past didn't excuse the evil he'd done, or the way he'd hurt the people closest to him. Surely there was a spot in hell with his name on it.

But he'd been given Nix anyway, and Ivan would thank whatever gods or devils had sent him every day for the rest of his very long life.

His demon. His soul. His perfect match.

THE END.

———

AUTHOR'S NOTE

Thank you so much for reading Inviting Bedlam! I hope you enjoyed this second book in the Demon Bound series.

And an extra thank you for giving our dear Vanya a chance! I know Ivan hasn't played the *best* brotherly role in past books, but you all know I love a redemption—I really couldn't help myself. And Nix, my sweet, mischievous baby. The chemistry between these two had me giggling at all hours, and I can only hope you had half as much fun reading them as I had writing them.

What's Next

Cooper and Chaos! I am so looking forward to diving deeper into the adorable, feral gremlin that is our chaos demon, and to giving our shy, self-contained Cooper a little shake-up.

And if you're too impatient to wait, you can read WIP chapters as I write them on my Patreon.

If you want to stay in the know, you can sign up for my newsletter for updates and news on upcoming releases. And I can always be reached by email if you just want to say howdy. I love, love, love hearing from my readers!

graebryanauthor@gmail.com

ALSO BY GRAE BRYAN

Vampire's Mate Series

Roman (Book One) – Danny and Roman

Soren (Book Two) – Gabe and Soren

Lucien (Book Three) – Jamie and Lucien

Johann (Book Four) – Alexei and Jay

Wolfgang (Book Five) – Eric and Wolfe

Colin (Book Six) — Colin, Fox, and Dane

Cassian (A Vampire's Mate Novella) – Blake and Cass

Demon Bound Series

Wreaking Havoc (Book One) — Sascha and Kai

Inviting Bedlam (Book Two) — Ivan and Nix

ABOUT THE AUTHOR

Grae Bryan has been reading romance since she was far too young to know any better. Her love for love stories spans all genres, and while her current series is of the paranormal variety, she knows she'll be exploring other worlds further down the line.

She lives in Arizona with her husband, who graciously shares space with all the imaginary men in her head. When not writing, she can generally be found reading more than is healthy, walking her monster-dog, or cuddling her demon-cat. She loves anything and everything gothic, strange, lovely, or cozy.

Find her online: graebryan.com
　　Join her Facebook reader group: Grae Bryan's Reader Den
　　Patreon: patreon.com/GraeBryan
　　Facebook: @GraeBryanAuthor
　　Instagram: @authorgraebryan
　　Sign up for her newsletter: graebryan.com/contact

www.ingramcontent.com/pod-product-compliance
Lightning Source LLC
Chambersburg PA
CBHW020619260626
47157CB00003B/1075